In a Peasant's Homespun Gown, Amicia Braved the Treacherous Path to the Cave Beyond the Waterfall . . .

Unaware that the outlaw Galen had already guessed her true identity, she hoped to gain his trust with tales of infamy at Castle Dungeld.

Galen's response was disappointingly cool. "My thanks for your visit," he said. "But the day is grown late and your family will be looking for your return."

"I want to be your friend." Unthinkingly, Amicia took a step nearer to lay her small hand against his broad chest in supplication.

Galen longed to respond . . . and in the next instant it occurred to him that here might well be the chance to frighten the maid into a sensible retreat. As if in proof, her soft lips parted on a satisfying gasp when he reached out to wrap her in his arms.

Never sparing a thought to the folly of her response, Amicia instinctively melted into his strong embrace. Undreamt-of sensations swept through her as he bent his head to taste the sweet honey of her lips. She wrapped both arms about his neck, tangled her fingers into cool strands of thick black hair, and drew the fire near like a moth determined to sacrifice itself to the destroying flame.

At last, Galen gently broke away. With a quick, blindingly sweet smile Amicia gave him a promise. "I'll see you on the morrow."

Galen's ploy had definitely failed . . .

Books by Marylyle Rogers

Dragon's Fire
Hidden Hearts
Wary Hearts

Published by POCKET BOOKS

Hidden Hearts

Marylyle Rogers

POCKET BOOKS

New York London Toronto Sydney Tokyo

An *Original* Publication of POCKET BOOKS

POCKET BOOKS, a division of Simon & Schuster Inc.
1230 Avenue of the Americas, New York, NY 10020

ISBN: 0-671-65880-8

First Pocket Books printing September 1989

10 9 8 7 6 5 4 3 2 1

POCKET and colophon are trademarks of
Simon & Schuster Inc.

Printed in the U.S.A.

To John,
My Brother and the Best Teacher I've ever had:
Thank you for convincing me that "I can!"

Author's Note

Henry II, King of England, Wales, Scotland, Ireland, Duke of Normandy, Count of Anjou, Maine, Touraine, Aquitaine, Poitou, and holder of Brittany and the Vexin built what came to be known as the Angevin Empire and endured the near constant rebellion of his four legitimate sons. After he died, two of his sons, Richard and John, followed him to the throne.

Richard wanted the power and prestige of the crown but had no interest in England beyond its ability to be the source of taxes to support his Continental wars and planned crusade. On his return from crusade, he was captured and held for ransom. John, acting as regent in his brother's absence, taxed the English people to an irrational degree, ostensibly to raise the ransom for Richard's release, which he never paid. It was left to Eleanor, the queen mother, to arrange for Richard's freedom.

After reigning ten years, during which time he seldom set foot in England, Richard died of an injury against which, with less arrogance, he could have protected himself. John took the throne and proceeded with a greed and petty cruelty that earned him the distinction of being one of the worst kings

England has ever known. The great Angevin Empire his father built, John lost. By the end of his reign in France he held only his mother's duchy of Aquitaine. As a result of his poor judgment and egotism he brought not only himself but the whole of Britain under the pope's interdict, which meant that for long years no church services, no burials in consecrated ground, no communion was allowed for his subjects. In a religious age this was a fearsome thing indeed. By his enmity with the French king, the pope, and his own barons he became the first English king since William the Conqueror, 150 years before, to be nearly (except for the occasional attempt at invasion of France) island-bound to Britain.

Moreover, on the plain at Runnymeade he opened the door to constitutional monarchy and sowed the seeds of democracy by putting his seal to the Magna Carta. A document of lasting impact despite the fact that it was not the first such charter, only the first an English king accepted under duress, and despite the fact that he repudiated it almost immediately. John's attempts to void the charter so infuriated a number of his barons that they invited the French to invade and replace John on the throne. At the same time others of the baronage, as opposed to John as they might be, could not but stand with him against any foreign pretensions to their crown.

A footnote in history tells us of an English knight named William who held a dense, nearly impenetrable strip of forest against intruders and near single-handedly halted the invading French in their attempts to cross and move deeper onto British soil. The common folk lauded him as "Willikin of the Weald."

John died little more than a year after signing the Magna Carta. During his reign he had not only alienated his English barons but—from the time he, as regent, demanded unreasonable taxes be paid to raise Richard's ransom—had oppressed the common folk. While tales of King Arthur and his court were written and sung as entertainment for the nobility, the common people found a hero of their own, a generous outlaw who came to the aid of innocent people whether noble or serf—Robin Hood. The earliest surviving written record of him is found in Piers Plowman, but it is certain that his legendary exploits had already been passed through several generations by the oral tradition of the average folk. His admirers among the common people were illiterate while the literate among the upper class were unlikely to enshrine such a man in their writings. The stories of his adventures have endured from that day to this.

During the early British Middle Ages all widows and minor children of deceased vassals, along with their inheritances, (and all of England was at the highest levels in vassalage to the crown) were the king's to dispose of as he willed. But had the terms of the Magna Carta been in effect and adhered to at the time this book opens (1199), Lady Sybil could not have been "denigrated" by King John's forcing her to marry the landless knight Gilfrey who was far below her social level.

Prologue

A scream rent the peace of twilight and echoed against the bedchamber's stone walls. Offered a moment of relief, the contorted body on the bed at its center slumped back, reed slender and limp. So fragile was the woman that her greatly distended belly seemed impossibly large as she gasped for breath and prayed for an end to the agony that neared a full day and night.

"Courage, Ladybird, courage." Anne brushed white blond hair back from a sweat-drenched face, laid the cool consolation of a cold compress against a broad brow, and silently added her heaven-bound pleas to those of the too beleaguered woman forced to endure this wrenching pain. "Soon it will be done." Voice a comforting croon that held more assurance than she felt, Anne added, "Soon the small one you've dreamed of for a decade and more will lie at your side."

Exhaustion hazed Sybil's pale blue eyes as she struggled to focus on her friend's concerned face. Anne had borne two sons already and had no fears of birthing the babe she carried now. Anne knew whereof she spoke. Anne's encouraging words she could

1

trust. Soon it would be done—Sybil's confidence wavered. Pray God both she and the child would survive.

Caught again in the jaws of a mighty vise, Sybil gritted her teeth against the ghastly cry welling up in her throat as if to confine it would be to lessen the coil of pain about her middle.

"Leave us." The man in the open door found he'd been neither heard nor even noticed by the tall, sturdy woman bent over the bed. The two castle-serfs, here at her request, glanced his way but when Anne called they turned immediately to do her bidding. It infuriated him. Castle Dungeld now was his and only by his generosity had Anne and her husband, Sir Jasper, been allowed to remain. He rued the decision intended to win some measure of acceptance from the widow he'd claimed as wife in order to possess her dead lord's fiefdom.

"Leave us." The harsh words sliced through the sudden quiet of the lady's momentary respite like a dagger and seemed to herald the laboring woman's next bout with agony.

Anne met Gilfrey's wrathful gaze unflinching and automatically stepped between his belligerent form and the bed, as if shielding its occupant from him. He'd been out on demesne business with his men when the lady's time had come, and those within the castle had specifically not sent for this man who was husband but not father. Yet here he was—an indefinable threat.

For ten long years Sybil and her husband, Conal, Baron of Wryborne, had wished for a child. When their prayers had been answered at last, they'd awaited this day with great anticipation. Anne was certain 'twas the wretched work of one of Lucifer's servants that had seen the baron dead before he'd seen their child. One of Lucifer's servants, and she feared she looked upon him now. Gilfrey's coarse brown hair, streaked with gray, framed a pock-marked face wherein a sour temperament had laid permanent lines of spite and turned thin lips ever down.

Narrowed eyes on the impediment before him, Gilfrey motioned another from behind his back as he spoke. "We will see to my lady wife's comfort." The words were a soft but undeniable command that Anne leave.

Anne's eyes widened at the sight of the filthy old crone who sidled from behind the new baron's beefy width. Near as much dirt encrusted Mag's claw-like hands as layered the tattered rags she wore for clothes. In horror, Anne slowly shook her head and glanced toward the woman again in the grip of pain. First sweet Sybil had lost her husband, then been forced to wed a man she loathed, and now this endless torture while her too-small frame struggled to produce the babe. How could she desert one so clearly in need of loving support to the questionable talents of these two. How when she was certain the man intended harm to any male offspring of his predecessor, a child who would have rightful claim to what Gilfrey meant for his own.

Taking the tall woman's negative motion as refusal to do as he demanded, Gilfrey snarled. "Begone and never dare deny my words again else I'll see you beggared and languishing in the streets!" He stepped forward, knocking the obstacle in his path aside with purposeful ease. The crone hustled in his wake as he strode to the side of the bed and peered between looped-back drapes at the woman so befogged by pain that she recognized neither him nor any other.

Recovering from the force that had sent her sprawling against a chest at the foot of the bed, Anne pushed herself to her feet, blue fire in her eyes—only to find herself flanked by a pair of Gilfrey's unsavory guardsmen. She had little choice but to depart although it felt like a betrayal of the woman who'd been friend since the day she'd arrived at this place.

As tall as her two escorts, Anne tilted her chin to

march from the chamber and down the broad corridor. Proudly ascending the cool, winding stairway built within the stone wall's width, she glanced sideways through a narrow arrow slit that did more to relieve the passage's gloom than the weak and fitful light of its oil-fed sconces. She caught a fleeting glimpse of a panoramic view. Blue waves crashed into white foam against the sheer rock base below while beyond the ocean's shifting patterns of shadow and light lay the green wall of a dense forest. Perched on the pinnacle of a steep isle, Castle Dungeld was a nearly impregnable fortress accessible only at low tide when lay revealed a narrow causeway between the island and the wild terrain of the mainland. A decade gone by she'd wed the knight in charge of the castle's garrison and been welcomed into its fold by Lord Conal's quiet lady. The only well-born women within its walls and for some distance beyond, they'd become close friends, just as were their husbands. Except for Conal and Sybil's disappointment in their childless state, life had been pleasant on this fiefdom of Wryborne—until a bare three months past.

One of Anne's escorts threw open the door of the small bedchamber allotted her and Jasper since he'd been reduced to a mere guardsman, so low a position in the hierarchy that 'twas an insult to an honorable knight. For Lady Sybil's sake alone they had stayed. At least they'd a private chamber, however cramped, and were not relegated to the large common room shared by other guardsmen one level below the great hall.

The door's ironbound planks swung closed behind her, and by the light of a single tallow candle left burning on a crude metal stand Anne sank down on the sorry bed's prickly straw-filled mattress. With neither fire nor window the room was cold and dark, emphasizing her bleak thoughts. Again she mourned the dreadful event which had seen such an abrupt change in the fortunes of Wryborne, the day when Jasper had accompanied Lord Conal to the forest

4

beyond the causeway to hunt. Their oldest son, Herbert, had felled his first deer—a feat making the day one to celebrate. Yet, at its end a seemingly numbed Jasper had sat slowly shaking his head, saying over and over that he and Conal had been merrily laughing, unaware of the dour gloom hovering near, happily praising the youngster's prowess, unprepared for sudden sorrow. His pained disbelief had echoed in the hollow repetition that there'd been no hint of the disaster about to curse the warm, sunny day with the chill darkness of death, no warning of the apparently stray arrow which with deadly accuracy had found a home in Conal's heart.

Neither Sir Jasper nor any other member of Castle Dungeld's hunting party had believed the ominously unmarked arrow accidentally shot, but there'd been no proof of treachery. Leastways none that could be taken to a king recently crowned and no friend to Lord Conal, no friend to the baron who had repeatedly stood against John when prince in his father, King Henry's, time or when regent acting in his brother, King Richard's, stead. Cheerful Conal, well-liked by his peers and beloved of the people on his fiefdom, serf and vassal alike, had precious few enemies. Indeed, there'd been no serious threat to his safety— save royal vengeance.

An insultingly short time after the baron's demise, Gilfrey had arrived with a writ from King John giving into his hands both the widow and her dower lands. That fact provided confirmation to all of Wryborne that their lord's death had been no accident but the result of a foul, murderous attack.

The disheartening gloom of her own thoughts increased Anne's fears for the woman above. She comforted her helpless frustration with the hope that Sybil's training as a postulant nun to meekly endure any ill that befell her, which had been a steady harbor during the recent upheaval of her world, would lend strength to see her through this as well. Concern for

Sybil soothed by faith in divine aid, Anne's mind turned to worry for the child whose birth was a threat to the new baron who stood close and waiting. Gilfrey had clearly been shocked when he'd discovered the bride the king had sent him to claim, the woman known to have been barren for a decade, was near to producing a possible heir. What wicked deeds did Lord Gilfrey think to hide by sending Sybil's faithful supporters away?

A mother herself, Anne paced like a caged lioness in protection of her cubs. Too distressed to join her husband at the evening meal in the great hall below, she prowled from one side of the cramped chamber to the other and back again. When a knock sounded, she flew to the door and found one of her former escorts on the other side with a call for her return to Lady Sybil.

Brushing past the messenger who'd not had time to step aside, Anne rushed down the winding stairs and burst into the lord's chamber. When she entered, Gilfrey turned from the window, watching with hooded gaze as she moved to the bed where Lady Sybil dozed. A tiny newborn's cries drew her attention to the cradle beside the bed. Pulling back a haphazardly thrown coverlet, Anne found a wee girl-child, yet unwashed and crying lustily. Anne glanced quickly around, relieved to see that the filthy crone Gilfrey had brought was gone. Pouring water from an ewer beside the bed into the waiting basin, she knelt at the cradle and began to wash the little body that kicked and punched against the foreign experiences of this new world.

As Anne wrapped the babe in fire-warmed blankets and laid her next to the mother, Gilfrey departed, satisfied with his work.

"Sybil," Anne softly called. "You have a beautiful daughter waiting to meet you."

Sybil struggled to lift heavy lids, intent on seeing the amazingly small being so hard to give life. At last weary eyes opened a fraction and a gentle smile curved pale lips. "So precious." The words were a mere whisper, more seen than heard above the healthy child's wails.

The new mother's smile seemed a reflection of the Madonna Anne had once glimpsed pictured in the cathedral at Westminster—pure and loving. Intending to lend privacy to this first meeting between mother and daughter, Anne stepped away and moved to gaze out from the window whose shutters Gilfrey had left open.

Warmed by relief for the newborn's well-being, Anne smiled in self-mockery at her peculiar fancy when she seemed to hear a faint echo of the babe's vigorous cries. As she absently stared into the murky night an unexpected break in the thick cloud cover sent a shaft of moonlight across the low tide–revealed causeway far below. A movement caught her attention. Eyes narrowed, she straightened to peer out. 'Twas odd. No one would willing leave the safety of the castle-fortress alone during dark hours, yet someone moved across that narrow pathway. A shadowy figure—not tall but a person either heavy or one with a bundle beneath flowing cloak.

ᜩ Chapter 1 ᜩ

Late Summer of 1216

Shhh, you'll wake Randolf." As Amicia sank down amidst tall meadow grass, her soft cautionary words slid into muffled laughter beneath the hand she pressed tight to sweetly curved lips.

By sending her off to pick berries of doubtful need for the evening meal, Orva had provided the excuse for this momentary freedom. In appreciation, Amicia had thrown her arms about the plump castle cook who looked like one of her own honeyed apple dumplings. Orva was an ally, and Orva understood Amicia's need for time free from the constant criticism in the dark shadow one man spread across Castle Dungeld, threatening to suffocate her. Given the opportunity for even a temporary escape, she'd run to fetch her friend, Kelda, then led the way over the causeway between island stronghold and the mainland's forest. They'd traveled up through dense grown trees to reach this meadow with its berry bush border. And all the while their serf-guardsman had lumbered along behind, a harmless giant of whom, truth be known, both girls were fond.

"Nothing will bestir Randolf now that the lazy oaf's fed and napping." In a show of courage Kelda tilted a softly rounded chin and squared sturdy shoulders while Amicia's restrained amusement found escape through the golden lights sparkling in her warm brown eyes.

At the sound of his name, the "lazy oaf" struggled through bleary layers of sleep to sit up. "You needs me, Mistress Kelda?" With slow determination he rolled to his feet and took a step toward them.

Dark blue eyes widened. "Nay—" Her voice came out a strangled squeak. "We're just talking. Pay us no mind." She smiled weakly and with feigned casualness waved him back to his shady spot beneath a tree clearly not distant enough.

Once Randolf had again settled into the welcoming shade beneath a huge oak, blue eyes faintly accusing, Kelda fell to the ground beside her friend. Although at crossgrain to her nature, Kelda ever sought to emulate the adventurous Amicia, but always 'twas she who got caught. It wasn't fair that, though she was a good hand's height taller and of more robust build, the slender Amicia was the courageous one. Not that Kelda minded being follower rather than leader. Following behind another was an infinitely safer position to be in, and she privately admitted her preference for security.

"You'd make a poor Maid Marian—getting caught every time." Amicia affectionately teased her companion.

"Right you are. I'm not destined to be an outlaw." Kelda lifted her chin and shrugged her shoulders in exaggerated unconcern. "Far rather had I be the fair Queen Guinevere at noble King Arthur's side." Grinning, she plunked an earlier-woven circlet of wild flowers atop her neatly coiled dark braids.

Amicia sat up, pushing tawny locks of free tumbling hair back from her smiling face and brushing spears of grass from the sleeves of her plain daywork gown. She drew her knees up, wrapped her arms about them, and rested her chin atop. Staring dreamily into green shadows, she consciously welcomed romantic fantasies, mentally replacing harsh realities with their hazy warmth. Always a pleasant escape and the more enjoyable after the previous night's rare visit of a traveling minstrel. All in the castle had avidly listened to him sing tales of a new hero, tales that provided fresh grist to the mill of Amicia's active imagination. The whole afternoon she and Kelda had been debating this Robin Hood's merits as opposed to the long-heralded King Arthur. She was proud to acknowledge that her stepfather's distaste for the common folks' hero influenced her own preference for the Wolf's Head. Even the passing thought of Gilfrey was a dreary blight on an otherwise bright summer day.

Seeing Amicia's eyes go dark as golden happiness faded, Kelda put into words what she assumed her friend was thinking. "'Struth, it matters little what sort of men we dream about. Others will choose those we must wed and with no thought to our wishes, least of all to the perfect love of the minstrels' songs." She disconsolately pulled the flower chaplet from her head.

"Saints' Tears," Amicia lightly scolded. "You know very well your parents will never force you to take for spouse a man you dislike." Amicia took the flower crown from limp fingers and with a cheering grin placed it again upon the other's dark head. If her smile was tinged with cynicism, 'twas not lack of confidence in the certainty of Kelda's future happiness that put it there. "You may not wed King Arthur or any other of royal blood yet marry a young and pleasing man you will, but if I do not wed a Wolf's Head, I'll likely be mated to some ancient dotard hungry for my dowry—but not until I'm a dotard myself."

Kelda's expression went solemn. Amicia had offered an encouragement she could not with honesty return. What Amicia had said was true. Amicia was seventeen already and she only a few months behind, both far beyond the age when most girls marry. Doubtless 'twas a fact, her parents would one day see her happily wed. But, although Lord Gilfrey constantly taunted Amicia with threats to see her soon bound either to a man infamous for cruelty or great age, he seemed determined to postpone any commitment that would promise the taking of her natural father's fiefdom to another at his death. The whole demesne knew was so. Often and loudly he'd complained about his lack of male heir leaving him with only the daughter of another man to inherit—as inevitable as the certainty that one day a husband would claim both it and her, yet something he seemed determined to hinder to the last.

"Don't go sorrowful on me, else you'll wreak desolation upon our precious moments of liberty." As Amicia issued the stern order, she shook her head and set a wealth of honey-toned tresses to dancing. The sun-streaked, unbound waves and cheeks lightly tanned to a warm peach tone were proof of her independent spirit—small rebellions against Gilfrey's repressive hold. "Leastways for a short while we've escaped the wicked Dark Lord," she whispered as if beckoning the other into an exciting conspiracy. "So, let's fly away to our secret haven." Amicia paused, tilting her head and arching her brows. "Mayhap along the way we'll find either your legendary prince or my outlaw of the greenwood."

Kelda couldn't resist the smaller girl's teasing invitation and rose, taking great pains not to again disturb their loyal guardian's rest.

Reassured by Randolf's steady snore the two girls crept quietly to where he slept and carefully placed their full berry baskets in the shade near his prone form. Once more Amicia led the way. At the edge of the forest's verdant wall she swept aside a tall fern's curly fronds to reveal the path lightly marked by repeated trips. Feeling Kelda close behind, a smiling Amicia quietly wound her way through the dense undergrowth. These excursions were proof of Kelda's affection, for nothing else could have driven the

younger girl into such woodland adventures, at least
not without an armed protector. Despite Kelda's
ineffective shield of daring, Amicia knew her friend
better suited to the warm safety of hearth and home.
And, had Kelda not insisted since they were toddlers
on joining in everything she did, Amicia would never
have invited her on such exploits.

Arriving at the mossy bank of a sparkling stream,
they turned to follow its meandering route. The gently
flowing water's bubbling melody grew louder and
louder as other shining trickles met and blended in its
ever faster progress until at last it became a soft roar.

Face white with tension, Kelda slowed to a halt
several paces short of the precipice over which the
water that was now a small river poured in a gleaming
torrent. While her friend held back, Amicia unhesitat-
ingly moved to the edge and gazed down. She loved
the wild beauty of water tumbling free, cascading
down to end its fall with a glittering splash in a pool at
the base, sending forth ever widening ripples until
distant rings calmed into the gentle waves caressing
mossy banks. Surely this was an example of the
serenity which was the rightful reward for a triumphant struggle against unjust restraints.

Sparkling droplets sprayed out on the downward
journey looked like precious jewels scattered by faerie
hands, beckoning her to follow and enter the haven for
her dreams, a cool place where for a short time the
world of pretend would shelter her. 'Twas the only
place beyond the corridors of her mind where she was
safe to indulge in fantasies.

She'd held them protected, shared with Kelda
alone, since the day in the castle stairwell when a
yuletide gift had been wrenched from her hands by
the captain of the guard, who was sotted with the
wassail bowl's liquid cheer. An aging friend of her
mother's had patiently carved a unicorn from a small
piece of green quartz and polished it to a glow as
bright as her dreams. The too merry thief, holding the

treasured piece just beyond her reach and stumbling more than once, had backed all the way up the steps to the battlements, taunting her for believing childish legends. Then at the top he'd held the symbol of her dreams out-thrust through one deep dip in the crenellated wall. Later a sober Oswald had sworn he'd not intended to drop it, but 'twas all the same in the end—dashed against the rocks below and splintered into a myriad of useless crystal shards—and she'd never forgiven him.

"Kelda." Amicia glanced back, restraining her impatience to descend. "You need come no farther with me. Wait here in the shade and soon I'll return."

Kelda gazed longingly at the soft green cushion of moss on the edge of the stream where the forest's tightly entwined branches provided an inviting shelter but shook her head. "Nay, if a little tidbit like you can climb down a rock wall, then one as big as I assuredly can." She'd not play coward before the friend she'd admired all her life. Besides, likely it was no safer to sit alone in the forest—too many predators about, either four-legged or two. Amicia might dream of meeting forest outlaws, but not she and not alone!

Amicia saw both the thinness of her friend's brave mask and the quick, apprehensive look cast into the shadowed woodland surrounding them. Guessing the truth of the other's thoughts, she again sought to ease her way.

"I'll move down to the ledge and wait for you. Then should something untoward happen, I can break your fall."

Kelda's skeptical eyes measured the other from tawny head to dainty feet and plainly revealed her disbelief in the smaller girl's ability to fulfill what she promised. "I'll be fine. I've done it oft enough afore."

Having no wish to belittle Kelda's deeds, Amicia did not remind her of how often she'd had to demonstrate the path's safety before her friend had attempted the descent to the entrance of their secret place. Impervious to the muddy stains the action would lay on her homespun gown and the scolding they'd bring, Amicia settled on the damp grass at the edge of the sharp drop and scooted nearer to dangle one leg over the rim, feeling for the toehold a short distance below. Once found, with slender fingers tangled in green blades, she lowered herself, face to the rocky wall. Welcoming the cool kiss of the waterfall's spray, she moved steadily downward to a ledge halfway between cliff top and pool, and wide enough to stand upon unaided while looking up to encourage her timorous friend.

Kelda closed her eyes, clearly offering a desperate plea for divine aid with a safe descent, and when they opened again determination darkened their blue depths.

Watching as the larger girl began the trip, Amicia, not for the first time, acknowledged how very different they were. Indeed, it was amazing that they were so close. Sir Jasper and Anne had raised their daughter as a well-bred woman aught be, but though they'd tried to instill the same virtues of quiet restraint in Amicia, they'd failed. Praise be that they, unlike her stepfather, blamed her neither for her lacks nor her impetuous nature. Rather they were amused, had even told her they were pleased that she took after her impulsive natural father, Baron Conal. Amicia was proud to have been found worthy of the father who, by all accounts, had been a warm and open man, well-loved by his peers and lessers alike.

When the two girls at last stood side by side, Amicia gave Kelda a wide approving smile, then carefully turned and moved straight toward the wildly tumbling river. It tickled her fancy that anyone standing on the pool's bank below would be stunned by the sight of two figures magically vanishing into the waterfall's shimmering spray. In reality they slipped inside a cave hidden behind the wall of rushing liquid.

Once inside their retreat, only dimly lit by the

shifting patterns of sunlight through water, Amicia glanced at the ring of stones in its center, a fire pit laid out by some long-forgot inhabitant.

"One day," she idly mused, "I'll bring one live coal in a small brazier and start a cheery fire." Amicia let fanciful visions of a cosy hideaway fill her thoughts as she spread out the poor homespun blanket not missed in the castle and smuggled here with little trouble. Aye, a cosy hideaway shared with her imaginary hero—a dark and handsome outlaw of the greenwood who avenged injustice and loved her with appropriate romantic admiration.

Amicia's words sank through Kelda's relief at having safely arrived, and she gave her friend a dubious look. "How, pray tell, will you explain the need for a brazier on a daylit berry-picking trip?"

"I'll say I'm going to cook the berries to brew my own fruit wine—or I'll pretend a desire to distill perfume from the meadow's abundant flowers." Such tasks could nowise be performed in the wild, but Amicia couldn't resist this gentle teasing of her easily gulled companion.

Skeptically watching as the smaller girl's soft hand smoothed the last corner of the rough cloth square, Kelda was certain the other was only fooling—almost certain. She feared Amicia just daring enough to attempt such a foolhardy scheme.

A faint rumble of masculine laughter rose above the sound of the falling river. Amicia's brows puckered, and without an instant's thought to possible danger she quickly moved to the front of the cave. Peering through a crystal wall of rushing water erratically shot through with white froth like the shattered edges of precious glass, not turning, she energetically motioned Kelda to join her.

The curiosity roused by her friend's fascination with the view overwhelmed Kelda's inbred caution. She eased forward until she stood only a step behind the smaller figure. One glance over Amicia's shoulder sent her scurrying back into the shadows of the cave's deepest recesses.

Barely registering the other's reaction, Amicia leaned further out. She strained to hear the words spoken by a tall, dark man whose striking appearance relegated even her dream hero to the realms of the merely average-blessed.

"Carl, you and Walter follow the pool's outgoing stream to the village of Brayston . . ."

Amicia's hands curled together with frustration when a small log caught in tumbling waters splashed into the pool and momentarily drowned out his words. Thoughts so recently filled with romantic tales of Robin Hood and fantasies of meeting such a one, inevitably if illogically, she wondered if some friendly sorcerer had given life to her dreams. These men below, were they, could they be forest outlaws? Excitement halted breath in her throat, and her heart pounded while she listened to talk all too oft swept away by the water's roar.

". . . valley at stream's foot while I . . . and through the forest . . . ocean's edge . . . the famous Castle Dungeld—from a safe distance."

The likelihood of meeting men same as those made legendary in tales of the common folk and sung of by foolish minstrels was remote. Yet even the remote possibility was so appealing that the few barbed twinges attacking the tower of her wistful hopes were soon vanquished. After all, what other purpose would bring strangers to the forests of Tarrant? People hereabouts were poor, and 'twas not a place frequented by wealthy travelers. Thus, it could hold no lure for common brigands. Moreover, these strangers were without identifying standard or the livery of any lord. The small but stubborn voice of reason refused to be easily silenced and argued, they had horses as surely Robin Hood did not. Mayhap, she dismissed even this discrepancy, these men were simply more skillful and by their success better outfitted—it *must* be so.

While questions mated with convenient answers rushed through her mind, brown eyes never wavered from the man who'd gone down on one knee beside the stream and in cupped hands lifted cooling water to his lips. His bent head hid an uncommonly handsome face yet gave a finer view of the ebony hair brushing the collar of his equally dark cloak. She'd never before seen hair so black that it reflected sunlight with a white gleam and wondered if it were truly as thick as it looked. Experience limited to the men of the castle guard and rare visitors, she hadn't realized a man could be so beautiful—not soft like a woman but stunningly masculine. When he looked up, she fell into eyes the same pale green as the crystal unicorn, and it seemed an omen. Here was the breathing, human embodiment of that creature of dreams.

Soothing liquid slid down a parched and welcoming throat. Autumn might be looming on the calendar of seasons but the sun was bright. (Although they'd ridden through a dim forest, muggy air laid upon Galen Fitz William as heavily as the chain mail that he traveled without for nearly the first time in his score and eight years.) At least they were finally on Wryborne lands. He only wished he knew precisely why.

Still on one knee at the pool's edge, he gazed around the quiet glade for the first time since Baron Conal's murder—he'd never viewed the hideous deed as a lesser crime. At foster with his parents' close friends, he and Sir Jasper's oldest son had been granted the privilege of accompanying the men on a hunt. The hunt which had culminated in the foul end to his foster father's life. As an eleven-year-old page, he'd been immediately summoned home to Tarrant. Although a break with traditional methods, his training had been completed by his father, Earl Garrick. It was a decision which had gone unquestioned, for a finer warrior or better teacher there never was and Galen had learned military skills second to none.

His father and King John were enemies of old; and, though the king dare not insult so powerful a lord, the earl had hesitated to place either his wife within the lecherous man's vicinity or his son within a king's vengeful power. Thus, Galen had accompanied the king on none of his oft-lost campaigns and had been given the opportunity to prove his worth at arms only in bright tourneys, mock games of war. That his father had faith in him Galen had never doubted, but many among his peers, mayhap jealous of such trust or more likely his inherited position and wealth, had not been so believing.

Staring blindly into his wavering reflection on the pond's gently rippling surface, Galen's mouth curved in a wry smile. Only when the baronage banded together and rose to force their reluctant monarch to reaffirm rights theirs from ancient times but by the king badly abused, had he been able to show himself more than the spoiled heir to the Earldom of Tarrant. Galen the son had proven himself an equal to his sire, the famous Ice Warrior. Together the two had fought common foes, then stood side by side on the field at Runnymede the summer past while John put his royal seal to the Great Charter. Unfortunately their untrustworthy king had almost immediately revoked the document, leaving his baronage so frustrated that some among them had invited the French to come and take the English throne by force—a rash step that neither Galen nor his father supported. Returning to their mighty fortress, they'd closely watched the conflict while quietly occupying themselves with caring for the lands and vassals of their fiefdom. Galen had rejoined the fray only once when foreign foes carried the fight too near, threatening the peace of Tarrant. Leading a mighty force, he'd driven the French into retreat from Tarrant's borders—a victory from which he'd barely returned when a strange letter had arrived from Castle Dungeld.

'Twas a challenge, this coming to the rescue of a fair lady and one made all the sweeter by the fact that it was in aid of his foster mother, a serene woman of moonbeam hair and gentle smile. He'd not seen her since that day close to two decades past when as a boy he'd bid farewell to Wryborne.

If only he knew what peril he and his small band, with neither metal armor nor shield of noble heritage, had come to defeat. Protected only by his skill and wits, 'twas an exciting challenge. Nonetheless, he'd have preferred a more specific description of the quest's purpose than Lady Sybil's simple message that danger threatened. Saints' Tears, why had she claimed she dare put no more into written words—leaving him to discover and vanquish a vague looming threat.

Gilfrey, her unworthy second spouse, was as much the enemy of Galen's parents as the king who'd given Sybil into his hands. Thus, well known and recognizable they could not openly come to their friend. Likely Gilfrey would have exercised his rights as husband and refused to allow any meeting between them. Moreover, their arrival would put the venomous man on his guard which, until they knew the source of the danger she feared, they must not do. To circumvent these obstacles, Galen had come as a common wayfarer, intending to neither claim nor deny any identity. A strategy planned to avoid the lies he'd been raised to believe were the worst of crimes and the biggest stain a man could lay against his honor.

Lifting another handful of water to his lips, Galen congratulated himself on remembering the perfect place to camp, a hidden haven where they could rest secure even should pursuers threaten. He chose not to share the news with his companions until they returned from assigned chores and smiling, pleased with the thought, he gazed up to the waterfall's midpoint.

Pale green eyes flashed with silver. Amidst the jeweled spray and shifting gleam of falling water intermittent glimpses of a beautiful face appeared. Sensible thoughts scattered beneath the enchanting sight. He shot a quick glance at his two companions. They'd had their fill of liquid refreshments and with no indication of a shared vision had returned to laughingly baiting each other.

Galen rubbed water-chilled hands over his face before looking back to the waterfall—only the image was gone. Still, the alluring fantasy shimmered un-dimmed in his thoughts. A water sprite? One of the spirits whom the ancients had believed ensouled all nature? He shook his head at so witless a notion. Once more he cupped his hands to lift a bowl of cold liquid but this time he buried his face within. The bracing chill failed to purge the image from his mind's eye—lovely and strangely familiar.

⊰§ *Chapter 2* §⊱

Best tarry no longer," Amicia whispered as the men at last vanished into the forest's green wall.

"Tarry, hah!" Under the strain of her growing tension, Kelda's response was nearly a hiss. "We've been trapped by your hero in the flesh—which surely proves how untrustworthy are these probable outlaws."

"Hardly their fault." Amicia struggled to restrain the grin trying to break free. "We took pains to hide our presence." Kelda shared with most others a suspicious view of strangers. Amicia stepped from the cave and carefully walked the ledge to the point where they'd descended. Certain they were now alone, with complete disregard for propriety, she hiked up the golden brown skirt of her simple garb and tucked its hem under the braided leather belt riding low on her hips, leaving her legs bare to the knee as she began the climb.

Kelda was fearful of being left behind and rushed to follow. Yet, not so brave as the smaller girl, dark blue eyes glanced apprehensively about the quiet, green-shadowed glade before she lifted her skirts and then only so high as absolutely necessary for safety's sake. With the unthinking confidence born of an oft-repeated action, Amicia's small feet sought and found each near-invisible hold in the rock wall. She'd wondered many times before who'd carved this vertical stairway to and from a hidden haven, but today the memory of silvery-green eyes outlined by lashes near as thick and black as the hair that framed a strong face, surely all of masculine perfection, left no room for other thoughts. Her imagination formed hazy romantic visions of the stunning man in heroic battle to save his lady-fair—herself, of course. A battle against injustice, against a most dastardly villain— Gilfrey. Who more dastardly than he? Wrapped in the world of fantasy, she was surprised when her hand came to rest on the plateau above but lost no time scrambling up. She wiped dust from berry-stained hands on skirts pulled free to modestly brush the ground once more.

"Pray God, Randolf hasn't gone to fetch help in finding us," Kelda gasped as she hauled herself up and stepped thankfully away from the precipice. "If the baron hears we've gone missing again, he'll blame my parents."

The probability rolled a dark cloud over Amicia's rosy dreams. Although she delighted in pricking Sir Gilfrey in any way she could, Amicia had no wish to see either Sir Jasper or Anne punished for her misdeeds. The possibility had simply never occurred to her. Victim of her own impetuous nature, all too often she failed to pause long enough to consider the possible results of her actions. 'Twas a fault she'd time and again sworn to conquer yet plainly had not. Giving her head a brief shake that set sunlight to burning on the streaks of gold in her honey-hued hair, she impatiently reminded herself that now was no time for self-recriminations.

"Then we dare not waste another moment." Amicia whirled and dashed into the dense undergrowth, heedless of foliage that dragged at skirts and thorns that scratched. Kelda followed close behind. The two breathless girls broke through the woodland's wall and tumbled into the meadow just in time to see a flustered Randolf on its far edge lumbering toward the outgoing forest path.

"Randolf, wait for us!" Kelda's desperate wail pierced the afternoon peace.

Expression torn between relief and irritation, Randolf turned to glower at the girls hurrying to his side with penitent smiles and pleading eyes.

"I'm of a mind to tells your father, Mistress Kelda, how you slipped away again so as I near had to call him to fetch you home—by boat." Likely the causeway betwixt mainland and Castle Dungeld's isle was near tide-hidden already.

'Twas a powerful threat, one which left both girls cringing. Randolf savored the moment of power although he was too fond of them to carry it out. Sir Jasper hated traveling by boat and did so only under dire need. Thus 'twas certain the girls would rue the day they forced him to such an action. And if not by Sir Jasper's irritation, then certainly by the baron's black rage.

"If we linger much longer," Amicia pointed out, "it won't matter as they'll have no choice but to send a boat for us all."

At the mere suggestion that his threatened woe might in truth occur, Randolf's broad, ruddy face turned a sickly shade of white—proof his had been an idle threat. Anxiety-frozen, Randolf stood rooted to the spot while Kelda moaned her dismay. Mentally leaping past the dread that immobilized her companions, Amicia spun to lead a race through towering trees and clumps of foliage. Despite the haste of their retreat when they arrived at the shore they found waves sloshing across the causeway. Amicia's shoulders slumped. Yet, never willing to easily admit defeat and determined that Sir Jasper not be made to do what he detested or Randolf be punished for an error of hers, she again lifted her skirts to the knee and boldly strode into the briny water. This immediate challenge drove from her mind all thoughts of the outlaw and his stated intent to view the castle from the sea's edge.

By the time she'd reached the far end of the natural bridge near lost beneath rising tide, the skirt she loosed once more was wet and clung damply to legs sticky with sea water. Moreover, her shoes squished unpleasantly as she ascended the narrow, winding path to castle gate. She'd doubtless have the devil's own time explaining both her distressing condition and her companions'.

While they passed under the day-raised portcullis and traversed the tunnel through the fortress's wide stone wall the low-riding sun drenched the clear sky with a pale rose glow. Amicia, intent on slipping unnoticed into the tower, saw neither the sky's beauty nor the strange horse in the stable into whose dark shadows she dashed. The low wooden structure that leaned against the towering curtain wall at one side of the entrance gate was large enough to hold the garrison's steeds and a great many more beside. She'd been told it had often been full while her father was lord, but such a possibility never occurred to her as visitors had been rare since Gilfrey had usurped his place shortly before her birth. Her attention focused on the exit at the stable's far end which opened no more than a few steps from the kitchen's rear access to the castle proper.

Reaching the portal not meant for common daily use, relief flooded through Amicia and in its wake left pleasure for the successful conclusion of a dangerous adventure, a near disaster averted by daring. As she stepped into a second dim hallway through thick stone, her satisfaction came to an abrupt halt.

"My lost lambs have come home—and none too soon." Exasperation strained Anne's normally cheerful voice. She knew them well enough to await a return so late at the back entrance.

Kelda ineffectually sought to hide from her mother the shoes whose wetness had turned to mud on the dusty path while Amicia—with a bright smile which she prayed would distract from their bedraggled appearance—drew a deep breath and spoke. "Orva sent us to pick berries for the evening meal."

"An unsuccessful quest?" Anne's brows rose above eyes that pointedly studied their empty hands.

Amicia's lashes dropped in momentary vexation. Not until that moment had she realized that in their haste to catch Randolf, they'd forgotten the filled baskets.

Kelda gasped, "We left them in the meadow!"

"'Tis a fine thing that Orva knows better than to count on your contributions." Anne slowly shook her head, patience sorely strained by worry over their close escape from bringing the baron's anger down upon them all, a risk too oft taken. Really, despite her sympathy with the young beauty's determination to never bend willingly beneath the hostility Gilfrey heaped upon her, Amicia must grow up and learn to think before she acted, to recognize that the dangers she tempted were a threat to others as well as to herself.

"We'll talk on the importance of carrying through with our responsibilities later." Anne saw a quick grin pass between the two girls and sharply added, "Soon!"

The girls recognized their error and quickly stifled their smiles. When two appropriately solemn faces were turned to her, Anne continued.

"Trestle tables are already being assembled for the evening meal so waste no time in washing—you've no time now for your usual bath—and donning appropriate gowns." They'd need to change out of homespun daywear in any event but, wanting them to know she recognized the evidence of their near too late return, Anne's narrowed eyes closely examined their drenched skirts and muddied hems.

Only one of the girls was her natural daughter, yet

she'd stood as mother to the other almost from the moment of her birth. After Sybil had been vilely robbed of her beloved Conal, the one-time postulant had seemed to lose all incentive to linger in the temporal world and instead retreated deeper and deeper into the spiritual realms she'd been trained to inhabit. Sybil's withdrawal had proved a most effective denial of Gilfrey's unworthy claims, but Amicia's impulsive rebellions were likely as much a response to a mother's remoteness as an instinctive, even understandable, response to a stepfather's cruelty.

Feeling as if they'd been granted a reprieve, however brief, the two girls exchanged another conspiratorial glance and turned to hurry up a narrow flight of stairs.

"Choose what you wear with care," Anne called after them. "And, Amicia, you *will* braid your hair and wear both a headdress and barbet."

Startled, Amicia stopped again, delicate brows lifted in surprise as she looked back at the older woman. Seldom did Anne insist on such propriety for a family meal.

"We've a guest. Leastways tonight a guest, although from this day on he'll be a member of our household."

"Who?" Questions gleaming gold in her eyes and thoughts filled with irrational pictures of the magnificent dark stranger sitting at her side for the evening meal, Amicia took a step toward the speaker.

The two expectant faces turned to Anne radiated the same extravagant hopes of a child at Christmastide and near brought her to laughter. Her lips twitched, but she restrained her amusement and shooed them off, thankful for a curiosity certain to lend speed to their preparations.

Determined to do what was needful and descend to the great hall in all good time, the two girls had reached the top of the steps and nearly bypassed the corridor's wide opening into a kitchen crowded with castle-serfs intent on their duties when they heard an unmistakable tut-tutting. A small mountain stood in their path, arms akimbo.

"Orva, we picked the berries. Truly we did." Kelda rushed to assure the frowning woman.

Amicia grinned at the rotund cook striving for a ferocious scowl but succeeding in appearing no more threatening than an irritated partridge, feathers plumped and strutting. She added an admission to the younger girl's words. "We left our baskets, full baskets, in the meadow." Her affectionate smile slid into a grimace. "But we'll go back on the morrow and fetch them." She hadn't left them behind apurpose, but might well have had she thought on it. Her grin returned and deepened. Should their evening guest not be the handsome outlaw, the forgotten baskets provided a fine excuse for again visiting the forest where she would seek a far more satisfying face-to-face meeting.

"That you will not, for I been warned to give you no more excuses to be gone." Orva wagged her finger at them but the admonishing effect was ruined when the stern glower accompanying it dissolved into her usual merry grin.

Laughing, Amicia hugged the well-padded cook, a gesture of true affection but also one that hid the determination to have her own way which burned in her eyes from one who would recognize it for precisely what it was. Both the kitchen and the tower stairway were located behind the great hall's dais and shared a common entrance to the huge room resounding with the clatter of tables being prepared for the coming meal. Their need for haste reinforced by the sound, the two girls hurried to the castle's highest level and entered the small bedchamber they shared adjacent to that occupied by Lady Anne and Sir Jasper.

Once inside the cramped room, while one girl poured water from the ewer into its basin, the other gathered up two cloth squares and both quickly rinsed away the dust of their day's adventure. Thus re-

freshed, Amicia faced a simple decision lent an unusual significance by the remote possibility of the dark
stranger as visitor. Anne had often muttered over the
severe limitations of a noble-born maid's wardrobe,
but never until now had Amicia been concerned by its
lacks.

"I wonder who this guest can be?" Kelda mused
aloud while changing into a deep blue camise. Pulling
a dove gray gown over head, she glanced behind to see
Amicia reach for a dress the hue of sun-blushed
peaches, and her eyes widened when she saw the
dreamy expression on the smaller girl's face. "Oh, no.
Surely not!"

"'Tis wool, I know, and a questionable choice."
Amicia purposely misunderstood her friend's dismay
and justified her selection. "But of a light weight and,
thanks to stone walls of such width, 'tis always cool
inside even when summer's heat makes a last stand."
Besides, she'd been told it flattered her creamy
complexion—a thing suddenly important.

Never had Kelda been successful in arguing sense
with Amicia. Now she did not even try, merely
shaking her head anxiously as Amicia slipped on a
fine linen underblouse whose long, tight sleeves would
softly ruche at the wrists. While Amicia added the
peach gown, Kelda loosed her dark locks from restraints disarranged during their hasty return to the
isle.

Soon both girls had brushed, plaited, and coiled
shiny braids into net crespins at the back of their
necks. After donning the cloth strips which smoothed
under their chins to outline young faces and the
starched head bands that held them in place, they
were ready to descend and satisfy their curiosity.

Bubbling with anticipation for an unlikely meeting
with her hero come to life, Amicia nearly danced
down steep stairs intermittently lit by wavering oil-fed
sconces. Kelda, forced by her natural caution to go
slow, followed at a more sedate pace. Still Kelda

caught up with Amicia who seemed frozen in the shadowed archway. The taller girl easily peered over Amicia's slumped shoulders and from behind those seated on the dais a short distance away saw the reason for her dejection. Dusty brown hair and a back which owed its breadth more to overabundant food than muscle definitely did not belong to the attractive outlaw. Amicia was clearly disheartened, but Kelda, leery of any extreme, was relieved. Didn't the priests teach that the Scriptures cautioned temperance in all things? Surely a man so exceptionally handsome as the stranger at the waterfall harbored some fearful and dangerous lack—mayhap in honor and all too likely in honesty.

Pushing disappointment aside, Amicia squared her shoulders and lifted her dainty chin. 'Twas best that their guest was not the one she'd hoped, elsewise he'd have to be a friend of her stepfather's and that would be even more disheartening. Nay, far better that the handsome stranger at the pool be truly a forest outlaw, a man by profession at odds with Gilfrey. That pleasant thought turned her mind to the fantasy wherein she and the outlaw joined to battle against injustice. Immediately she began devising schemes to see this fantasy become as real as her hero. As a first step she must find some method to win free of castle restraints and escape to the forest on the morrow. The challenge revived her spirits and enabled her to bravely meet this visitor who'd been given the chair she normally occupied on Gilfrey's left. Amicia marched toward the dais. He was more than welcome to the position she had never enjoyed.

While Kelda slipped past to join her parents at the midpoint of one long line of lower tables, the lady of the castle looked up from her seat at the right of a never-accepted husband to meet Amicia's smile. Lady Sybil's fragile fingers wrapped about the heavy gold crucifix lying on the black garb of mourning she'd never put off as if 'twere an amulet against evil. 'Twas one more barrier between her and the man whose wicked spite had curdled so long within that it had turned to sour acid, eating him from inside out.

"You're late," Gilfrey growled, glaring eyes stabbing at his prey.

Although a lover of adventure and willing risk-taker, Amicia wasn't nearly so courageous against human foes as others supposed, but never would she admit the lack. Merely had she assumed a mask of false bravado so oft everyone believed it real, never seeing the maid quivering beneath. Knowing that if ever she allowed fear to break the facade she wore, she'd be left defenseless, Amicia called on talents honed by experience and gave her constant tormentor a cheeky grin as she stepped up and started to pull back the chair at her mother's side.

When Amicia moved to take the seat next to her, Sybil felt the girl's tension. She admired her daughter's valiant spirit and wished she dare see that Amicia understand they each, in their own way, rebelled against a common oppressor. Lowering her gaze to hands now palm-joined, Sybil prayed that one day she could explain her decision to never lay in Gilfrey's cruel hands a weapon so potent as a mother's love. She prayed, too, for strength to continue hiding it behind a religious fervor that, though true, did not exclude her child.

"Not there," Gilfrey's snarl was low but impossible to ignore. "Sit in the chair next to your usual place, as you will from this night on—while my son sits at my left."

Amicia had been prepared for a visitor meant to become part of the household, yet she was startled by the announcement of his identity. Her lady-mother was Gilfrey's first and only wife. Thus, 'twas plain that this son was not of legitimate line and his presence an intended insult.

A mocking sneer spread Gilfrey's thin lips wide. Sybil might have withdrawn so far from the world as to suffer no discomfort under his deed, but Amicia recognized and felt the affront. It was enough to gratify him—for the moment. He'd wait and in silence savor the impending execution of his ultimate vengeance.

Amicia watched cruel satisfaction grow in Gilfrey's expression and wanted nothing more than to tell him precisely what type of venomous snake he was. Yet she knew it would only delight him with the knowledge that he'd succeeded in irritating her. Instead she gave him a smile of blinding sweetness and moved to the high-backed chair he commanded she take.

"As always, kind sir, I appreciate your providing me with the boons I most earnestly seek. A seat at the table's far end is truly the answer to earnest prayers." Her words were soft and the thread of amusement at their core lent just the right touch of mockery to deflate his self-contentment—like a gentle breeze which with the slightest puff scatters a dandelion's fluff. Happily her tormentor's rage-blurred eyes failed to see fingertips turned white by the strength of their angry hold on chair back or notice that trembling knees stole grace so that she nearly fell into her seat.

Pressing palm-joined hands against pale lips, Sybil watched the exchange of unpleasantries from beneath lowered lashes. Here at this table was the future Gilfrey had taunted her with, and there was so very little she could do to forestall its fulfillment. Tell her loyal friends, Anne and Jasper, could she never. They'd no power to do more than she herself, but too likely they would try—earning a harsh punishment. Only could she earnestly pray Merciful Mary, Mother of God, to intercede on her child's behalf, to see that her message safely reached Tarrant and the powerful friends she'd had no contact with since Conal's death. Moreover, for a rescue quest blessed with success, she'd pledged to enter a convent and fully commit her life to God's service.

Platters bearing a fine selection of foodstuffs were

delivered to the tables by castle-serfs. No well-born men, not even his vassals, chose to send their sons to Gilfrey for tutoring. Thus, unlike most noble homes, there were no pages to serve. None of the four at the high table spoke for a time after the task was complete, and then it was Amicia who turned with a forced smile to the young man supposedly sharing her trencher but who, in little more than a moment, had seemed to inhale the whole.

"It seems we are not to be formally introduced, so I must tell you that I am Amicia, and ask what you are called." From the corner of her eye, she saw Gilfrey go rigid and was pleased that her softly barbed words had pierced his armor of self-complacency to sting with their reminder of his lack of social skill. It added a warmth to her smile which widened her companion's light blue eyes and momentarily robbed him of speech.

With a mouth crammed full of crusty bread, the one no longer an adolescent yet still struggling to be a man answered, "Fa . . . r . . . d."

The sound was so garbled that even had she not been startled by the rude sight, Amicia wouldn't have been able to understand.

The poor creature recognized his error and turned a brilliant crimson. Swallowing hard, he attempted to correct his mistake. "I am known as Farrold." He burned with embarrassment and couldn't meet the beauty's surely sneering gaze.

Ever a defender of the misused, Amicia's soft heart bled for Gilfrey's unlikely weapon, and she tactfully carried on as if naught had gone amiss. "Farrold? 'Tis an unusual name."

His blush deepened.

"I like unusual names," Amicia calmly continued. "It seems to me there are far too many Stephens and Henrys. When you call out, six people answer. Far better to be unique."

Farrold peeked at her suspiciously. Few proper-blooded and still fewer beauties bothered be kind to one bastard born. Yet her gentle smile was sincere and won his trust in an instant. Before he knew what he was about, a shyly smiling Farrold was telling her of the small freehold where he'd been raised.

While Amicia appeared to listen patiently, her errant thoughts wandered to a tall, dark man whose lean grace and penetrating gaze was all that this unhappy boy was not and likely could never become. That glimpse of her ideal, though brief and seen through falling water, was impossible to drive from her mind.

Farrold's smile faded into stern lines when he spoke of being sent to foster in one of King John's lesser fiefdoms. The emotionless words made it plain that the experience had been an unhappy one although he proudly stated that he'd won his spurs and had been honorably serving in his foster father's garrison when called to Castle Dungeld.

Unnoticed, Gilfrey listened while Farrold quietly spoke of his fostering. Hearing every forlorn word, he steamed. He'd teach the sapling boy to show less than due appreciation for what had been given. After all, he could as well have left the unwanted brat to a serf's lot. Gilfrey nearly wished he'd followed that course. Only the then-secret plan to claim a barren widow as wife and the resulting fear that he'd have no legitimate son had driven him to do more. Aye, a poor excuse for a man Farrold might be, yet the only chance Gilfrey had to complete the all-important vengeance he'd plotted, nay, carefully nurtured for near three decades.

"Mayhap you would care to give my son a tour of my demesne on the morrow?" Gilfrey's emphasis of what belonged to him was meant to grate on Amicia's nerves and succeeded, but through long practice she hid her instinctive distaste.

"A fine idea." And a fine idea it was, Amicia wordlessly affirmed. Knowing that even Orva couldn't provide her with an excuse for slipping off into the wilds, the prospect of using her stepfather's suggestion for doing what she was elsewise forbidden pleased Amicia no end. "Kelda and I will happily ride out with him."

The golden sparks of laughter in Amicia's eyes and the wide grin that seemed to harbor a secret jest pricked Gilfrey with a discomfort he could not identify, an inability which irritated him the more.

·⋙§ *Chapter 3* §⋘·

Amicia's plan was going exceedingly well. As she dropped over the precipice near the cascade of glittering water, the warm sun on her back and the cool spray on her face intensified her excitement and anticipation. When the dawn added yet another perfect day to the stretch of a late-season spell of exceptional warmth, it had seemed a positive omen. Her good fortune had held when Kelda proved more agreeable than expected to the task of keeping Farrold occupied during their afternoon tour. Moreover, the young knight had seemed to neither notice nor care as she slipped away from where he sat with the plainly admiring maid. She should have known Kelda was smitten by her determination to wear a fine linen dress in a flattering periwinkle blue rather than the sturdy homespun normally worn for days in the wild. But then her own choice of garb, a homespun gown dyed a deep forest green, had been dictated by her certainty that a well-born woman would be unwelcome to an outlaw.

She'd no doubt that the outlaws would return. The secluded glade was too perfect a haven for them to pass by. And when from her secret viewpoint she saw them arrive, she meant to step from the cave and invite them to share its ideal cover. Surely they'd be grateful, and how better to begin the friendship she sought. Distracted by pleasant possibilities and in haste to give them life, Amicia wedged her toes into the wrong crevice.

"Whoa." Unsteady stone gave way. She instinctively flattened herself against the rock face while her foot and a scattering of rocks slid freely down. Heart pounding so hard it drowned out even the water's soft roar, before she'd fully realized her danger, Amicia thankfully found herself resting on the narrow but solid ledge leading to the cave entrance.

Crinkling her nose against the pungent odor of damp earth disturbed and greenery broken by her clutching fingers, she gingerly eased away from the suddenly untrustworthy wall, and glanced down. Hoping the dirt her garb had gathered in the descent could easily be got rid of, she brushed a palm over the worst streaks and smiled as they disappeared. Time enough once she was safe inside to clear the rest away. Shafts of sunlight filtered through the towering trees edging both the pool below and the cliff top above to gleam on the falling river toward which she carefully moved.

First passing from bright daylight into the flickering shadows beneath tumbling water, Amicia then turned into the cave whose cool gloom momentarily blinded her. Without pausing for eyes to adjust, she stepped confidently forward—and into an unyielding wall, one not of cold stone but of living flesh. She jumped back. Only the two iron bands which of a sudden fastened about her upper arms and jerked her tight against a broad expanse of hard muscle saved her from a violent end to the foolish action that near toppled her into the water's downward plunge.

"God's Teeth, child. Think before you act!"

The deep velvet voice rolled from the chest beneath

Amicia's ear. An experience so oddly exciting that she wanted only to cling to the source, at least until her pulse ceased its fearful thundering. Two near fatal accidents in so short a span of time were more than even her adventurous spirit could deal with.

Finding himself in the arms of a maid who clung like a limpet, Galen was disconcerted. He'd come to the cave entrance expecting the return of young Walter only to be the receiver of a tempting bundle of soft curves and honey-silk tresses. Seldom in his life had he been uncertain what action to take and never with regard to a member of the frailer half of humankind.

"Galen!" Carl's call was a teasing admonishment.

Lifting his hands, palm-up, on either side, the one addressed demonstrated his innocence of the implied wrongdoing.

Amicia recognized the laughter in this new voice for the jest it meant and went still, arms falling limp and blush-heated face bent. When the man who had rescued her stepped back, she stared intently at the soft leather boots clinging to muscular calves as if to look higher would be the final humiliation.

Galen saw her embarrassment and was ashamed of his part in its cause.

"We meant no harm," he murmured, lifting her chin with his fingertips.

Amicia looked straight into light eyes whose silver-green color even the cave's twilight interior could not steal. They were as penetrating as the sharp splinters of crystal her shattered unicorn had become and their dangerous, breath-stealing power made it imperative that she protect herself or reveal all she meant to hide. Thick lashes dropped to break their hold, and she responded to his comment without taking time to consider the wisdom of her words.

"I know, but I am unused to . . ." Her voice trailed away. No village girl could have arrived at her age without experience of bantering far more earthy.

Instead she refuted his first words to her. "I'm seven-teen and not a child." Against the amusement in his eyes she looked down.

Galen grinned. Her last statement sounded like nothing so much as the petulant child she'd claimed not to be. "Seventeen—aged indeed. You have my apologies. My only excuse is that these smudges brought too clearly to mind my childhood joy in building castles of mud."

Strong fingertips again brushed her face, this time tracing a trail of dirt across her small, straight nose and petal-soft cheek. Uncommonly lovely, like a bright lily only just opening its petals to the sun. Galen found himself with a strong impulse to retrace the path, to hold her face between his palms and search the tempting curve of her lips for the nectar sweetness surely hidden within. Impossible! He with-drew his hand as if it had been stung by a bee hovering protectively about the precious hoard.

Amicia peeked from beneath lowered lashes at the man who'd filled her thoughts and dreams since the moment she'd first seen him. Catching her glance with a gentle smile, he stepped back and swept his hand palm up in a wide and elegant arc. The exaggerated gesture earned a merry laugh as Amicia lifted her skirts a fraction to sink into a curtsy before accepting his invitation to move toward the fire-ring now har-boring dying coals.

"Are you the owner of the blanket we found folded in the back, the one who claims possession of this haven?"

Looking back over her shoulder, Amicia nodded. Galen, his companion had called him. Galen, a fine name, a name perfect for a romantic forest outlaw. Moreover, with his midnight black hair, mysterious green gaze, and the uncompromising masculinity of sun-bronzed face and tall muscular body, clearly he was perfect or as near to as mortal man could be.

To Galen the maid's lambent, half-closed eyes

seemed filled with seductive promises an innocent couldn't possibly understand, even less fulfill. She was dangerous, at least to his honor and peace of mind.

Even had Galen not watched the day past as the impetuous maid lifted her skirts to plunge across the sea-covered causeway to the castle, he'd have known who she was. Not her name. That he had yet to learn. But her parentage was clear. Though dainty and unquestionably feminine, her tawny hair and golden brown eyes were a replica of his beloved foster father. Only the unexpectedness of the waterfall's vision of beauty had momentarily kept him from making the connection. By the time she'd begun her crossing to Dungeld's isle, he had known who she was. What he hadn't expected was her return. Any noble-born female, particularly a virtuous maiden, should run screaming from strange men, not seek them out— alone.

Horrified to realize she'd been standing mute, openly studying him as no well-bred girl ought do, Amicia rushed into speech. "I come whenever I can slip unseen from the village." No time better than now to surreptitiously convince them that she was of the common folk, like they. "But because I live with my parents on a small holding beyond its outermost boundary, I've no need of the cave at night and you are welcome to its use." There she'd both given herself a new background—she'd seen such a farm more than once—and made the magnanimous offer she'd planned.

So, Galen acknowledged, she thought to keep her true identity a secret, as if with her soft hands and classical features she could be a peasant. Still, he held his peace and motioned her to sit on the blanket neatly folded at one side of the fire pit as he questioned her with apparent casualness. "Your parents have no objection to your solitary wanderings?" He couldn't picture the pure Lady Sybil sanctioning her daughter's lone wanderings.

Amicia took her time settling on the square of homespun, seeking just the right words and just the right offhand tone to deliver them in. "If they knew, they might."

Galen hid his amusement for the girl's unhesitating confession of untamed ways.

Intent on sounding natural, Amicia failed to notice the wryness of Galen's smile when she continued with as broad a hint of her desire to join their exploits as she dared. "They are far too busy to recognize my preference for the wildwood, for the excitement in the adventures it offers—as you surely know."

The maid's last statement startled Galen, and his dark brows rose. Knew what? What did she think had brought them here?

Amicia saw his unspoken question and was flustered. Had she erred in referring to their forest pursuits? "I mean—you're here when surely if you could, you'd stay in the village or the castle or the—" Beneath a steady stare growing ever more intense, she stumbled to a halt, drew a deep breath, and plunged on. "I've listened to the tales of Robin Hood, and I believe his virtues unquestionable. So brave and just and—" Falling deeper and deeper into a bog of her own making, Amicia's mouth snapped shut, and the eyes above that firm line went soft with a plea for understanding.

At the mention of Robin Hood, comprehension broke like sunlight through the fog her muddled words had created in Galen's mind. Sweet Mary's Tears! She thought they were outlaws! Albeit, just and romantic. To the heir of a powerful earldom, this was a title of dubious honor. Stunned speechless, a rare event, he left his companion to answer the maid's awkward statement.

"'Tis certainly wise of you to so quickly recognize our sort." Under the girl's assumption and his friend's stunned response, Carl was hard put to restrain the grin tugging at the corners of his mouth. Lacking

Galen's awareness of their visitor's true identity, he'd no compunction about using her offered cover to their advantage—what better excuse for their presence in the Wryborne forest?

As Carl spoke, Galen heard the trap close around him. It was hard enough on a man who held truth and honest dealings as the highest goal to travel in disguise among strangers. But, now he would be drawn into acting out a total charade with his beloved foster father's daughter.

In relief Amicia flashed a brilliant smile upon the man she looked at clearly for the first time. He was near as tall as Galen, mayhap a decade older but with hair as warm a brown as his laughing eyes.

"He is Galen and I am Carl—who are you?" Carl, too, had been taught the virtues of being direct by Earl Garrick, Galen's father.

"Amicia." The answer was immediate, and only after it was said did she fear it possibly ill-done. She nibbled anxiously on the full curve of her lower lip. 'Twas an uncommon name and if spoken hereabouts any would tell them it belonged to the daughter of the castle's lady, the one who was the fiefdom's heiress.

Still towering above, Galen studied the young beauty from luxurious hair, unbound as no well-bred woman ought publicly be seen, to the toes of small feet peeping out from beneath her carefully arranged skirts. Though seventeen was an advanced age for a female to be unwed, she was plainly an innocent. In truth, naive enough to take foolish risks and offer strangers dangerous temptations all unknowingly. Aware that she was as noble-born as he, but unable to admit to either heritage, he desperately wondered what earthly subject they could talk of?

As the silent moments lengthened, Amicia, too, wondered what to say until struck by an idea's weak but hopeful glimmer. In the same hour that she and her two companions had ridden out from the castle another had departed as well. And that person had carried a burden which would likely be of interest to men of Robin Hood's mold.

"Gilfrey of Castle Dungeld is a truly wicked lord. He makes the people's life a misery whilst taking what little they have for his own." She looked hopefully into the two faces gone suddenly expressionless. Surely she could tempt them to linger here by providing them not only with the perfect retreat but also with a deserving target for their worthy pursuit of justice for the common folk. That it would also fulfill her fantasy of a handsome hero battling her oppressor, the Dark Lord, was no bad thing.

Once again Galen was amused by the girl, though he hid it well. Did she not realize that no serf or common freeman would call a lord by his given name? She clearly hadn't thought out her assumed identity's true position in the world, but then probably she'd no experience by which to know its ways. Galen couldn't decide whether this maid was the danger they'd been asked to resolve, a part of the problem, or simply an impulsive creature too likely to expose the whole to those within the castle. Whatever the case, he assuredly could not trust the truth of their identities to her, and they would all be best served by her immediate return to the castle's safety.

"Gilfrey respects not even the church," Amicia continued, unaware of her hero's dilemma. "The lady of the castle, who once was a postulant nun, gives all that she can to the Abbey of St. Jude on the hill beyond the village. But no sooner does her offering enter hallowed walls than a tax collector arrives to claim the whole for unpaid taxes."

Galen straightened imperceptibly. Was this the danger that Sybil had written of? Did she ask aid in seeing the abbey protected from such noble thievery?

"As I traveled here, the abbot who visits her weekly passed me by on his return to the abbey. I saw the bag attached to his saddle and heard its jingle so 'tis certain he returns with her donation." Looking expectantly into Galen's eyes, Amicia was disappointed by their lack of emotion.

"Our thanks for your visit," Garrick said, and the hand he held out left her little choice but to comply. "But the day is grown late and your family will be looking for your return."

Amicia glanced quickly toward the cave entrance and was horrified to find the sun glowing bright through falling water, a certain indication of its lowness in the sky. Having achieved her goal and more, she'd not realized how long she'd lingered.

"Aye," she hastily agreed. "I must go but will return to see you again."

"It would be better for us all if you did not." Galen's response was immediate and heartfelt, although the words cost him an unaccustomed pang of regret. She was a unique female and, as one who'd known many well, he knew of how few that could be said. He'd like to have had more time to learn what made her react as least expected—lifting her skirts to lead the way through dangerously rising tide, seeking out strange men, and who knows what further risks she'd take without a moment's hesitation. He was intrigued; and, had they met as the social equals they were, he'd have pursued the answer. But then, perhaps someday they would.

"I want to be your friend." Amicia's eyes were dark with the pain of rejection, and she unthinkingly took a step nearer to lay her small hand against a broad chest in supplication.

Carl's gentle snort preceded a sotto voce comment. "Did she wish to be my 'friend,' I'd be inclined to let her."

Galen shot the man unaware of her true identity a quick and quelling glance. In the next instant it occurred to him that such an action might well be the very thing needed to frighten her into a sensible

43

retreat. As if in proof, Amicia's soft lips parted on a satisfying gasp when he reached out to wrap her in his arms and draw her alluring curves near.

Finding herself suddenly close against the tall, powerful body sent a tremor of shocked delight over Amicia. Never sparing a thought to the folly in her response, she instinctively melted into his strong embrace. Undreamt-of sensations swept through her, robbing her of sensible thought, of anything beyond awareness of his warmth and strength and the feel of the heart beneath her hand accelerating to the same quick, pounding pace as her own.

The enticing woman-child willingly nestled in his arms set Galen's blood ablaze. When her small pink tongue darted out to touch a softly bowed upper lip, silver flames flashed over her with the power of lightning, and he surrendered to temptation. Bending his head, he tasted the sweet honey of her lips, a finer nectar than ever he'd dreamed existed and one he feared addicting.

Lost in the haze of a mindless response, Amicia melted closer against its source. She wrapped both arms about his neck, tangled her fingers into cool strands of black hair as thick as it looked, and drew the fire nearer like a moth determined to sacrifice itself to the destroying flame.

"Hmmm—time for me to be gone," Carl muttered as he moved to step beyond the couple so entwined they cast a single shadow.

Galen's head jerked back at the sound, and the cool breeze of sanity swept over him with a realization of the folly to which he'd succumbed. Tightly closed lashes shielded him from the unexpected passion he'd found smoldering in a core of innocence as he moved away from the delicious form, untutored but pliant, attempting to break the dangerous embrace.

Amicia, far too inexperienced and much too deep into her own responses to recognize the threat he was striving to protect her from, helplessly followed, burying her heated face against the rapid rise and fall of his wide chest. Galen gritted his teeth but knew 'twould be cruel to desert the fire he'd kindled while it yet burned in one new to its hungry heat and consuming ache. Thus, he held her lightly, resting his chin atop flower-scented tresses and slowly brushing calm solace up and down her back.

When Galen stepped away and Amicia followed, they'd effectively blocked Carl's exit path. Certain that this was not the time to interrupt, he silently retreated into the shadows beyond the fire.

Struggling through the whirling smoke of desire, Amicia returned to the reality of strong arms. She was content until she realized that the caresses he gave her were those of a father for a child and nowise satisfying now that she'd experienced the flames of excitement he could ignite if he chose. Although determined to return and seek the core of the dizzying firestorm, she knew by the glimpse of a rose glow beyond the watery wall that the sun was perilously near its day's end when the tide would truly have risen. She'd have to run the whole way and then only the horse left waiting with Kelda and Farrold would save her skirts from another drenching as she again crossed near too late.

Amicia backed away and with a quick, blindingly sweet smile gave Galen a promise. "I'll see you on the morrow."

Galen's ploy had definitely failed. More than failed, he acknowledged. It had been a disaster—for them both. She was a most assuredly dangerous child—a danger to herself and a serious danger to his peace of mind. He opened his mouth to counter her words but she'd already slipped out.

Giving a low whistle, Carl said, "A potent package, hmmm?" Having come to stand behind his clearly thunderstruck friend, he stroked his chin and sighed with exaggerated regret. "Would that I had met a pretty peasant so willing."

"Aside from the certain truth that your wife would

see you suffer for such a deed," Galen's smile was a grin, "that pretty maid is an innocent—and no peasant."

Carl grinned at Galen's reference to his Maida's likely reaction to any such event, but tilted his head questioning the last part of the statement.

"Think again on her appearance. Have you never seen another much the same?"

Like dawn sundering the night, Carl's eyes widened and his mouth dropped. Snapping it shut a moment later, he shook his head in wonder. "They are eerily alike."

At the point where the forest path opened on the meadow, Kelda paced to and fro awaiting Amicia's return, pray God soon. She'd wrung her hands so oft and so harshly that they'd grown sore, while under her breath muttered imprecations alternated with fervent prayers. There were times when she could cheerfully strangle Amicia. Twilight was already upon them, and after the past day's near disastrous late return, she'd expected the other girl to pay more attention to the all-important time of tide-turning.

"Surely we ought to set out for the castle without further delay," Farrold urged, trying to hide his anxiety. "Wouldn't it be better for us all if they need send a boat for one and not three. What earthly benefit is there in all being penalized for the irresponsibility of one?" Farrold had carefully chosen the most logical argument he could think of to convince his pretty companion of the wisdom in saving leastways themselves from punishment. His father would be furious, would think them irresponsible when in truth it had been only the lovely heiress. "I don't mean to see Amicia suffer, but 'twas her choice and not ours so why should we pay the price." Nervous strain thinned his earnest voice.

Kelda paused to look at the young man holding the reins to all three steeds. He shifted awkwardly from

foot to foot, and she felt guilty on Amicia's behalf.
Farrold had more reason to fear than either of them.
As he'd quietly explained during their afternoon of
laughter and serious talk, while a legitimate son's legal
rights allowed him to occasionally flout parental authority, an illegitimate son was dependent upon his
father's good will for advancement and could never
do the same.

"Mayhap you are right. We can tie her mare here
where Amicia will find it when she returns. Then, if
the sea has not risen too high, she can overtake us." To
Kelda it felt like desertion but Farrold was right,
'twould be to no purpose for three to suffer for the
actions of only one.

With quick, smooth movements of more grace than
any earlier demonstrated, Farrold separated the reins
of Amicia's horse from the others. He gave their reins
to Kelda, freeing his hands to securely fasten the
dappled mare to a sapling sprouting in the shade of a
giant tree on the forest's edge. He then helped Kelda
mount her steed and speedily climbed atop his own.

Riding slightly to the rear, Farrold intercepted
Kelda's uneasy glance back and gave her a smile of
mingled reassurance and appreciation. Flinging a
thick braid twined with sapphire ribbon over her
shoulder, Kelda shrugged as if it were of no import
and turned toward a rose-hued horizon.

They rode madly across the disappearing causeway,
laughing like children as their horses' every stride
splashed them with water. But the joys of freedom
died in their throats as they approached the foot of the
winding path to castle gate. A dark figure waited there,
arms folded across barrel chest and meaty shoulders
stiff with fury.

Although unable to quickly move legs ever swollen
and afflicted with fierce aches that worsened his
temperament, the moment the two riders were within
reach, Gilfrey lashed out to knock Farrold from the
saddle and into the rapidly rising sea. "You will learn

the folly of laughing at my commands," he snarled down at the boy fighting for balance amidst shifting waves. While the boy sought to rise from his awkward sprawl, Gilfrey moved his cold, narrow gaze to Kelda.

Ride-soaked and shivering under a once gentle breeze turned chill by the baron's ire, still Kelda had sense enough to dismount, putting the animal between her and the furious man.

"Don't blame her." Farrold pulled together what little bravado he could muster to defend the girl who had listened to his woes with compassion. He nearly gained his feet only to be thrown to his back again by an incoming wave of unexpected height.

Ignoring the stabbing pains the action lent, Gilfrey whirled to roar at his ungrateful whelp. "You dare command *me?*"

Although close once more to success in his struggle to rise amidst wave-receding and momentarily shallow water, Farrold fell back under the force of his father's ire. "We were ready to leave in all good time and only lingered to await our companion."

Kelda gasped at the sudden defection of her erstwhile protector. She'd left Amicia behind to accompany Farrold for the sake of shielding him from punishment, but never had she expected him to save himself by pointing the finger of accusation at the other girl. No matter that it was a fact painfully clear by Amicia's absence.

Farrold saw Kelda's shock and cringed at his own cowardice. He hadn't wanted to disappoint her of all people. Now he'd shamed himself by condemning near the first female in his life who'd lent a sympathetic ear and uttered no word of ridicule for either his birth or his less than polished manners, less than perfect form and face. All before this maid who'd amazingly offered an even greater understanding, almost approval. He shot Kelda a glance pleading for forgiveness.

The baron reached down to grasp a soaked collar

and jerk from the wave's hold a pitiable, drenched creature who looked like a half-drowned cat. "Take your horses and begone." Gilfrey tossed his disdained son to the dirt path at the girl's feet. "But remember my anger is not a thing to tempt lightly."

Soft heart aching for the youth whose fate was held in cruel hands, Kelda helped Farrold scramble up. In their haste to obey the harsh command, through rapidly dwindling light they did not see the approach of a distant figure.

Splashing great spurls of water a dappled steed plunged through the waves. With fine disregard for safety, the rider urged the horse into a full gallop across the narrow and nearly obliterated causeway.

"You witless fool! Almost you drowned my mare!" Gilfrey shouted. Beneath unreasoning fury with this ever unwelcome reminder of his predecessor, the earlier arrivals were completely forgotten.

"Mayhap," Amicia called to the human obstruction standing full in her path. "But you'd have thought it a small price for ridding yourself of me." Amicia's eyes flashed with the golden fire of a daring courage this man never failed to rouse in her, and she rode the horse straight ahead until even the implacable baron had no choice but to step aside or be, at the least, pushed from the narrow path into the rising tide.

"That price and tenfold more," he snarled as she passed. "Yet, 'tis my curse to know that you will outlive me." He loudly called a fierce punishment upon the rapidly departing back of the dainty nemesis he couldn't quickly follow. "But never again will you risk valuable horseflesh with your untamed ways. 'Twill be more than the stable serfs' lives are worth to see you mounted without my leave."

Amicia hid her distress over his threat to future meetings with the exciting outlaw beneath a mask of bravado. Steadily continuing on the upward path, she purposefully let her head fall back and mocking laughter echo against the steep sides of the rock isle. If the haunting sound were tinged with more bitterness than natural in the voice of one so young, its goal was accomplished. It gave wordless voice to her proud refusals to be humbled by her foe. It was her cry of freedom and smote him with more discomfort than any blow she could physically render.

❦ *Chapter 4* ❦

Galen shifted in search of a more welcoming spot amongst tall ferns and dense bushes clumped at the base of a massive oak. Mayhap the maid had stretched the truth in order to impress supposed outlaws? It seemed all too likely as either he or one of his companions had watched the humble abbey from this spot, convenient if less than comfortable, for near two days without sight of a suspicious approach.

The creak of a cart's turning wheels cut short the song of a robin in the branches spreading above. Another simple farmer come with a share from his meager supplies to give the good fathers? More than one had passed by on the narrow, rock-strewn path a short distance from where he crouched. A farmer or one of the troubled villagers who sought spiritual comfort for physical ills. The sight that met Galen's cursory glance had him leaning deeper into the sun-dappled barrier of leaves for a closer look. Of a certainty the cart was a small two-wheeled farm design and pulled by a sorry-looking mule, but the driver perched on the vehicle's seat was suspiciously well-fed amidst a demesne whose inhabitants, those he'd seen thus far, looked a gaunt and hopeless lot. And though the man's garments were of plain design,

51

they were of a finer weave than homespun. Galen's experience in a noble's methods for shielding his own from greedy thieves left him with no doubt but that here rode the baron's tax collector.

Galen waited motionless until the cart and its driver disappeared beyond the stone wall surrounding the abbey. Only after peace had returned and the robin's song resumed did he rise to his feet and give a series of short, low-pitched whistles. In a moment Carl stepped from the woodland on the rough path's far edge to watch as Galen swept one hand from left to right to indicate the lane's incoming path and then pointed at the abbey gate. Carl slowly nodded before moving back to vanish again into forest gloom.

Sinking once more into shielding foliage, Galen silently acknowledged that he owed the impulsive girl an apology for doubting her words, and when he saw her again he would tell her so. Pray God not! He gave his dark head a sharp shake, intending to return errant thoughts to rational control. Although the summer sweet maid's passionate response had convinced him that his plan to frighten her into sensible ways had been a dismal failure, it assuredly had succeeded in planting her tempting beauty firmly within his mind. And though it now appeared he'd driven her from the folly of forest wanderings, he'd discovered it exceedingly difficult to drive her from his thoughts and impossible to restrain her visits to his night dreams.

The tantalizing memory of lush curves nestled trustingly in his arms was interrupted by the sound of wooden wheels striking the stone-littered pathway. He peeked through the green lace of fronds unmoving in summer stillness. The cart's beefy driver had clearly fulfilled this errand many times before and any apprehension he might once have felt had been lulled long ago. Looking neither left nor right as he entered the woodland's shadowy cover, the man broke into an off-key and bawdy song. He was allowed to travel a goodly distance into the woodland, far enough that neither his song nor his cries for aid could be heard by the abbey's gentle inhabitants.

The huge trees on either side of the narrow pathway spread their branches overhead to twine so tightly together that they permitted no more than occasional shafts of sunlight to break through. An odd rustling in the leafy cover ahead caught the driver's attention. His song broke off mid-word as a stranger dropped to block the lane, drawn sword in hand.

"Sir Robber, I am a poor farmer," the cart's occupant whined, sweat beading his upper lip.

"A farmer mayhap." Carl's laughter scoffed. "But poor you are not."

"Does the baron pay you with fine cloth or food aplenty?" Galen coldly asked from behind as with a flashing motion his dagger sundered the thin leather strip holding a pouch at the self-proclaimed farmer's waist. The clinking sound of it falling into his waiting hand earned a smile of satisfaction.

"Nay!" Too late the unprepared man's hands clutched at thong ends dangling empty. And again too late, he realized that while dropping to the ground, its thief had smoothly removed the dagger from a sheath he'd thought well hidden inside one boot. Left defenseless, his wail of disgust turned into a colorful curse on them both that ended with a threat. "The baron will find you and demand a dreadful price for this villainy."

"We tremble in terror." Galen grinned mockingly as he tucked his opponent's dagger into his own boot.

"I think I've found myself a new occupation." Carl's eyes gleamed with amusement as he hoisted himself up into the cart's back and clamored over its small load of grain-filled sacks to pull their prey's arms behind his back. "'Tis an easy way to win the riches I deserve."

Galen laughed at what he recognized as a jest while moving to stand in front of the furious tax collector who doubtless thought the same words a threat. While

Carl bound the man's hands with the length of leather cord left useless at his waist, silver-green eyes steadily met iron-gray. Watched with a glare that if 'twere honed metal would render a mortal blow, Galen opened the smooth bag and poured a small mound of copper coins into his cupped palm. "Aye, you are—or leastways will be—a very poor and possibly much abused man. I doubt the baron will be overly generous with you for this day's labors."

Too familiar with his lord's vicious spite, the bound man's face went white, yet within moments impotent rage flooded it with ruby color. "Only if the baron is generous, will you lose no more than your hands for this deed." The words were gritted out between clenched teeth just before Carl gagged their speaker with a strip of coarse cloth torn from an emptied grain sack and then used another strip to fashion a blindfold.

Galen and Carl knew that unseeing darkness and silence would increase their foe's apprehensions. Thus, without pity for a man greedy enough to take all that his suffering peers possessed for the sake of his own reward, the two assailants spoke no further word. Rather, they roughly placed the unsavory varlet atop grain sacks in the cart's rear. Then, to fulfill the plan laid out at the start of their two-day watch, Carl tied his steed to the cart's back, climbed to the driver's seat, and set out to deliver the vehicle and its occupant to where the forest edged ocean shore. The rising tide had assuredly obscured the causeway link, but when the baron realized his expected henchman had gone missing, he'd send guardsmen in boats to find him.

Before his cohort and the well-loaded wagon had disappeared down the narrow track, Galen retreated into the woodland's dense greenery to await the coming dark of a near moonless night. He blessed his good fortune when he found a patch of thick grown grasses in the midst of a tight ring of trees and gratefully lowered himself to the welcome ease of nature's pillow. To gauge the time he had to wait, Galen gazed up through gently rustling leaves at a small patch of sky. Even as he watched, the dome's pale blue seemed to blush under the sun's low descent.

Pink deepened from rose to magenta while the deepest of indigo blue blurred the horizon's dark line. Ever awed by nature's magical display, Amicia stood on her toes the better to lean through a dip in the castle's crenellated wall for a wider view. Such serene beauty lent a peace to her spirit that had been sadly lacking during the two days since Gilfrey had forbidden her to leave the castle, a restriction which had nearly driven her mad—likely his goal.

Shaking heavy honey curls, Amicia concentrated on the vivid scene of subtly shifting hues to push back the distressing thought of her stepfather. When, by the Dark Lord's edict or restraints of foul weather, she was unable to escape to the mainland's waterfall haven, this was her favorite retreat. To fulfill the obligation owed his liege lord, the baron had sent the majority of his men to fight the king's battles, leaving this a near deserted and peaceful site. Only one guardsman watched from the curtain wall encircling the island fortress. It was unnecessary that there be more. Any foe's army must await low tide and then approach unprotected and single file across an open stretch of sea.

"There you are. We've been looking for you everywhere."

Surprised, Amicia turned to find Kelda rapidly approaching, Farrold at her heels like an obedient puppy just as, whenever free of his father's demands, he'd been since their afternoon in the meadow.

"Your outlaws have struck the abbey!" Kelda announced in a righteous disapproval tinged with smugness for her right reading of the stranger's unscrupulous character.

Amicia's heart sank. *"My* outlaws? Struck the abbey?" Surely Galen hadn't used her talk of gifts to the church for the purpose of stealing the wealth for himself before even Gilfrey's man could. The possibility sent a shiver of cold over her.

Strictly holding her attention from the abrupt edge so close, Kelda ignored Amicia's emphasis of ownership. "They stopped Denby as he left the abbey, and took his money pouch!"

Relief restored Amicia's warmth and provided a gentle smile as she quickly glanced about to be certain the guard captain who'd taken this watch stood out of hearing range on the wall's far side before softly arguing her friend's unjust accusation. "So they didn't attack the church but merely retrieved what Denby stole from the holy fathers. Doubtless 'twill be returned to them," she airily asserted.

Startled by this talk of outlaws—as if they were acquaintances, even friends—Farrold's jaw dropped.

"Will they, I wonder?" Kelda looked skeptical of surely untrustworthy men but shrugged. "Mayhap they would, if they'd time, but the Dark Lord has dispatched men to comb the woods for these dangerous intruders upon the peace of Wryborne."

"Peace, hah!" Amicia derided. "The peace of oppression, of starvation, and poverty are nothing worth preserving."

Suddenly both girls realized before whom they spoke. Wide blue and rebellious brown gazes turned upon their hapless observer.

Farrold blushed under the sudden attention. They feared to offend him with their talk of his father—needlessly. He shrugged and awkwardly reassured them, "Though he be my sire, he is near a stranger to me. Seldom have I seen him. Indeed, before I was summoned here, only one time."

"Once?" The shocked girls asked in unison.

"Once." Farrold's nod sent a lock of straight brown hair down across his forehead. "When he came to take me from the family who'd raised me from a babe and deliver me to the castellan of Salisbury Tower—where, with the good-blooded sons of royal vassals, I began my training for knighthood."

Unexpectedly, to his own deep self-disgust, here amidst strange surroundings and in the company of two whose approval he desperately sought, memories of the boys' neverending taunts for his base birth overflowed the dam of false unconcern he'd built long ago. The belittling words of his peers had stolen what small physical grace he possessed, leaving him a bumbling page, then a clumsy squire whom no knight willingly accepted for service. 'Twas not, as it should have been, by virtue of just reward for skill's attained but rather by command of the king that he had been knighted. He was all too aware what woe it meant upon anyone dependant on his military prowess for safety. Against these bleak facts Farrold's face closed into a stiff mask while his eyes burned with pain.

Although Kelda misunderstood the reason for it, she felt Farrold's anguish. The emotion roused her protective instincts. For once forgetful of the frightening heights on which she stood, Kelda moved nearer to him. "Your family let him take you?"

"Though they were as dear to me, they weren't truly my family and had no say in the matter." Farrold was quick to defend those he loved. "Baron Gilfrey is of good blood while they, though free, are mere farmers."

Honey-brown eyes had widened at the depth of disapproval in Kelda's strange question. Amicia curiously studied the dark-haired girl who knew as well as she that 'twas common practice for well-born sons to be fostered in another's home.

Kelda sensed her friend's scrutiny and knew the reason for it. She'd accepted the action as natural when her much older brothers, now knights wed with families of their own and living on other fiefdoms, were sent to foster. But, though a small child at the time, she'd known they'd looked forward to that great day while Farrold seemed to have been taken against his will. Her chin tilted defensively yet she didn't allow her attention to shift from the earnest youth still speaking.

"They said that I must be thankful he'd arranged a finer life for me as neither they nor theirs could ever aspire to be more than farmers tilling the soil for another's wealth. Yet I've wished many a time he had left me on the farm in peace and happiness." Farrold cringed guiltily. He sounded like an ingrate and rushed to explain. "I've learned the debt I owe my father for seeing to a better life for me. I know I must do my all to please and repay him for arranging for my future as few noblemen do for their low-blooded whelps."

"You wish he'd left you on the farm?" Kelda asked, so startled by the unfamiliar concept that she heard no more.

Embarrassed by his own words, Farrold flushed a fresh and shining ruby hue and was thankful that the ever-deepening shades of dusk would conceal a measure of the color. He shouldn't have told this right-born maid his low-bred preferences. Now he could only try to justify his position. Standing unnaturally straight, he announced, "I'm not a murderer and didn't want to be trained in the killing arts." His firm statement faded into a sheepish admission, "I don't even like to hunt."

"What then would you have done with your years?" Amicia asked, curious about this attitude beyond her experience.

"Rather than killing, I would see things live and grow. Far better to renew life than to see how quickly what took years to nurture can be cut down with sword or blackened with fire." The intensity in a soft voice grown strong demonstrated Farrold's sincerity.

"Why didn't you tell Gilfrey so?" Amicia questioned. Seemed to her the only logical thing to do.

Farrold's brows rose in horror. "Tell him what an

58

ingrate is this mongrel cur who is no more than an unwanted accident? Refuse an offered gift? Nay, I must never forget the debt I owe my sire—first simply for my existence and once again for permitting me a finer life than to toil in the fields, an animal owned by men." He spoke vehemently, a vehemence covering his trampled dreams.

Amicia realized she'd no right to question Farrold's thinking. She recognized the impossibility of an illegitimate son standing against the sire who held his fate in his hands. He was desperately uncomfortable, and Kelda clearly ached for his woe. Thus, Amicia sought to smooth the spirit rasped by their thoughtless queries by shifting the focus from him. She looked again to Kelda and returned the conversation to the outlaws and their pursuers.

"You say the baron goes out to hunt my hero?"

"Aye." Kelda gratefully accepted the change of subject sure to give Farrold a welcome relief. "They depart at dawn."

Amicia's brows rose. Low tide would not reveal the causeway until some little time after the sun had risen. "They mean to take the boats?" She was surprised. Few in the garrison were fond of the water crossing although the stable on the outcropping of the bay's far curve housed a full complement of horses. There was no question of such an expedition during dark hours. Mayhap born of his own wrongdoings, Gilfrey feared possible foes lurking in the night to strike him down, and he would never venture from his fortress in less than full light of day.

Kelda was quick to repeat the plan the bragging baron had loudly outlined to men gathered in the great hall. "Lord Gilfrey believes they'll catch the outlaw departing from the abbey if they arrive early enough."

Amicia grinned. "Then he, too, believes my outlaws intend the coins not for themselves but for the abbey?"

"Oh!" Kelda's eyes widened. She hadn't thought that far. A puzzled frown puckered her smooth forehead. Why would the baron think it so?

"If Dungeld's garrison goes out early on the morrow, then I go now while the tide is still low to warn Galen aforehand." Amicia spoke her thoughts aloud, determination glowing gold in her eyes.

"What?" Kelda gasped, horrified. "You mean to cross the causeway alone on a night with no moon and go to a man of questionable honor?" Too many layers of emotion crowded into so short a span of time were confusing.

Amicia gently laughed at the other's amazement. "I assuredly would not ask either of you to again risk the Dark Lord's rage."

"But what of you?" Kelda nearly wailed. "You risk not merely the baron's ire but the wild beasts in the dark forest and, worst yet, the Wolf's Head who is surely the most dangerous of all!"

Dangerous? Aye, the tantalizing memory of silver lightning flashing from green eyes, of a fiery kiss, and the shocking excitement of strong arms proved it true—yet worth any risk.

Kelda saw her friend's dreamy smile. Her unease intensified, but after days of listening to Amicia sigh over her Galen's striking eyes and handsome face, she knew any argument from that direction was lost before it had begun. "If you won't consider your own safety, then what of mine? What am I to say on the morrow when only I descend for the morning meal? What defense have I, who mama will blame for failing to prevent your going or failing leastwise to warn of your intent in time to see you forestalled?"

Witless fool! Amicia derided herself. She'd no wish to cause Kelda or her mother ill, yet once again she hadn't paused to consider what price her actions might demand others pay. But, she brightened, a problem once seen can be solved. There was always a way. Biting her bottom lip she looked back to the horizon where only the faintest rose glow marked the edge between the indigo blue of descending night and the black horizon.

Through the growing gloom Kelda noted the other's furrowed brow and congratulated herself on successfully arguing the proposed action's folly.

"Tell them I'm not feeling well." Amicia whirled to direct the other girl. "Melly will help. Have her curl up in my bed and pull its curtains closed. Then, if your mother comes to check on me, you can tell her that after a sleepless night I'm resting at last. She may peek but will not disturb." Amicia leaned closer and, seeing the skeptical anxiety on a softly rounded face, reassured and cajoled. "You know she won't insist on waking one ailing, and I'll return as soon as the causeway is passable. I swear I will."

Kelda had grave fears for the right reasoning of this plan but knew herself unable to prevent the adventurous girl from doing whatever she pleased. Moreover, her discomfort was likely a result of her own timid nature and, thus, a shame to her.

"I've no desire to bring woe or even worry to you or your mother," Amicia earnestly explained. "But neither can I allow my greenwood friends to fall to a threat from which I can save them."

Kelda was embarrassed that she'd used selfish thoughts of her own comfort to fight against such a courageous action. If Amicia was brave enough to attempt so heroic a deed, surely she could do this small part to support her.

"I'll find Melly if you'll fetch a cloak. 'Twill be chilly before dawn. And Farrold can keep Oswald distracted."

Although a guardsman on the curtain wall had yet to challenge a lone figure crossing the causeway, Amicia was quick to say, "A wonderful notion." She wanted to move into action before Kelda had a chance to reconsider. Realizing that Kelda assumed she meant to sleep in their hidden cave, she was glad she'd not told the other girl about the outlaws' use of it. Had she done so the younger girl would never have agreed to lend aid. Kelda, in misguided protection, might even have gone to Lady Anne to see her departure prevented.

"I swear I'll find my warmest cloak before I slip down the back passage and out through the stable while the castle serfs are occupied clearing the great hall and cleaning the kitchens." Amicia sent the other two a blinding smile and hurried away, preventing either from putting forth a further objection, possibly one harder to dismiss.

"Be careful," Kelda softly called after the slender retreating back. When they were young she'd thought it was Amicia's beauty that gave her courage, but as they grew she'd realized that Lady Sybil was lovely, too, yet serene, tranquil even in the face of adversity. Still, she'd never been able to dismiss the link or longing to be as pretty and brave as Amicia. "I wish," she sighed her thoughts aloud, "I could be as strong and daring as she."

"I'm glad you are not," Farrold quietly averred, startling the maid who'd nearly forgotten him there. "Amicia *is* beautiful, but so are you in a comfortable way."

Kelda found his description a compliment of dubious merit. Farrold saw her doubt and rushed to explain his questionable praise. "Amicia is like a spirited horse—exciting, unexpected."

Though doubtful about his description of her, Kelda was positive Amicia wouldn't appreciate being compared to a horse, however beautiful.

Farrold saw her deepening frown and doggedly continued. "Not all men enjoy hurtling through life with such a companion, first tilting one way and then another, racing headlong only to halt abruptly and dash back the way you've come." He slowly shook his head. "Nay, no such upheavals for the likes of me. Far rather had I to live quiet and comfortable with a woman who shares my love of a peaceful hearthfire."

Kelda's eyes glowed with pleasure for words that had proven a finer compliment than any she'd ever thought to receive. He had described precisely the future she'd dreamed of in the deepest corners of her heart, a future she would treasure.

Having spoken his piece, Farrold was embarrassed by her silence and immediately cleared his throat. "Best you do as you promised while I join Sir Oswald, although what we've to talk about I don't know." Farrold peered through the almost total dark to the bulky shadow still on the parapet's far side. The man was decades older and a seasoned warrior who likely had little use for the young and inexperienced.

Kelda smiled her gratitude for his willingness to do what she'd suggested without consulting him. "Just ask Sir Oswald about his last campaign with King Henry. He loves to tell about his heroic deeds, and likely you'll have more trouble getting him to halt than to begin."

⊷§ *Chapter 5* §⊷

From the tax collector?" Bushy brows rose so high they near joined the thick white hair ringing the speaker's head as he incredulously studied the pile of copper coins gleaming against the dark wood of a use-smoothed table.

The priest's shocked words held a note of honest dismay that added to Galen's unease. Already had he been surprised when, after being given entry to the abbot's small and austere chamber, he'd discovered his host to be a familiar figure from his early years on Wryborne lands—an unforeseen problem. Although merely a youth struggling to leave childhood behind when last they'd met, should the hood of his cloak fall back he was certain Father Pieter would recognize the boy he'd once tutored.

"We know Lady Sybil sent a donation to you, one which the baron's minion came to take back," Galen quietly stated, careful to keep his identity hidden within the hood's shadows. "We acted to right that wrong."

"A worthy cause." Father Pieter nodded while above a gentle smile his eyes gleamed with the quick laughter Galen remembered. "But unnecessary."

Despite suspicions earlier roused, Galen instinctively lifted his chin against the other's words. At the action his cloth shield dropped away, leaving his handsome face revealed to the flickering light of foul-smelling tallow tapers clustered atop a metal platter on the table's far end.

The abbot stepped forward, amusement draining from his face. Much shorter than his guest, he peered up at the stranger who was not truly a stranger. Unmistakable mist-green eyes proved that the promising boy he'd once known had reached adulthood, exceptional childhood beauty hardened into the uncompromising masculinity of a strikingly handsome man. The abbot closely studied the frame that once had lengthened too rapidly for flesh to keep pace but now was formed of well-proportioned muscle and would tower over most. Moreover, on entering he'd moved with the lithe grace of one in perfect physical condition. The subject of the extended examination stood steady and confident until at last the aging cleric nodded his approval, the white ruff of his hair waving as if in agreement. All in all a worthy heir to the famed Ice Warrior.

"Why are you here on Wryborne lands, my son?" the abbot asked at last, going right to the heart of the matter as had always been his way.

With affection Galen wordlessly acknowledged his old mentor's habit but countered with another question, a puzzle presented firstly. "Why is the return of a wrongfully taken gift unnecessary?"

Accepting the younger man's prior right to an answer, the priest's lips took on a wry quirk as he spoke. "Lady Sybil and I are not so simple-minded as a certain cunning lord believes."

He'd never met the man, yet Galen had no trouble recognizing Baron Gilfrey in the description—his parents had described him just so.

"A man both wicked and sly, he possesses an

inordinate conceit and cannot believe those of purer intent able to circumvent his will. Thus, our goal has been remarkably easy to achieve. Merely does the lady give thirty marks each time, and when the baron's 'minion' comes to retrieve her gift, I return to him the same bag—with fifteen inside.''

Galen blinked at the expression of benign innocence on the abbot's bland face. As a child he'd thought of the slightly built priest with his laughing eyes as a mischievous angel, but never had Galen suspected him capable of such devious ways, even in the pursuit of pious goals. At the same time, it soothed his conscience and reinforced the possibility that good ends excused the withholding of truth, even to the extent of allowing misconceptions to take root and grow in another's mind.

"Never has it occurred to either the baron or his 'minion' to ask if I have given them all I received.'' Father Pieter sighed in mock regret then went solemn in truth as he added, '' 'Tis plain they believe that I, same as near all others on these lands, am too fearful of their earthly power to risk their ire. They fail to understand that I answer to a higher authority. One who has surely blessed our paltry endeavors to relieve the painful poverty with which the wicked have assailed folk hereabouts.''

The abbot stepped away to perch atop a small stool on one side of the table while waving his guest to another. He waited until both were as comfortable as the simple wood seats allowed before continuing. "Though our noble thief has no fear of stealing what is meant for the church, apparently he dare not question the honesty of its custodian. A strange paradox but a fine thing, for were he to ask, my vows would compel me to speak only the truth.''

Galen nodded his acceptance not only of the abbot's honesty but of his whole plan to outwit the wily baron.

The warm smile most oft upon Pieter's face returned. Yet, having honestly answered his guest's question, he now demanded answer to the one he'd posed. "What brings you to Wryborne after all these many years? And why have you not gone to the castle as noble guest but rather skulk in the dark like some forest brigand?"

Galen grinned. How different were people's views of such men. While Amicia thought of him as an outlaw and romantic hero, Father Pieter—rather Abbot Pieter—saw his actions as those of a skulking villain.

Stalling for time to consider the wisdom of sharing his secret with this man, Galen absently lifted a coin from the pile on the table between them and skirted the issue. "In battle I've put to the test all the fine skills Lord Conal and my father taught me—and won."

Steady silver-green eyes glanced at the listener who'd gone solemn with an unspoken query. Galen knew the other wondered on whose behalf he'd fought; and, returning his attention to the jealously sought metal round on his palm as if it were of great interest, he quietly answered. "Little respect have I for our king, but less for the French. Although one year past I stood with my father on the field at Runnymede to insure that John put his seal to the Charter, when a group of fellow nobles invited the foreign prince to our country, we neither of us supported them."

The abbot had joined many churchmen in applauding the movement to force a reluctant king's reaffirmation of the document that put some limits to royal rights and insured the respect of religious orders. But he, also, believed the barons had gone too far when they sought the leadership of a French prince. A vital problem and reason for the darkness which had fallen upon the land, yet none of this was answer to the question he'd asked.

Unspeaking, Abbot Pieter lifted his brows in an action the younger man recognized as his former teacher's patient demand for the pertinent response. The sharp mind this learned man had praised in a boy came to a quick decision. He'd share the tale of his quest with the abbot. What better source had he to learn the true purpose behind a desperate plea.

"Shortly after I routed a group of invaders who carried the fight too near Tarrant, a message arrived from Lady Sybil—the first communication received from her since the day I left this fiefdom so many years past." Surely, Galen hoped, here was someone who could explain the cryptic words. With the lopsided metal circle shining between thumb and forefinger, Galen paused to watch his host closely, but no glimmer of understanding lightened the age-lined face before him. 'Twas disappointing. Mayhap he'd not been specific enough. "The gentle lady stated that danger loomed and begged us to intervene, yet she did not tell us the nature of the threat. I have come in answer to her plea, but can accomplish little without knowing the need. What evil have I been summoned to quell?"

No response was forthcoming, and Galen let the coin drop to clink against its fellows. Abbot Pieter merely looked puzzled. When Galen spoke again frustration roughened his low voice. "Surely you have some knowledge whereof she writes?"

"Since the wicked event that sent you away, life has grown bleak and hard but little changes from day to day, year to year. What Lady Sybil could possibly seek of you, I do not know. She seldom concerns herself with aught but the state of her soul—and the plight of the people. From the first she has quietly worked with me to lessen the misery of the common folk near crushed under the heavy yoke of Gilfrey's tyranny and the king's avarice. They've little to eat, rags to wear, and more than a few lack the strength to survive the storms of winter in the bitter cold of their wretched hovels."

Galen straightened. Did his foster mother merely wish tangible help for her people? It seemed unlikely, yet his warm memories of her soft heart and loving spirit made it a possibility.

The abbot saw his friend brighten and was quick to deny the false hope. "Though what we accomplish is but a pittance lost in the gaping void of Lord Gilfrey's malicious greed, 'tis no worse this day than a year or even a decade past."

Which, Galen acknowledged, meant it could hardly be the reason behind her desperate plea. His mouth tightened against the loss of another hope.

The strong man's disgust with being blocked by an invisible foe—lack of information—was plain to Pieter, and he offered what little support was in his power to lend.

"Since I left Castle Dungeld to join the abbey, there's been no true priest within its walls."

The quiet statement broke Galen's preoccupation with the task that seemed to grow more difficult with each failed strategy. No noble residence he knew of lacked at least one cleric to perform daily masses and act as scribe for its lord.

Pieter saw the puzzled expression in silver-green eyes and hastily explained. "When Lord Gilfrey arrived, he had a cleric among his company and felt no need for my services. Unfortunately his man is so poorly educated that he's barely able to put word to parchment and possesses neither true loyalty to the church nor deep love of our Lord." Abbot Pieter's distaste for the facts strained his voice. "Few among the castle's inhabitants are willing to seek religious guidance from him and come to me. Lady Sybil, however, has chosen to withdraw from worldly concerns and prefers never to venture beyond the castle walls. Thus, once each week I attend her there."

Attention straying again to the problem of an unknown goal, Galen gave his host only polite interest.
Pieter's laughing grin returned like sun from behind
fleeing clouds, and gently prodded a distracted mind
down the path he'd laid. "In the confessional we are
alone, so totally alone that what is said reaches no
other ears."

A slow smile of satisfaction spread across Galen's
firm mouth. Privacy was a rare and precious virtue
seldom found within the tight confines of a fortress.
He leaned toward its benefactor as if speaking to a
fellow conspirator, which in truth the abbot had
become.

"Tell her I've arrived and will do all in my power to
aid her cause if she'll tell me what is needed. Assure
her that I am hers to command, yet only by knowing
the cause have I hope of forestalling what she fears."

The abbot nodded even as he cautioned, "I was on
the Isle of Dungeld only two days past and cannot
return for near a sennight without rousing suspicion."

"An unfortunate delay," Galen said as he rose to his
full height. "But worth the wait."

Abbot Pieter stood, bumping the table as he did so
and sending the piled coins sliding down to spread in
a wider arc across its surface. The motion caught
Galen's eye. He lifted the discarded leather bag, and
scooped the unwanted coins inside.

"So that you may with perfect honesty tell the baron
that you have none of the confiscated wealth, I'll take
these away with me."

The aging man's face reflected such an odd mixture
of relief and distress that Galen nearly laughed. "Nay,
father, I do not intend to enrich my own pocket. You
know as well as I that I've enough and more without
taking at the expense of either the church or another
lord's starving serfs. Rather will I see these coins used
to provide those in need with a measure of what they
lack."

The abbot beamed his approval of this rare noble able to put a limit to his greed and consider the anguished poverty of others. Yet, if Galen meant to go to the common folk, he'd find a group with little reason to trust a person unknown and would need a sign of worthiness to win even the opportunity to prove himself. Bending his head, Pieter removed his rosary without disturbing a single strand of white.

"Godspeed and take care." In a gesture of good will and support, the older man extended to the younger what at first glance seemed a simple string of black beads. But if the eye followed its downward flow, a rich and distinctive crucifix was found—all of gold and set about with jewels of ruby fire.

Galen was warmed by the respect his former instructor in right ways was plainly offering. Without need of words to define its intended use, he solemnly nodded as he accepted the loan of this precious religious emblem. After tucking it safely away, he said, "I will remain hidden and return here one week hence." He moved away, opened the door, and ducked beneath its low frame to disappear into the anonymity of night shadows.

A gleam of light sundered the darkness, and Amicia sighed with relief as a towering silhouette bent to step through the square of momentary brightness. When the door closed, cutting off the light, from her vantage point on one of the lower limbs of an elm a short distance inside the woodland's edge, she was left to visually search through near impenetrable gloom. At last she saw movement—a figure approaching—but restrained her impatience and forced herself to wait until it drew closer.

Patience was not Amicia's strongest virtue, and quiet waiting sorely strained what little she possessed. After leaving Kelda and her admirer behind on the parapet, she'd set out on her planned mission without delay. Once over the narrow causeway between Dungeld and the rocky shore she'd quickly moved through the colorless forms of the night forest, trying to bring reality to the weak hope that if her warning were delivered with haste, she could return before the tide rose too high for a safe return.

To prevent nameless fears of unseen foes from weakening her courage, she'd concentrated hard on her objective—only to find the waterfall's cave empty. A few moments of growing anxiety inside the damp cavern had convinced her to abandon her initial plan to await Galen's return within its relative safety. She was sure he'd gone under cover of night to restore the stolen gift to the good fathers. Refusing to linger and give cautious thought to the wisdom of her action, she'd set out to intercept him on the return path. The excitement of a dangerous adventure was easier to deal with than the tension of idly waiting for another to complete a daring deed.

You were a fool to let your thoughts wander, Amicia scolded herself. Now she'd lost sight of the shadow she meant to intercept. It was frustrating. Bracing one hand against a branch above, Amicia leaned forward to better see the path not far away.

"Oh-h—" As the limb swung wide Amicia's short yelp of dismay echoed in a forest suddenly gone still. She tumbled to the ground. Fortunately her soft landing amidst the thick padding of ferns at the tree's base prevented physical injury, but it did nothing to ease pride bruised by the inelegant heap of tangled cloak and skirts she'd become. A fact made all the worse by the parting on one side of a foliage wall and the unmistakable light eyes gleaming down at her. Amicia wanted to scream in frustration but hid it behind the brave smile she gave the man who reached down to lift her as easily as if she were a child.

Galen's amazement at the sight of the well-born beauty so clearly fallen from a tree, shredded leaves still clumped in her curled hands, quickly turned to vexation with her for another unexpected and ill-advised arrival. Unaware that the cloak pulled loose by the fall remained on the ground, Galen stepped back into the path and lowered her feet to solid earth. Still, he held her slender shoulders between his hands, torn between kissing her senseless and shaking a measure of sense into her. Sweet Mary's Tears! What was Lady Sybil thinking to allow her daughter such dangerous freedom? And if Lady Sybil had developed such a preoccupation with religious concerns and the serf's plight that she failed to see the headstrong girl's doings, surely Anne should protect her lady's daughter from the folly of wild actions. 'Twas a puzzle for which he could not demand answer without revealing his true identity and past ties to Castle Dungeld.

Tone roughened by the impossibilities of the whole situation, he demanded, "What are you doing out here in the forest during the darkest hours—and alone?"

Amicia's dismay in so graceless a meeting faded beneath the flaring of a quick temper. "I risked my own safety to bring you a warning."

Galen's brows rose but his cold expression changed not at all, and he chose not to ask the obvious.

"Fine." His lack of response was an insult! "The baron is welcome to you!" Amicia jerked free of his hold and whirled—or attempted to do so. A thorn bush caught at her skirts, imprisoning her in its prickly hold. She immediately turned toward the spiny culprit and gave a sharp tug, but acting with more irritation than care she only succeeded in seeing her gown more firmly entangled.

"Wait or you'll tear it," Galen cautioned, moving to stand directly behind her. "Let me help you free."

Indignation at his attitude toward the perilous chances she'd taken on his behalf was not lessened by his offer of aid, and Amicia tried to pull away.

To restrain the angry girl, Galen wrapped one arm about her waist and drew her back against his wide chest while leaning over her shoulder to better see as he sought her release from the bush's grasp. Such intimacy, however pure the motivation, was a mistake. The maid's wildflower scent tantalized his senses almost as much as the downward view of alluring curves, soft and so temptingly near.

The strength of the arm holding her and the heat of warm muscle at her back arrested breath in Amicia's throat and strangled all her fine temper. Thinking to recover her dignity by blocking off the sight of the hand efficiently dealing with her captor, one thorn at a time, she let thick lashes drift down. A tactical error that she discovered only when already too late. In a darkness without even the distractions of shadows and moonbeams, she was all too aware of the man so close his night-black hair brushed her cheek and found herself leaning pliant against his powerful body. She feared that by his nearness, by the arm binding her so tightly, he could feel her heart pounding and would know the heavy beat due neither to fear nor to anger but rather to heated memories of the last time she'd stood wrapped in the fiery circle of his embrace.

When the beauty melted against him like wax to candle-flame, Galen's hand went still on snagged cloth. He felt her tremble, heard the tiny catch in her breath, and his blood caught fire, racing through his veins with the speed of windswept flame. His head turned the whisper of distance required to bury his mouth against the satin curve of skin between throat and shoulder.

Amicia felt as if she'd been branded—a welcome mark of fire—and arched her throat into its heat. Sensing tantalizing pleasures just beyond her reach, she nestled her head against the broad shoulder while a soft moan escaped tight constraints.

The aching sound was more than Galen could resist. He justified sampling her honeyed nectar with the lie that he had restraint sufficient to then see sweet play end. Yet, in his impatience for the taste he loosed the last thorns' hold on her skirts with less care than intended. Stepping back, he turned her full into his embrace, hands sliding beneath her cloak to stroke slowly up and down her back, caressing and pulling her tempting form ever closer. His hungry mouth gently brushed hers, enticing her lips to part, and when they opened to the heat of joining, the kiss immediately deepened, whirling Amicia into a chasm of fiery sensations.

When she instinctively lifted her body into the hard curve of his, Galen felt the limits to his control drawing dangerously near. So much for his lauded iron will. More of this wild maid's untutored yet irresistible enticements and he'd lose the ability to see her chastity remain intact.

Amicia was beyond rational thought, too deep into the well of new and addicting pleasures to comprehend the honorable motives behind his attempt to push her away. To her his action seemed an unbearable rejection, and she fought free of his restraining hold to burrow against him again.

A low groan broke from Galen. Her innocence was even more dangerous than he'd thought—constantly presenting him with such temptations as he couldn't possibly be expected to long resist.

Hearing the rough sound through a smoky haze of passion while at the same time feeling him tense to reject her once more, Amicia twined her small fingers with his much larger ones to prevent them from putting her aside.

The feel of soft hands, unused to toil, served only to reinforce the fact that this naive seductress was both a virgin and well-born—two insurmountable barriers between him and the satisfaction of a forbidden desire. He was neatly trapped between his hidden identity and hers. A man of honor, he could not take what she seemed willing to give—'twould be a betrayal of his dead foster father. And more, for all her wild actions, Amicia was clearly too innocent to know what she invited by this escapade in the wooded dark. But he with his considerable experience should surely have no difficulty in controlling his responses. A fine and rational argument that did nothing to douse the fire raging in his veins. Indeed, it merely intensified his frustrated irritation. Disentangling his fingers, he cupped her shoulders and gently but firmly held her away.

"What danger does the baron threaten me with?" After the aching moments just past, Galen's voice was husky as he looked down into a smoldering golden gaze full of confusion.

Still lost amidst the cinders of a hungry fire, Amicia found no meaning in the words. To Galen the sight of the obviously well-kissed beauty was far too tantalizing, and he stepped abruptly back from more danger than he dared risk.

Pulse loudly pounding in her ears, Amicia struggled back to sanity. She was embarrassed by her inability to return from passion's fiery valley with the same ease as he. Plainly he'd not found her as exciting as she'd found him, had not shared the same depth of delight. The mere possibility fanned a small flame from the coals of her temper, and its bright light cleared the haze from her eyes.

Galen's smile was curiously one-sided. That she found his hard-won restraint insulting was clear, yet he'd no doubt she'd be frightened indeed if he'd fully taken the gift she was irritated with him for rejecting.

The fact that he seemed to find her emotional state entertaining did nothing to cool Amicia's indignation. Though its warmth was the last thing she needed, she pointedly turned her attention from him and bent to retrieve her cloak. Straightening, she squared her shoulders before answering his question in a voice whose weakness irritated her more.

"Gilfrey rides out at dawn to hunt you down for interfering with his tax collector." Beneath the power of light eyes that seemed to penetrate the dark, Amicia had failed to adequately consider the words she spoke.

Imperfectly hidden, amusement deepened the groves on either side of Galen's lips. Did this girl not hear what she said, how she betrayed her identity? Who but one of Castle Dungeld's own could know what the baron planned? And more, who but one of close bond, however unwelcome, would name the baron Gilfrey—not this time alone, but near every time she'd spoken of him?

Of a sudden, Amicia realized a portion of her error. As too oft in the past, she'd spoken without thought but quickly sought to give a believable source for her knowledge. "My—my sister Melly is maidservant to Wryborne's heiress who told her it was so. When she came home by the night tide, Melly told me, and I came directly to seek you out so you may be prepared when the dawn arrives."

If he hadn't known who she was, he might have believed her—except that she hadn't explained her use of the baron's given name.

"I thank you for your risk on my behalf, and in gratitude I'll escort you safely to your cottage on the village's edge." He waited, wondering what excuse the inventive girl would find to waylay his honorable offer.

Amicia's smile froze. While behind it her thoughts whirled with this new challenge, she refastened the dark cloak at her throat. For the first time in her life she failed to find a suitable answer.

Galen watched delicate brows knit above the unnatural curve of passion-swollen lips and felt guilty. His offer was sure to force her into a polite rejection and dangerous night spent alone and unprotected in the forest. He quickly recanted his action.

"Better yet that neither of us risk traveling to the village at so late an hour—too many night creatures might take exception to our intrusion into their world."

Happily, Amicia didn't realize how revealing was her deep sigh of relief and brilliant smile. "'Struth. Creatures both human and beast. I fear the poachers who hunt in the dark would be even less understanding than their animal counterparts."

Galen returned her infectious smile and offered a seemingly harmless alternative. "We share the secret of the waterfall's cave making it only fair we share its haven tonight."

Amicia was suddenly aware of how very near she'd come to willingly surrendering innocence. By her actions had she not given Galen just reason to expect her to fulfill their wordless promise by spending the night alone in his company? A reasonable expectation doubtless any true village girl would willingly satisfy. Alarmed, she looked up, and the crescent moon now risen high above shadowy treetops revealed the apprehension in deep brown eyes.

"Doubtless my two companions are already asleep inside." Galen's reassuring smile brought Amicia only an inexplicable disappointment. "They'll be surprised when they awake and find themselves hosts to such delightful feminine company." That the maid was caught between relief and regret proved she suffered as much from frustration as he and the fact eased Galen's irritation. Maintaining a perfectly gracious smile, he offered Amicia his arm.

Studying Galen closely, suspicious of the innocent smile below light eyes gleaming with amusement, Amicia put her fingers atop his forearm and let him lead her toward their destination. She refused to ask why he deemed it safer to walk to the cave than the village. No use in the question when she'd really no other choice, even if she wanted the one that would leave her fending for herself in the dark and take her the sooner from his company.

❧ *Chapter 6* ❧

Slowly Amicia drifted up from the purple depths of slumber to the lavender haze between full sleep and wakefulness. Pleasant dreams of the welcome fires in the circle of powerful arms faded into a misty awareness of falling water and the cave it hid. She turned her head and felt the gentle rasp of the cloak Galen had rolled into a pillow and placed beneath her cheek before lying down at her side and laying his own atop them both. Just before heavy lids opened in search of the man, the sound of an unfamiliar whisper came to her ear.

"But who is she?"

"A fine question, Walter." Amicia recognized this quietly laughing voice. It belonged to the man named Carl, and it continued. "You weren't here when our outlaw leader's admirer last appeared."

If the second speaker was Carl, then his questioner must be the young third member of the band whom she'd seen at the pool's edge that first day.

"Outlaw?"

Although the stunned question was little more than a gasp, after Carl's soft words it seemed to fill the cave's tight confines. Yet, its comparative loudness was not what puckered Amicia's brows but rather the

wealth of disbelief it held. Why? Though she'd been
the one to give them this description, Carl had confirmed it true. So, what was the reason for this unmet
third's surprise? Did he simply choose not to think of
their praiseworthy actions in such terms? She went
unnaturally still, fearful of interrupting what promised to be an interesting conversation.

Within an hour of rising Galen had given up the
battle to keep his gaze from the sleeping maid, and
when a frown disturbed the perfection of her face, he
saw that she was wakeful. Stepping between the other
men, he pointed at the feminine figure too rigidly held
to be sleeping still. Quashing the guilt for instructing
an impressionable youth to join in a lie, he mouthed
an order to his squire to go along with the ruse.

As bewildered Walter nodded, light from the fire pit
struck glints of red in the straw-toned hair brushing
shoulders angular with the quick-growing bones of
adolescence. He'd willingly follow any directive given
by the lord he much admired. Nonetheless, he was
most confused. True, they'd specifically come unan-
nounced and without material proof of proud heritage, yet how, he wondered, could anyone fail to
recognize in Lord Galen's noble face and bearing the
well-born man he was. That anyone had mistaken him
for some ill-begot outlaw was a most unbelievable
notion.

Galen moved to kneel at the dainty beauty's side—
where he'd spent a sleepless night, too aware that the
alluring form that had so recently curled in sweet
surrender against him lay only a handsbreadth away.
Forcing his mind into less evocative channels, he
concentrated on the fact that the sun was well up and
she must be up and soon on her way home. "Amicia,"
he quietly called.

The sound of her name on Galen's lips was a
beckoning music that Amicia could not resist. Rolling
to the side, on one arm she lifted toward its source.
When heavy lashes half-rose, she found herself a scant

breath from the man so recently the focus of wickedly sweet dreams. Caught in the snare of a silvery-green gaze that pierced the cave's constant twilight gloom, memories of the dark hours' brief embrace echoed in the heartbeat once again pounding at a furious pace. Her world seemed to shrink until it held only them two.

In the darkened depths of her eyes Galen saw the same fiery images, and when peach-sweet lips parted on an inaudible moan, he slowly leaned down. So intent on again tasting their delicious forbidden nectar was he that only Carl's muffled spurt of teasing laughter woke him from the momentary trance. He abruptly pulled his head away, an unaccustomed heat warming his face. God's Blood! Blushing like some untried boy!

"Come, a breakfast of tender roast quail awaits." The mundane words were formally spoken but his low, husky voice brushed a velvet caress across Amicia's senses while the brilliant green fires burning in his gaze wielded more power over the woman than he knew. He rose and offered Amicia his aid in rising, but she looked at the proffered arm with such longing that her desire to be wrapped within its embrace was unmistakable. Galen's jaw went hard with the self-control demanded to keep from answering her untimely temptations. Leastways, he comforted himself, her back was to his companions. Thus, they'd not viewed the seductive sight of heavy-lidded eyes, parted lips a breath from a kiss, and sleep-mussed, tawny mane. Though assuredly no danger threatened her from either the happy-wed Carl or the young Walter, he was unwilling to share the vision with any other.

Amicia scolded herself. By the age of seventeen no village girl would be so clearly smitten. Still, although she moved to sit primly upright, her gaze followed the line of his still outstretched arm up to the muscular expanse of a green-wool covered chest, strong throat, intensely masculine face, and stunning eyes. She gulped and recanted her assuredly wrongful assessment of a village girl's abilities. Never would she believe any woman drawing breath could be less than overwhelmed by him. Forcing a strained smile, she laid stiff fingers lightly atop the fine wool of his sleeve and silently ordered herself to leastwise pretend some small measure of maturity. The need was reinforced when, as he helped her to stand, she caught a glimpse of two pairs of curious eyes upon her.

Galen had felt Amicia's admiring gaze slide over him as surely as if it had been a physical caress. Most women had the experience to shield their interest behind coy words and sophisticated smiles—the better, they mistakenly believed, to trap him into the permanent giving of what he would not. Amicia was far too naive either to know the strength of her allure or to recognize the danger in her vulnerability to him. Only by virtue of their hidden identities was she protected from his hunger—and even that restraint had its limits.

"The noontide hour fast approaches." Wanting to turn the maid's potent gaze elsewhere, with his free hand Galen waved toward the cave's mouth. Bright daylight sparkled beyond the waterfall door but the sun had risen too high to send beams slanting through its liquid barrier.

Amicia bit her lip, castigating herself for allowing personal matters to waylay her attention from important obligations owed to others. She'd given Kelda a promise to return with all possible haste, had put her friend at risk of Gilfrey's ire. By midmorn she must cross the causeway, return to the castle-isle before her absence was discovered. But how? Again, her lack of forethought threatened others. She should have considered this problem before, while there was time to devise some worthy ploy. Now her thoughts froze beneath the sudden fear that Galen would insist on escorting her safely home—to that wretched imaginary cottage on the village edge. Saints' Tears, she wished she'd not gotten so carried away as to create a specific description. She'd been fortunate indeed that he'd not forced her to answer his offer of the past night. Too likely today he would.

Although Amicia stared straight ahead, Galen saw the dilemma stealing golden lights from her eyes and immediately sought to soothe the worry from her path. "As you warned, the baron and his men crossed by boat at dawn."

Apprehension grew fourfold in the anxious face lifted to him, and Galen cursed himself for stating his meaning so awkwardly. He shook his head and hurried to clarify his words. "From a safe distance we watched as they passed by on their way to the abbey, then almost certainly the village. Proof, you'll agree, that the village path is unsafe for a lone woman to travel."

Amicia nodded, fearful of where his comments led. While Galen doubtless referred to the dangers faced by any woman who traveled alone ('twould take one feeblewitted indeed to risk the road while a party of rough men trained to war were about), she acknowledged the danger in being caught by her stepfather. But then she'd no intention of traveling in that direction. The problem was how to go the other way without alerting Galen.

"Thus, once you've eaten I'll accompany you—"

"Nay!" Amicia immediately refused the apparent suggestion that he walk into a situation far more dangerous for him than for her—and one both unnecessary and unwanted. Her mind raced, seeking some rational argument, but found none in the muddled morass her thoughts had become.

"Not to your cottage on the village edge," Galen continued, unfazed by her rejection. "I suggest that you would be far wiser to join your sister at the castle. By the time you've eaten the tide will be out, and while the baron uselessly hunts his prey, you can safely cross to his domain. Then only when he and his guardsmen are again within the fortress, need you venture forth—in company with your sister and the escort surely she has."

Amicia's relief lent an enticing warmth to her smile. Green fires flashed so vividly in Galen's eyes that her gaze fell away, recognizing the danger she incited and cursing herself for faltering before the thrilling contact.

"One day—" His words were so low only she could hear them, a threat she took as a promise. The pleasure in eyes gone to honey was unmistakable when they rose to linger on his mouth 'til he could taste their sweetness. Frustration with the restraining company of others warred in his mind with the certainty that only their presence protected her from what he'd sworn he'd not do.

Feeling Galen's tension and divining its source, she glanced at the cave's other two inhabitants. Carl was grinning while the boy, surely no older than she herself, looked disapproving. Did he think her some obliging village girl free with her favors and condemn her for it? Righteous indignation rose. How dare he censure her when, in the company of outlaws, he was clearly not so virtuous himself. Yet, how else but that he should see her that way when she'd gone to great lengths to convince them she *was* a village girl? Her night spent here with strange men gave adequate reason to question her virtue. She felt her cheeks heating to a rosy hue.

Galen saw her embarrassment but could do nothing in front of her to correct Walter's wrong interpretation. Another trap laid by hidden truths, and it brought a dark scowl to his suddenly cold face.

Carl watched the others with a curious expression. He was amused by the sight of his noble friend emotionally falling victim to a woman for the first time, if the naive and headstrong maid could be termed that. He wished Galen's parents could share the view. They'd made no secret that they hoped their son would wed and be about the business of providing the next generation of heirs, although he'd repeatedly told them he'd yet to meet the female he could bear waking to see day after day. Earl Garrick was patient and could hardly be else when he'd waited so long himself, but Lady Nessa grew increasingly anxious. Aye, they'd delight in seeing their ladycharmer son caught in the toils of a tiny, untamed woman-child. The utter misunderstanding between the two intensified his amusement, but he jauntily stepped forward to lighten its murky flow.

"Milady," Carl's exaggerated bow would have bordered on insult but for the teasing gleam in his eyes. "Your meal awaits." Both hands swept to one side, directing her attention toward the spitted quail turned golden by the slow burning coals of the firepit below. "If our honored guest will take her seat, our leader's squire will serve."

Galen gave the unrepentant Carl a scowl of displeasure for his reference to Walter's true position while Amicia sank into a curtsy as exaggerated as the bow, assuming both title and manners a meaningless jest.

The man's friendly grin soothed Amicia's discomfort. Responding to it without thought, she didn't pause to realize that by such elegantly executed mannerisms both demonstrated a long experience in their usage.

"Gentle sir, I most gratefully accept your kind invitation to dine." The savory odor of roasting meat reminded Amicia of how long it had been since last she'd eaten. She moved forward and, with all the grace Anne's years of careful training had taught, settled on the upended stump placed on one side of the ring of stones. While hunger rumbled in a most unladylike manner, she waited, arranging her skirts daintily about her small feet safe from possible sparks from the flame-blackened pit.

Walter looked in confusion between the lord who had silently bade him go along with the maid's odd assumptions and the man who'd plainly named him squire. From behind Amicia's back Galen slowly, firmly shook his head. Walter shrugged, stepping into the fire's ring of light to reach for the spitted bird. He quickly freed several strips of the golden meat and offered it to the beauty who watched in anticipation.

Hearing sounds behind, Amicia assumed the two older men had turned their attention to other matters and thus she was safe in quietly questioning the one known as Walter.

"Have you been with Galen long?" she asked, as hungry to know more of Galen as to enjoy the succulent roast in her hands.

"Since I was eight." Walter's voice was strained by his fear of saying more than he ought. 'Twas the truth but not all. He *had* been in Castle Tarrant since the day when he was eight that his parents had taken him there to foster with its earl. Yet, he'd not been oft in Galen's company until at the age of twelve he'd won the honor of being his squire. A proud day.

Amicia heard his strain and nibbled her lower lip. She hesitated to further offend him by asking when their forest hiding days had begun. Instead she tried to put him at ease with a simple comment. "It must be a pleasant life—surrounded by creation's beauty and free of other's restraints." She was unaware of the wealth of longing in her final words.

Having no idea how to answer, Walter gave a weak smile and mumbled a wild excuse to move away from the lovely stranger's curiously familiar presence.

Left to her own company, Amicia devoured the roast quail with a delicate ferocity, unaware of the quiet communication taking place at the cave's mouth. Walter joined the two men standing where the falling water's gentle roar would mask low-spoken words.

"Has this girl visited Castle Tarrant?" Walter asked,

brows knit above a frown of concentration. Surely he'd remember any visitor so pretty, though not if they'd met during his days in his father's keep. But, how could that be? His family's lands were far from here.

Galen smiled wryly while Carl presented the boy with the same puzzle he himself had earlier been given and successfully solved.

"Close your eyes, picture her face, and compare it to those near to you in our castle home."

A pale green gaze closely watched as the young man obeyed, his face creasing with a fierce concentration. A moment later Walter's eyes popped open, and his jaw sagged in stunned recognition.

"Aye, a lady she is, Walter," Galen confirmed. "But to guard the success of our guest, we dare not reveal our own good birth. Rather, for her safety as well as our own, we'll let her believe her version of our purpose, even will the actions we take on the people's behalf support her theory." Aye, once trapped in living a lie, he could only work to see some good come of it.

Walter's eyes widened at the planned behavior so uncharacteristic of his lord, but he nodded his willingness to do whatever he was commanded.

Taking a small cloth square from a stone outcropping near the entrance where it had been left to dry, Galen leaned out to hold it under falling water. Wringing it out as he went, he moved around the outside of the firepit until he stood opposite the maid daintily licking her fingers. Self-derision gave his smile a faint twist. Walter, even Carl, might believe the reasons he gave for his action to be wholly unselfish. Himself he could not deceive. The need to prove himself all that the naive beauty dreamed of rose more from a desire to impress her than for any altruistic purpose—save the absolute determination to see Lady Sybil free of the unknown looming danger.

"If you're done, best we be off to set you on your path to Castle Dungeld."

Amicia looked up. To her thinking, she was too small when standing, and now, seated so close to the ground, Galen towered above. The shadow he threw stretched across the cave floor and climbed the wall behind as if intent on overawing her with his impressive size. She met the penetrating power of eyes gone again to green flame, and breath caught in her throat. Smiling weakly, she gulped before reaching out with fingers she hoped he'd not notice were already embarrassingly damp.

Twisting the cloth between her hands, she rose too fast and tripped on her own hem. A blush stained her cheeks with discomfort for the clumsiness displayed. Even as she prayed he would think the color due to the fire's heat, he proved it unlikely by stepping around the ring of stones to steady her with a strong hand on either shoulder.

What was it about this man that stole her natural grace and left her a bumbling fool? She need not even glance his way to know the answer to that witless query—had she not repeatedly enumerated his attractions from toes to thick black hair?

Looking down at the top of a tawny head fire-brushed with gold, Galen sensed her tension. He wished he could as clearly tell whether it was born of embarrassment alone or tinged with an awareness of him as deep as his own for her. A useless question that he must neither seek answer to nor waste time pondering when it would only increase the strain. He cursed himself for a fool. He who had been pursued by many—and had willingly fallen but never lingered long enough to be trapped by sensual snares—had suddenly gone as moon-eyed for a sweet face and lush form as ever had any callow youth. And all for an untamed maid current circumstances decreed he could not have. Gritting his teeth with self-derision, he forced the hands on her shoulders to push her a step away before loosing her and inclining his dark head toward the outgoing way.

Amicia's heart thumped uncomfortably. She was dismayed to once again have proof that he could easily set her away when all she wanted of life was to nestle against the wide chest that had been no more than a hand's breadth away. Shame for her weakness hardened into temper as she turned and marched toward the cave entrance.

Had Walter not earlier learned her heritage, he'd have known it after one glance at the golden flames of determination flaring in her eyes. He quickly stepped out of her path.

When the young man abruptly ducked away, Amicia was struck with regret. She'd not meant him to pay for the ill-temper raised by her own mistake, and she gave him the same blindingly sweet smile that had stunned Farrold when first they'd met. Walter's brows flew high and his mouth again fell open. A beauty he'd seen from the first but the potent heat of that smile rivaled the sun, and in it he was sure lay the reason behind his lord's odd behavior.

Although Galen had bent to retrieve the pillow-rolled cloak Amicia had forgotten, he, too, saw the smile she gave the boy and frowned. Jealousy he would not admit. Such emotions were for the weak-willed, and he was not that. Still, he coveted all such sights and wished for the power to see them reserved for him alone.

Intent on proving herself more capable of physical prowess than she'd recently displayed, Amicia lightly stepped from cave mouth to hidden stair. Only as she stood at the point where she ever descended and ascended did she pause to realize that in order to safely navigate the climb, she must lift her skirts and reveal a shameful length of leg. She glanced quickly over her shoulder and found Galen waiting just behind. No help for it. What needs must, must be. Brushing a mass of tawny hair back from her face and shaking it to fall in heavy waves past her waist, Amicia took a handful of skirt, tucked it beneath the low slung belt of braided cord riding her hips, and began to climb.

Galen hadn't paused to consider what lengths might be necessitated by such a leavetaking, and his eyes widened at the unexpected sight of a shapely bare calf a scant distance from his eyes. He looked up and caught a glimpse of delectable thigh. Lord, had no one taught this maid what may and may not be done before a man? Were she his, he'd be certain she knew it full well before any other was blessed with the vision. Unbound hair was rebellious, this was reckless. The wordless berating of a lax teacher succeeded only in reminding him that he had certainly been taught better than to take advantage of another's lack—no matter how strong the temptation. Forcing self-control he turned his attention to the rock wall's hand and toe holds. He'd known the dusty dents carved in stone from such an early age that he little needed to give the deep concentration bent upon them.

Once standing atop the cliff, Amicia hastily jerked her skirts down while Galen heaved his much larger body over the precipice. She turned toward the path she and Kelda had blazed between cave and meadow, but Galen halted her with a soft touch on her arm. When brown eyes glanced back over a slender shoulder, he motioned her to follow him and headed straight for a green wall. Amicia questioned his sanity for risking so rough a trail but dared not argue for fear he'd question the source of her knowledge. To her surprise, once he'd pushed aside the weeping ends of a willow branch and moved a few steps beyond, there was a path, years overgrown but discernible.

By this new way through the deep shadows of dense trees, lush forest greenery soon gave way to the shore. A shore Amicia deemed too quickly come to. Desperately searching for an excuse, any excuse, to again meet this exciting man, it never occurred to her to wonder how he'd come to know the route. Rising waves lapped at the causeway's edges. She must hasten across to relieve Kelda of the worry that doubtless had her pacing their chamber—yet how could she go when it might mean the end, might be the last time she'd see Galen.

Amicia gazed over the pathway through a sea which in its shallow reaches was near the same shade as Galen's eyes. Torn between regret for leaving and anxiety to reach home quickly, she barely noticed when he settled the dark cloak she'd have forgotten about her shoulders.

"Hurry or the incoming tide will block your path," Galen urged, concerned for her safety—and hoping that with her distracting influence removed he could concentrate on solving the problem of getting the coins to the people without the baron's interference. Besides, surely someone in the castle had missed her. To reinforce the importance in seeing her gone, he reminded himself that were it known she'd been out all night, 'twould be the end of her fair name, a prize she must never lose in shame.

"I'll leave," Amicia nodded, "as soon as you've given your oath to meet me on the morrow at midmorn."

Galen shook his head. 'Twould be madness—an endangerment of his quest and a risk for her, both from her stepfather and from him.

Amicia promptly plopped down atop the soft pillow of a green fern, golden brown skirts spread around her like the petals of a flower, and met his surprised gaze with a saucy tilt to her chin.

"Meeting again would be madness." Galen spoke his thoughts aloud, but more firmly added, "It was you who brought the news that I am hunted."

Amicia impulsively lifted his hand between her two much smaller ones, and took a chance, praying her shaky instincts had a firm base. "Tell me you wish never to see me again, and I'll go. But if you cannot, then I won't leave 'til you've promised I may come again to the secret haven we share. You need not leave the cave's protective shield—I'll come to you." Amicia waited, heart thumping in fear of his answer.

Raised by parents committed to truth, Galen had always met uncomfortable questions with implacable silence—a tactic that would not suffice with this open girl. Yet, untrained to deceit, he knew himself unable to meet her direct brown eyes and successfully lie. Gazing down at the soft, pale fingers clinging with determination to his much darker, sword-callused hand, he ruefully shook his head again.

"Not at the cave and not on the morrow, I've work to be done." It was all too possible that she might inadvertently lead his foes to the cave and see its perfect hiding spot revealed. He closed his mind to the fact that on the next few days low tide would occur at midmorn and by refusing to attempt a change of that point he ignored the only likely opportunity to defeat her.

"Then the day after," Amicia persisted. "And in the meadow at the end of the path I nearly led you across."

Galen didn't speak, but Amicia took his denial of the location and date as his only objections, and accepted his ensuing silence as agreement. She jumped up to throw her arms about his neck, rise on her toes, and give him a quick kiss on the chin, the highest she could reach, before fairly dancing to the causeway's beginning.

One last time before setting out, the impetuous girl turned to offer a cheery wave. Then, like the enchanted water sprite he'd thought her when first seeing her face through the waterfall, she seemed to float across the narrow path bound on each side by the sparkling sea. Staring intently at the alluring sway of the slender figure with a tumble of tawny hair glowing against her dark cloak, Galen wondered how he'd allowed his will to be turned by so guileless a maid after he'd withstood the schemes of famous beauties.

He had been a fool! Never had a woman interfered in his actions—'twas unmanly and, with important work to be done, he could nowise afford to surrender to such witless ways. How had he been tricked into agreeing to meet this hopelessly headstrong child–woman? Too likely the action spelled doom for his important quest—all because he'd allowed his response to her to fog the clear thinking and to melt the ability to freeze personal emotions for the sake of higher causes which his father had early taught him. But the blame was his, and he must take it; and not, like too many weak men did, lay it on a woman. Moreover, he found that although he regretted the circumstances under which they'd met, he couldn't regret meeting the exceptional girl. Lips clamped with determination, he turned back toward the forest and the tasks awaiting his return.

Before speaking, Kelda carefully looked up and down the corridor. This topmost level of the castle contained only the chamber she shared with Amicia, the one belonging to her parents, two vacant, and a long-unused chapel, yet she feared being overheard. Her mother had been sending messengers to ask after Amicia's health at increasingly frequent intervals.

"If she doesn't soon return, Farrold, we're bound to be discovered and I fear the prices both she and I will pay. Mine the lesser—I'll only be punished for abetting her deed while Amicia's good name will be despoiled." Feeling helpless, Kelda gazed into the earnest young man's eyes.

Farrold felt equally as helpless. He was small comfort, he knew, but he couldn't argue the certainty of that fearsome end to the beauty's wild deed should discovery come. To be gone without chaperon all through the night would lay a stain upon Amicia's good name that no man of honor would overlook.

Even the prize of her great dowry could never whiten the blotch on one so easy with her ways. 'Twas too great a risk to wed a woman who'd possibly gift a spouse with heirs of questionable sire. And if no man would wed with her, then needs be she enter the convent where the daily restraints of religious life would inevitably wear her wild spirit down.

On her companion's face Kelda saw the questioning of Amicia's morals and straightened in quick defense. "At least she is doing something to stand bravely against the one who would control our every move while I sit safe in my chamber."

Farrold recognized the mild rebuke, and it smote his tender pride. 'Twas bad enough that he'd been left behind when his father set off to hunt the outlaw. A telling choice that made clear the low esteem in which his father held him. "I, too, am left to safety while others take up an adventure." He spoke aloud. Then, as if ashamed of the criticism he'd long ago learned to never turn on his sire, he quickly added, "But I am willing to accept the decision for, as I've said before, I prefer a quiet life to dangerous adventures."

Kelda was sorry for flaring up at him. She'd known since discovering him lingering about the kitchen fires early this morn that he'd been wrongfully slighted when important matters arose. And from the baron's point of view the choice had been poorly made, for by the conversation Farrold had overheard between the two girls the night past, he knew more of the outlaws than any other among the garrison's number.

"The quiet life which I, too, prefer." Kelda's tone was quiet and succeeded in its goal of soothing Farrold's ragged spirit.

"Aye, 'tis why I so much enjoy your company—" Farrold gave her a nervous smile. "Nay, I more than enjoy your company, I wish it would always be mine." There, he'd spoken aloud the dream that—since the first morn they'd remained in the meadow while Amicia slipped away—had daily grown stronger.

"To be ever together would be the fulfillment of my heart's desire," Kelda softly responded, lashes shielding a gaze too shy to see how he reacted to her bold answer. That they'd known each other for less than a week made no difference to her certainty in the rightness of this match.

Farrold was delighted. Here was a thing he'd not ever thought to find, a sweet maid who honestly wanted to spend her life with him—a base-born and graceless knight of no certain future.

"Mayhap 'tis possible. By other's lights, we've neither of us great prospects for the future. The son of a baron I am, but by birth unable to inherit, while you are the child of an honest and worthy knight, yet one of no great standing."

Kelda had long since worked this out in her own mind, and her smile widened with pleasure to hear him put her fondest hope into words. As Farrold took her fingers carefully into his own slightly trembling hold, she peeked up through still lowered lashes and found him slowly bending near. She tilted her chin and willingly yielded her mouth to the gentle brush of his. 'Twas warm and welcoming, a commitment made and sealed.

⤳§ *Chapter 7* §⤳

Amicia let out a long-held breath as she silently slipped through her chamber's ironbound door. She'd made it safely across the causeway, through the stable, and up the back stairway without anyone questioning the passing of a dark-cloaked figure.

"At last!" Kelda took Amicia's hands and fairly jerked her into the room. "Hourly my mother's sent a messenger to ask after your progress."

"She didn't discover me absent?" Amicia gasped. Her brown gaze flew to the bed in time to see Melly spring out from its drawn drapes, relief plain in her awkward haste.

"Best I hurry to the kitchens," Melly quickly muttered. "As 'tis I been gone so long Orva'll whack me for certain sure." She rushed to the door and made her escape before either of the young mistresses could dream up some further mad scheme.

Amicia watched the meek girl's escape, nibbling her lip. So involved in her strategy to circumvent the Dark Lord's wicked plans had she been the night past that she'd failed to consider the cost of her plan to the faithful Melly. She must go and speak privately with Orva before the cook had opportunity to chastise the girl.

"I see you've a care for Melly's troubles on your behalf, but apparently none for my discomfort. I had to lie to my mother at the day's first meal and return false messages all the morn long. She's awfully concerned for your health."

Amicia's eyes widened at the unexpected assault by a friend and constant supporter. Though she knew herself prone to act rashly, in this instance she had weighed her actions. She'd already explained to Kelda her belief that the protection of Galen and his companions from imprisonment, even maiming or death at Gilfrey's hands, was of more import than another's worry. However, her conviction of the greater good to be served by the former, did nothing to lessen her discomfort at being cause of the latter.

Before she'd waded through her own guilt to question the reason behind Anne's unusual concern for the simple headache she'd expected Kelda to use as excuse, the door unexpectedly swung open. Anne stood in the portal, hands on hips and brows raised as she let her gaze slowly sweep from Amicia's tangled mane down her cloaked figure to muddied shoes. Words were unnecessary.

"I'm feeling better now," Amicia said hastily. "I thought a brisk walk across the parapet might blow away the lingering web of pain." She rubbed fingertips against temples and then combed them through her wind-tossed mass of tawny silk. "Pray pardon, I should have brushed my sleep-mussed hair before I went." She let the cloak drop haphazardly across the chest at the foot of the bed.

A faint and skeptical smile curled Anne's lips. It was useless to question further when a longed-for opportunity had come and passed. Still, Anne wanted the girl to know what she'd lost. "A pity you were so ill when Lady Sybil desperately wanted you to join her early this morn."

Amicia's shoulders slumped. Her mother had called

for her. Her mother—so serene that 'twas as if she existed on a higher, spiritual plain—had never asked anything of her. A fact which made the rare summons all the more significant.

"She swore the matter," Anne continued, "was of the utmost import."

Amicia's expression was bleak as she met Anne's penetrating stare. They both knew her mother would never speak an untruth, not even by exaggeration. If she'd said it was of utmost import, then of utmost import it had been. But even had there been no specific purpose at all, it was a missed chance to begin a bridge across the gap between.

"But," Anne unhappily continued, "the messenger we sent to summon you repeatedly returned with the news that you were too sick to be roused."

"I'll go to her now." The guilt she'd experienced earlier was proven to have been naught but an uncomfortable pricking by comparison with the sharpness of regret now stabbing into Amicia's heart. By the ever increasing amount of time she'd spent in prayer these past few weeks her mother had demonstrated a growing unease. An unease for which even Anne had been unable to learn the source.

Anne caught Amicia's arm as she sought to hurry past. "Your willingness comes too late. The baron learned that she'd sent for you—doubtless from Mag." The downward curl of distaste on her lips was merely a reflection of the opinion shared by most in the castle of the creeping crone who served Gilfrey. "She moves about so stealthily we none of us know when we are watched." Anne shook her head sharply as if to scatter the other's unpleasant image from her mind and leave clear the view of a more important problem. "He went into the lady's chamber, and when he came out announced that she'd made a request to be left in solitude for a sennight to fast and pray."

"Surely," Amicia frowned her bewilderment with

Anne's restraining hold, "if she wanted me this morn, she'll welcome me now." Gently shaking off the older woman's hand, she reached for the door's cold latch.

"'Struth," Anne agreed with a quiet defeat in her tone that held Amicia back more effectively than any physical restraint. "But Sir Gilfrey has posted Mag to guard the door of her privacy—a worthy goal, if sincere. But never have either Gilfrey or Mag entertained such pure intents. Thus, despite Sybil's recent worriment, I doubt 'tis accurate. Moreover, your mother would be far more like to confide such decisions to me than ever to her unwanted mate."

Amicia sagged against the hard planks of the still-closed door as if it were a physical manifestation of the barrier now between her and her mother. "Then I failed my mother's simple call." It hurt.

"Until seven days hence." Anne nodded. "And pray God the wicked man allows enough sustenance to reach our lady that she survives the fast he will doubtless enforce." Fast, huh, Anne silently derided. More likely 'twas punishment for whatever purpose lay behind the countess's call for her daughter.

"Right-ho, Galen," Carl called out.

Smiling ruefully at the sight of proud war horses reduced to the menial chore of pulling a crude farm cart, Galen stepped into the narrow dirt lane from where he'd impatiently waited amidst the cover of thick brush. And a long wait it had been though a welcome adventure after three days spent confined in a damp cave while the baron and his men trooped back and forth through the forest in ever increasing frustration. Three days confined, save for his dangerous, low-tide visits to an empty meadow.

"You had no difficulty in purchasing the grain, I see." Galen's dark head dipped toward the bulging bags piled high behind Carl as he reached out to wrap his hand about one horse's bridle.

"As you thought, the miller was more than pleased

to supply grain to any buyer with the coins to pay—apparently there are too few about able even to trade for his goods or services."

"Then we've completed the first step in our plan." With the lithe grace of one used to constant physical activity, Galen moved around and vaulted up to settle on the driver's seat beside his friend. "The miller has the coins he needs. Of more import, the coins were earned through his honest toil, leaving the baron unable to claim 'tis a gift from outlaws who stole them from him, justifying his seizing of them."

Carl glanced sideways to meet green eyes gleaming with silver satisfaction, and he grinned with the shared enjoyment of thwarting the villain who'd usurped a good lord's place. "His grain he sold me, along with this sorry excuse for a vehicle."

"'Struth, 'tis sorry indeed," Galen agreed, casting a critical gaze over the cart's warped planks. "But doubtless it will be welcome to some impoverished farmer. Now, if Walter has succeeded in quietly passing our summons throughout the village, we've a gathering of curious people to meet."

Expression going solemn, Carl nodded. "And we pray the diversion we set up for the baron and his men will keep them occupied near the shore 'til we've done."

"Assuredly we pray, but I've greater faith in the heavenly intercessions of the good fathers at the abbey who support our cause." Support their cause Abbot Pieter and those under his rule surely did, even to the secret stabling of great and all too noticeable destriers amongst their humble donkeys and placid horses.

Trust the abbey's supplications Carl did, yet nourishing a deep religious faith beneath his merry nature, he believed their pleas for divine aid no excuse to lessen his own. He quickly crossed himself and offered up a short but earnest prayer to the patron saint of charity before snapping the reins to urge sorely slighted steeds on with the journey.

As they traveled down a narrow, rutted path that carried them past the quiet village and on toward their goal, the two weary men who'd been up most of the past night sank into a companionable silence. Praise God, the craven fools of Dungeld's garrison hadn't the courage to spend a night outside the protection of castle walls, and certainly not enough to risk dark hours in a forest known to be inhabited by outlaws. Were it elsewise, Galen and his companions wouldn't have had the opportunity to lay the false trails meant to lead their pursuers on a long and fruitless chase. A giant maze had been laid for the baron and his men to follow through dense woodlands of ominous shadows and hidden stumble-holes opposite their "outlaw" foes' true destination. Only after hours of difficult travel and frustrating paths to nowhere would they discover its end—on the beach near its beginning. 'Twas a game which, hopefully, would distract them long enough for Galen's band to complete their errand of mercy.

As seemed to have become Galen's habit during any moment his thoughts were not demanded for strategy or survival—and there'd been many such moments during days in the cave's eternal twilight—his attention drifted to the very real memory of the untamed beauty. Amicia was utterly unlike any other woman he knew. She never did the expected nor, despite her diminutive size, easily bowed to another's will. Foolishly brave and clearly lacking any intent to snare a wealthy, important lord for mate, she was very unusual indeed.

The sun-dappled forest ahead faded while in his mind arose images of tawny hair alternately burnished by sun or polished by moon, of eyes flashing gold that melted to soft honey brown, of petal-soft lips that tasted of passion's sweetest nectar. The images' temptation was not lessened by their lack of substance. Rather their power was increased by his frustration at being unable to satisfy their call—an unfamiliar emotion and one that spawned a mighty impatience to sunder the restraining cords of false identities, cords holding him from honorably seeking her for his own.

Days of disappointment when the partner in a promised meadow tryst did not appear and nights spent in dreams of stolen kisses and the ache of hunger they left had reinforced his wish to come as heir of a great earldom and claim her as his well-born bride. A wish impossible to fulfill so long as his quest went unfinished—impossible and dangerous both to the quest's outcome and her well-being.

A stray shaft of light pierced the leafy roof of entwined branches to gleam over the black head Galen shook to free it of the untimely visions. Seeking a diversion, he asked, "Isn't the glade just around that rock outcropping?"

Carl gave his friend a puzzled glance. Having chosen it himself, 'twas strange Galen questioned its whereabouts now. But then, a smile dawned, Galen had become a moody stranger of recent days— missing that tender maid, no doubt. Turning his eyes to the space between one horse's ears and clamping his lips tight together, Carl restrained his amusement. It was a fine jest that the renowned lover had been captured by a wild innocent all unknowing of her great feat or the many who had tried with wiles more practiced and failed. Holding his voice emotionless with great difficulty, Carl answered.

"Aye, and by the many prints laid in the dust of our path, I'd say as there's many who've heeded Walter's call."

Galen recognized the carefully monotonous tone for the controlled amusement it meant but to speak of it would only deepen Carl's curiosity and open a subject he meant to see closed. They continued in silence, Galen's dark brows riding low over green eyes flashing with such fierce silver lights that Carl deemed it miraculous they'd not struck the forest with the devastating fire of a lightning bolt.

"They're here!" Under Walter's great relief his voice cracked, but for once he barely noticed this repeat of its embarrassing tendency. As commanded, he'd summoned the villagers, more specifically the head of each household. They'd come but during the wait had grown restive, milling about the small glade, trampling an area of tall grass and new grown bushes. Then, moments ago they'd begun to demand the meaning of his foolery.

Creaking over ruts and brushing through the wild undergrowth reclaiming ground once lost to make room for a now abandoned hovel, the cart rumbled into the clearing's center. As the crowd fell back several young saplings were crushed. Galen rose to stand on the cart's seat so that all could take stock of him while he slowly looked from one hollow-cheeked and underfed man to the next and saw the mingling of distrust and curiosity in their eyes.

He spoke with quiet deliberation. "Though a stranger in your view, I am a friend to the people of Wryborne. In support of my claim I bring Abbot Pieter's rosary." From a pocket behind his wide belt, he pulled a string of black beads from which glittered a ruby-jewelled gold cross. "He entrusted me with this holy emblem so I might demonstrate to you his trust in me."

"Aye, but for what reason did you summon us here to this place in the wilds?" The speaker was near as tall as Galen and, as none gainsaid his words but rather murmured their agreement, was clearly the village leader.

Pleased to have found the one man who could speak for all, Galen jumped down from the wagon's seat to meet the man on the same level. "I am called Galen. By what are you known?"

"Edgar." The answer was brief and, despite the fact that he was so gaunt the bones of his wrist showed beneath the ragged cuffs of sleeves too short, the man met green eyes steadily while calmly waiting for their possessor to state his purpose.

Confident of his ability to rightly read a man's character, Galen found a liking for this leader who was neither servile nor belligerent. "The bags of grain in this wagon's back are fresh from the mill and meant for you and yours."

Like a cool breeze across drought-burned land, a murmur ran through the gathering. Their expressions were filled with a painful hope at war with suspicion.

"What price do you ask for this generosity?" The leader's voice was tense. He could feel his fellows' desperate wish to believe, yet strangers—most particularly generous strangers—were too possibly seeking to buy support in evil intents. And, once given, a support that would leave the innocent to pay the price for villainous actions.

"Only that you take the grain, use it, and speak of the gift to none beyond Brayston's outlying boundaries."

The village leader's eyes narrowed. Clearly the well-dressed stranger asked that they allow no word of the gift to reach the baron or his minions. It would seem an easy promise to give, as such an action would earn them naught but punishment for failing to pay the heavy taxes on such goods, taxes that would take near the whole. Yet, his trust was not easily won and the voice of skepticism asked if that was this Galen's intent—to see them punished? But to what purpose? After all, hadn't the stranger the goodwill of the abbot whom he did trust, and who would never aid a wicked cause, nor lend support to a plan that'd see them suffer at the hands of the one who'd usurped their good lord's place.

Decision made, Edgar solemnly nodded. Then, gray-streaked hair brushing bony shoulders, he turned and motioned the villagers to form a line. Reassured by their leader's acceptance, they moved to obey, and soon Carl was handing out the sacks of grain one by one.

Galen watched, fearing the hunger-weakened men unable to carry the weighty bags to their homes. Concern for them darkened the eyes above his friendly smile to the same shade as a shadowed forest and melted the wary men's suspicions. As those passing close by began offering tentative smiles in return, Galen realized that his mere act of giving had provided them with renewed strength.

Only after the last of man from Brayston had been given his share, hoisting the bag over a shoulder and starting down the recently laid pathway of trampled greenery between glade and village did Edgar approach the cart still holding several grain sacks.

"Have you a way to use this?" Galen lightly tapped the wagon. "Without drawing your enemy's spite?"

Edgar studied the tall stranger whose appearance seemed too plain a proof of good birth for him to feel easy. "Why do you wish to bestow such bounty upon we poor folk of a tiny village of little import?"

Galen smiled slowly, appreciative of this man's ability to stand unfaltering before him—few of the common folk could for more than a moment. But then, though clearly he suspected, Edgar had no way to be certain about the noble heritage of the man to whom he spoke.

"A fair question, friend." Galen nodded. "I have secrets to keep, but none at your cost. I swear by the Holy Cross that you and I share a common foe and that my quest means trouble only to him and never to you."

Directly meeting the intensity of a pale green gaze, Edgar was at last convinced of the stranger's honesty and for the first time gave an answering smile. "We've a fair-sized meeting hall where the cart can be hidden when needful."

"Then take and stow both it and the surplus grain

there now. The baron leads his men on a hunt for human prey and likely will come to search here."

"'Tis done." Edgar was not a man for unnecessary words and after his brief agreement merely turned toward the retreating back of a villager who'd clearly been lingering within earshot. A wry smile curved Galen's lips as he noted the strained patience in the instructions called out for the village's ox to be fetched.

Galen was surprised by Edgar's reference to an ox. The massive animals were expensive to purchase and expensive to keep if only by the tax they called the owner to pay. While on better-managed demesnes a lord might provide them to see his fields more productively worked, it was hard to believe that here men so plainly poor possessed such a beast.

Glancing from Carl, who was busy loosing the two mighty steeds from the humble cart, to the giver, Edgar saw Galen's perplexity. His answering grin mocked. "'Tis a beast we of the village share, the only one to survive the murdering baron's greed." He shrugged. "By conspiracy we keep its existence a deep-hidden fact."

The cynical smile that laid creases in Galen's sun-bronzed cheeks held an odd quality of amazement as well. He was well enough acquainted with the subtle deceits in court politics, and had nothing but disgust for the schemes built of lies and meant to attain greater power or wealth. But, on Wryborne he'd found a priest, nay, abbot who felt justified in circumventing the truth—if not lying by false words—and simple men concocting complicated strategies to fool the man who'd usurped their beloved lord's title and lands—a small, silent but doubtless satisfying victory over tyranny. It was becoming ever clearer that there were circumstances that made right the use of an untruth's wrong. A possibility Galen welcomed for the ease it lent a sorely strained conscience.

"I applaud your creativity," Galen said. "And if there is aught I can do to aid your endeavors, I'll willingly try."

Edgar tilted his head to the side, questioning the offer's sincerity. "But for help how would we find a stranger who comes from nowhere we know and disappears into the same?"

"Another fair question," Galen grinned in acknowledgment. "Do you know the pool at the foot of the stream's waterfall—between the seashore and your village?"

Edgar nodded, sunlight picking out the gray threads in his hair.

"At dusk and then again the following dawn send a child to the pool's edge and there have him whistle three times before returning to his own hearth. I or one of mine will come to you as soon as may be."

Edgar nodded again, without expectation of finding a need to make the call but appreciative of the other's willingness and offer of trust like to that which he had given. For the first time in near two decades of unjust oppression Edgar felt less alone and more hopeful for the future. Smiling faintly, he watched as the two strangers mounted freed steeds—which looked to be as fine blooded as their riders—and disappeared down the track by which they'd arrived.

⋐§ *Chapter 8* ⋧⋑

Please, Randolf, please." Amicia's soft entreaty was heartfelt, and she unknowingly squeezed the huge serf's arm between her small hands.

By the bright light of flames stoked for the day's work in fireplace dominating one wall of the great hall, Randolf looked down into brown pools of hope and felt his determination to keep the wild maid safely within the castle slipping away. "I'm taking the boat, and you know you hate boats." It was a desperate protest which even as he spoke he knew would do no good.

"Hate boats?" Amicia looked indignant. "I've no distaste for boats. You've got me confused with Sir Jasper. He hates boats, not I."

"But mistress—" Randolf postponed the admission of a clear defeat. "Only am I going to the stable on the shore's far end to fetch sacks of feed for resupplying the castle's stable and to make certain the lads there put out an adequate amount for horses what'll return sore weary and hungry at dusk."

"Don't you see?" Amicia squeezed Randolf's arm even harder. "With the Dark Lord and his company out on their futile search for what they'll not find, this is the perfect opportunity for me to slip away—just for an hour or two," she wheedled. Randolf looked to be wavering in his conviction, and Amicia pressed her advantage. "I'll take my dark cloak and huddle beneath it, blending in amongst the bags you take to fill with feed, and none will be the wiser. The only one who purposely would spy is dutifully guarding my mother's door."

Four days had passed since Amicia was to have met Galen in the meadow, and she was desperate to be again with the epitome of all her romantic dreams. In truth, far more than merely her hero come to life. He was real enough to melt her soul with his passion and thrill her heart with his gentle words and concern— all for her rather than the property and title the heiress to Wryborne would bring her spouse. The fiery embraces he'd shared with the simple village girl he thought her to be left her naively certain that 'twas she herself who held his interest. Moreover, the wonderful tale Melly had carried to her of his kindness in providing for the people of Brayston only increased her admiration and certainty that he was the romantic outlaw of the greenwood she'd taken him for from the first.

Randolf was so accustomed to Amicia's disrespectful name for her stepfather that he thought nothing of it. Yet 'twas that very part of her statement, that ill-considered reminder of the baron's frustration at being consistently outwitted, which deepened his fear of this proposal. Unfortunately, however, his trepidation provided no effective argument against her appeal to join his journey.

"You've got to promise," Randolf demanded, "you'll not run away and stay gone so long we both incur his wrath." She'd done such a thing so oft he knew it was near certain to happen no matter her oath.

"I promise, Randolf." Amicia gave her glowering friend a bright grin, although beneath the exaltation in winning her goal she suffered more than a pang of guilt for the untruth it was. There was no other way, she justified the bold-faced lie. He must perform his chore while her purpose for the trip lay in the meadow some distance beyond. A fact that left her no choice— really.

Randolf was never fast in his reasoning, yet Amicia feared that by the same unusually strong instincts that made him a good hunter and trustworthy guide he might see her lack of honesty. To hide her unease she put on her sweetest smile and hurried away, cheerily promising to fetch her cape and meet him at the dock where the lightweight boats were moored.

Rushing from the momentarily quiet great hall and halfway up the spiraling stairwell, Amicia came to an unplanned halt. Only steps from the dim archway opening onto the next level's corridor, her way was blocked by two engaged in a tender scene. Kelda's fingers were twined through brown locks while Farrold, his back to where Amicia stood, held Kelda's welcome warmth close. Despite her recent experience of such thrilling embraces, Amicia thought these two were foolish to stand in a passage so oft used.

When Farrold broke their fervent kiss, though nearly of a height, Kelda buried her face in the crook between his neck and shoulder. "I swear," he whispered urgently, "as soon as my father is done with his mad hunt for the elusive outlaw, I'll go to him and beg that a marriage between us be arranged."

Kelda took a short step back, cheeks tinted pink by shy pleasure as she looked into Farrold's earnest face and returned his promise with another. "Then I will pray hourly for a swift end to the chase and do all in my power to aid the capture that'll see it concluded."

Amicia gasped. For the first time in their lives, she and Kelda stood committed to opposing goals. She'd risk any peril to see Galen and his men escape the baron's snare while her friend had just vowed to see them chained in the castle's dungeon—or, worse, dead by the Dark Lord's command.

At the sound so near, the couple turned, terrified by the thought of discovery.

"You frightened us," gasped Farrold, who'd thrust Kelda behind the shield of his back.

"I didn't mean to," Amicia assured them, mustering an innocent smile of contrition in hopes they'd not realize how much she had heard. "In haste, I rounded the corner without care and near bumped into you."

Kelda studied her friend suspiciously. Too well she recognized the bland smile that oft hid truth or mischief. Yet, it was possible that Amicia had suddenly come upon them and been startled. Kelda couldn't be certain if that was so or if Amicia had overheard a promise abhorrent to her. The thought of the break between them, that the fulfilling of her stated intent would bring, was painful. But surely the thrall in which the Wolf's Head held Amicia was the true danger, and by seeing it sundered she was more a friend than a foe. Amicia's night journey alone was foolish, nay, dangerous and such meetings were best ended before they came to a dreadful conclusion.

Full of self-righteous intentions, Kelda stepped from behind Farrold's back. "I'll go above with you."

"No need for you to halt your—visit," Amicia laughed, praying her teasing tone would fool Kelda.

Kelda's earlier blush deepened into a rosy glow, which Farrold found charming. "Amicia is right," he argued. "You'd needn't rush away. Although I must leave to join Sir Jasper at the tiltyard, I'd enjoy your company on the walk there." Farrold liked Kelda's father very well; and, as they both had been slighted by the baron who chose to leave them behind while he hunted his foe, the older man had offered Farrold the opportunity to hone his battle skills.

Farrold was unaware of the undercurrents between the two maids, but his plea tipped the scale. Amicia could have kissed him herself when the other girl nodded her assent. Kelda was near the only person able to prevent her from departing with Randolf.

While the self-absorbed couple turned to descend, Amicia dashed up the narrow steps two at a time. Fearing she'd already been too long waylaid, that Randolf might have grown weary of waiting and left her behind, without entering the bedchamber Amicia snatched her cloak from the peg just inside its door. Impatient but forced to go with more care in the descent, Amicia hurried down, slipped past the kitchen to the back stairway, and arrived at the outbound door. After stepping out, rather than proceeding on her usual path toward stable and castle gates, she ducked into the low opening of a small tunnel through the wide stone wall. Exiting from its far end, she braced one small hand on rough stone and carefully walked the narrow dirt path skirting the back half of the tower's perimeter until she came to the point facing the open and deadly sea.

At this height the wind seldom seemed to blow at less than gale force, and she exercised great caution while moving from the security of the stone wall to a stout rail. Clasping the rail so tightly her fingertips went white, she peered down the wooden steps zigzagging to the bottom of a near vertical rock face. She saw Randolf, a small figure far below, and was relieved. Now all that remained was to navigate this ghastly stairway. Randolf had said she hated boats, and she had truthfully said she did not. She'd no terror of boats—she'd a terror of this sole method of reaching them. Every instinct urged her to retreat, but she tilted her chin as if daring fate and with forced courage began the descent.

The fierce wind wrapped her long cloak and skirts tight about her legs making each downward step a struggle, yet she persevered though gripping the railing with such strength her hands soon felt numb. Often she'd derisively asked herself how she could fearlessly scramble up and down a sheer wall beside a tumbling torrent of water yet turn to a quavery mass of terror at the prospect of this journey. She knew the answer was one that merely proved how childish were her fears. It was upon these rocks that her precious crystal unicorn had been smashed to useless, nay, dangerously sharp slivers. In the past she'd comforted herself that only in the unlikely event that the mighty fortress of Dungeld were under attack would she need to navigate these steps, which groaned and swayed with each gusting slap of nature's invisible hand. Now, to preserve the continuation of her much more precious living, breathing fantasy, she'd willingly risk it.

"I'd almost given up on your coming," Randolf called out when the maid neared the end of her descent, down where the wind's fury was less and would not carry his words away.

Concentrating only on safely lowering one foot after another, Amicia forced a smile of false bravery upon stiff lips, a smile that added no warmth to her fear-paled countenance. That smile remained frozen in place until she thankfully stood flat on the narrow dock fastened to the isle's stone base, and thereupon became a brilliant beam of warmth. "I had to overcome one small impediment, but now I'm here and we can be on our way." She scrambled into the boat and pulled her hood close over her face as she settled beside a stack of empty bags.

Randolf stepped in, pushed free of the dock, and began to row. His uncommon strength soon had them rounding the isle and cresting foam-topped waves that aided his intent by tossing them toward the mainland.

One out-jutting end of the half-circle shore whose center was bisected by the causeway revealed at low tide was their goal. Once they'd reached it, Randolf jumped into the briny water and pulled the small boat well up onto the rocky strand. Amicia quickly climbed out, and soon her companion was occupied with single-minded devotion to the task of hauling empty bags to be filled into a three-sided building. The horses of Dungeld's stable were rotated between here and the isle-castle's stable. Every member of the garrison possessed two steeds—one to be ridden out from the castle and another in this stable for those times when it was inconvenient to wait for the tide's release of the causeway path. Each stable was provided with a full complement of stable-serfs to see to the right care of the great beasts, but 'twas the strong Randolf's appointed chore to regularly load the heavy supplies and row between the two, keeping each provided with all that was needed. He took great pride in the strength that had seen him given such a singular honor and toiled hard to fulfill it well. Concentrating on the careful doing of his responsibilities, he didn't see his small companion pull her cloak close and disappear into the forest's green wall.

Amicia nibbled at her bottom lip even as she steadily weaved through bushes rich with summer's ripe growth, avoiding thick clumps of grass whose long blades could tangle about her feet and bring her progress to a bruising if momentary halt. She'd never before had reason to find her way to the meadow from this point. Without the need to go unobserved, she'd have walked across the open shore to where the causeway began. From there 'twould have been a simple matter, but from amidst these towering trees whose branches interwove above and the dense undergrowth below it would be all too easy to lose her bearings. The one thing she knew for certain was that she must climb to the meadow's higher level. Thus, she turned away from the sound of crashing waves and moved straight ahead. Before long a smile of satisfaction replaced her worried frown. The land had begun to show a decided incline. Decided indeed, for within a very few steps it was necessary to tuck her skirts beneath the low-slung belt and use her hands to grasp any conveniently placed foliage to pull herself up. The great energy expended was rewarded when at last she scrambled onto a suddenly flat area.

As she pulled her skirts down to again brush her

toes, Amicia peered through the prickly leaves of a tall-grown holly and found herself not on the meadow's edge, not anywhere familiar. Delight gleamed gold in her eyes. The inaccurate pathway that had ended in a wrongful destination was no misfortune to her.

"'Struth, a succulent meal you'll make, my pretty bird," Galen purred in mock seductiveness. "A few more turns and we'll taste the pleasure." He suited actions to words, rotating a spitted pheasant strung between the two forked branches he'd driven into the ground on either side of a fire not large but hot.

Leaving his companions in the cave's safety, Galen had ventured out to track the men who tracked him—far safer to know where your enemy lies. But, when the baron paused for a midday meal in the empty meadow just over the rise, once again Galen's hunger had urgently reminded him of the right to warren given his father and heirs by Baron Conal. By that gift from a friend he'd the legal right to take small game anywhere on Wryborne lands. Of course, if caught he couldn't claim that defense without revealing the whole quest—and before even he fully knew what it was. Nonetheless, it had been excuse enough to keep himself and his companions fed with more than the supply of salt-dried meat and dark rye bread that they'd brought on their journey. The delicious smell of roasting pheasant made his stomach growl, and he wrapped a hand about one end of the spit, lifting the prize from the heat. It had been some time since he'd set the bird to cooking and longer since he'd lost sight of the baron and his men—a dangerously long time.

A rustling sound in the bushes bordering the glade caught Galen's attention. He froze. The sound was too loud and too erratic to be born of the gentle breeze. With the instincts of a battle-tested warrior, Galen instantly tossed the spitted bird to a clump of lush grass and whirled with weighty broadsword firmly clasped between his hands. Honed metal raised menacingly above his head gleamed as he met his foe—a petite and wide-eyed maid who stared in fascination at the deadly threat poised to descend upon her.

"Never come upon a man by stealth and *never* from behind!" Galen lowered his arms and resheathed his blade. "Too many there are who will strike in defense without first pausing to question the fool who erred."

Amicia's heart was thumping at a mighty pace, but she tilted her chin and boldly met a blazing green gaze. "I climbed the hill and didn't realize you were here until I was upon you." She'd used much the same words to explain her reaction after stumbling into Kelda and Farrold. But whereas earlier they'd been a lie yet accepted, now they were sincere and still inadequate.

Faced with a foolhardy courage possessed by no woman he knew, admiration tempered Galen's irritation. He'd seen the fear in deep brown eyes, yet she stood firm against his anger. For all he deemed it important to curb her wildness, his slow smile played traitor to right logic and revealed his approval.

Stunned, as ever, by the power of his smile to melt her vexation and turn well-ordered thoughts to a muddled morass, Amicia could think of nothing remotely intelligent to say. In truth, the attention of this incredibly attractive man had rendered her as mute and silly as a moonling serf-girl besotted with a stable boy. Once again she'd given Galen reason to think her a weak-witted fool.

Dropping her gaze to break their long and breath-stealing visual bond, Amicia's eyes fell upon the abused pheasant. She walked over to lift it, dust a few green blades from its golden skin, and carefully poke as if to test the meat's progress. "This won't be done through for an hour or more." That she hadn't the least experience by which to make this judgment he needn't know. She restored the spit to its proper position atop the two forked branches. Feeling unequal to meeting the green gaze so heavy on her, with arms wrapped about her middle, she stared down at her handiwork.

Galen moved to stand just behind Amicia and studied the sun-burnished silk flowing in rich waves down her slender back, a thick glory again defiantly unbound. He desperately wanted to bury his fingers in its luscious mass and draw her soft enticing form back against his own hard body. Regret deepened his voice to dark velvet as he spoke. "I've been here too long already and must continue tracking my foe." Before she could question his purpose, he explained. "To know where they are is to stand prepared."

Without stepping away, Amicia turned her head and looked up. Light rippled over the golden strands in hair swinging to one side. Forcing her voice to remain emotionless despite the lump of disappointment threatening to block her throat, she merely offered a logical comment. "Then find something else to eat, you must." Having overcome great difficulties to meet him after long days of trying, she desperately wanted him to stay with her—leastways for a while.

Although she'd not complained or even argued for time spent together, as she had that day on the shore, Galen read the plea in the brown depths of her eyes. For all his great training and harsh experience in the impassivity demanded of successful fighting men, Galen again fell to defeat at the hands of a young and tender maid.

"For near a sennight they've searched in vain—mayhap for an hour more they can do without an unseen escort." Galen waved a beaming Amicia into the shade beneath a towering oak. Accompanied by the murmur of a gentle breeze ruffling the leaves overhead, they lost count of time as they talked in carefully chosen words of such mundane matters as favorite foods and colors and of great events like the king and his battle against first his barons and then the French invaders. Only once did either come dangerously near to admitting a true heritage and that when Galen unthinkingly spoke of his presence on the field at Runnymede while John put his seal to the charter.

"You were there?" Amicia was deeply surprised and straightened from her half-reclining position. What circumstance could have put an outlaw on the possible battlefield between royal and baronial forces?

Stretched full out on a comfortable cushion of thick grass, Galen didn't stir. Although cursing himself for the pride that had led him to voice such a claim, he remained apparently relaxed while under the guise of ease he quickly covered his error. "The barons were anxious for the aid of any strong fighting man." It was the truth, and he could say it without fearing any trace of shame for a lie revealed. "The earl I supported welcomed my aid full well." That, too, was true. His father had been proud of his heir's wholehearted support.

"I see." Amicia nodded. She'd no reason to question an explanation so firmly stated. "And do you support still the barons' cause?" Afraid of what opinions he might read in her gaze, she bent her attention on the deep runnels her fingers plowed through green blades.

Galen saw the once steady and uncomplicated foundations of their conversation shifting hazardously. This was a very serious political question and though the maid would likely never know the long hours it had taken to reach his decision, he carefully stated his position. "I support the tenants of their cause, as I supported them when written in the charter signed by the king. But I do not support the actions they've taken—the summoning of a foreign prince to our shores."

"Then you will fight at the king's side?" Amicia asked. Gilfrey was a great supporter of King John, whom she found loathsome—always standing too near and trying to touch as no man save husband ought. When they were "blessed" with a royal visit, she'd early learned to be conveniently ill while her mother retreated to prayerful fasting, and Anne took her daughter to visit distant relatives. She didn't know what the charter's tenants were, but she'd privately cheered when the king had been forced to bend beneath the will of his baronage. Yet, she had wondered if they'd not gone too far when, by virtue of rare visitors and overlapping gossip vines, tales of invading French forces wended to them on this distant coast. Until then Gilfrey had kept to himself this reason behind why an overmeasure of guardsmen from Dungeld's garrison were still posted with the king.

"I would fight the French who arrive in ever greater numbers, but fight my fellow Englishmen I would find difficult to do. Thus, I am here and not where even now battles are being waged." All humor had drained from Galen's face, leaving it as cold and icy as the North Sea—an expression those who knew his family well had no difficulty in identifying as the son's legacy from a father known as the Ice Warrior.

The sharp blast of a hunting horn shattered the peace. Galen leaped to his feet and dashed into the shadows of the woodland opposite where Amicia still sat. Though slower to respond than he, she rose to rush after him, following his path of crushed grass and haste-broken shrubbery.

Weaving through natural impediments in as direct as possible a route to the cave, Galen damned himself for allowing personal joys to interfere with his duty to protect his own. If his companions had fallen to danger because of his failure, he'd never— Nay, he'd not allow possibly unjustified guilt to cloud the clear mind needed to meet the dangers a horn blast assuredly portended. Literally breaking through the forest wall, he arrived at the pool to find Carl anxiously pacing its edge, hands clenched with impatience.

"Has some danger befallen Walter?" Galen demanded of the unsuspecting other's back.

Carl whirled. "Nay, he's gathering our weapons from the cave."

"If he is not in danger and you clearly are not, why then risk the horn?" Tension still high, relief for his friends' safety warred with anger at their apparently needless use of an instrument likely to summon more than they wanted to come.

Focused on his leader and barely noting the girl who'd followed behind, Carl explained. "A young lad came to this spot and whistled three times before pleading for help with tears pouring from his eyes. Put us in a quandary whether to leave our secret haven in his full view or wait. Then afore we'd settled on what action to take, he ran back into the woodland heading toward the village."

"I'm sorry I questioned your decision." Galen regretted his unjust criticism. Carl had never demonstrated else than good judgment nor had the man ever acted as rashly as he himself had so recently done. Walter arrived, carrying both his own sword and Carl's, and they'd no time to waste. "We must go quickly yet with caution," Galen directed, expression sliding into cold self-disgust as he explained the need. "We don't know where our enemy lies—a lack for which I am to blame."

Only as Galen swung around to depart did he realize that Amicia had followed him. He waved the other two males to go on ahead, leaving him a private moment, only a moment, to speak with her. "We almost certainly move into danger, and you must return to your own people—now." Neither speaker nor listener spared an instant to recognize what Galen's words revealed: awareness that the village was not her home.

Amicia stood motionless. Though Galen had claimed responsibility for the danger in not knowing where the enemy was, she was well aware that the true blame for his failure lay at her feet. She'd drawn his attention away from that serious duty. Accepting her guilt for deepening the peril into which he walked, there was no question of her deserting him now. Yet, acknowledging herself to be a dangerous distraction whose life honor demanded he protect at possible risk to his own, she nodded her apparent assent and stepped back to leave his path clear.

In the lead, Galen easily tracked the boy's route. With Walter in the middle and Carl guarding the rear of their path, they soon arrived at the edge of the forest ringing Brayston.

Smoke billowed from a fire-blackened pile near the center of a cluster of simple huts—clearly once a home of thatch and wattle speedily reduced to ashes. Grim faced, the three "outlaws" silently watched mail-clad men dismount to crumble what little of charred walls remained upright. Atop his massive steed Gilfrey's sneering laughter drifted over all.

A choked sob followed by a fierce sniffle shifted their attention. Galen turned to see Amicia part shielding fronds and sink to her knees beside a brave boy giving way to racking tears. Though irritated that again she'd ignored his command, he welcomed the maid's easy empathy with a sorrowing child. She gathered the shaking form close, patted his back, and murmured comforting words of no meaning until he'd recovered his control. Then, pulling back, he scrubbed his flooded cheeks with the cuff of his homespun shirt. Caught in his distress, the boy barely recognized his comforter as the daughter of the castle's lady and had no thought to spend on wondering at her presence. 'Twas a fact unimportant when viewed next to the wickedness at work in his village. He rose and faced the men to whom he'd been sent seeking aid—too late.

Aware that now when the boy had regained hard-won composure was not the time to bruise youthful pride with the comfort of a man, Galen spoke to him with quiet respect. "You came to us for help against this villainy?"

The boy nodded and strands of tangled hair clung to cheeks still tear-damp. "My father, Edgar, told me what to do and I done it." The child's voice was strained by the struggle to hold back further tears.

Once more Galen glanced over the distressing scene, certain that the baron had chosen the village leader to use as an example with which to frighten others into submission. "'Tis your home they burned?" he asked, although he knew the answer.

Bargaining for time to master his voice despite his inability to slow the tears again dripping down his cheeks, the boy nodded again.

"And with the fire they brought a threat?" Galen's curiously flat words masked a growing rage as he watched cruel men mount and follow their leader from the place they'd destroyed.

Drawing a deep, ragged breath, the boy spoke to Galen. "They says they're certain we know but are hiding the outlaw's whereabouts, and that for each day we fail to lead him to your lair, they'll burn another home." He'd instinctively known that it was this man the others obeyed though he'd not have been able to define the wordless air of command that clung to him.

Galen looked down into the boy's courageous face and gave him a smile. "What are you called, son of Edgar?"

"Davie, sir."

"You are a valiant lad, Davie, and I salute you." Galen laid closed fist on his heart and gave a brief bow. "Moreover, I believe I've a solution to the threatened woe."

The boy's eyes widened with both pleasure in the man's approval and surprise for his claim.

"Go to your father and tell him first to spend the time between now and the darkest hour of night loading provisions into the wagon and whatever else any cannot bear to part with. Then when that hour arrives, he must yoke the ox to the wagon and bring it and all in your village to the glade of the grain-giving." Galen saw the boy's confusion and his smile deepened. "He will know where I mean."

Although Davie's eyes were still red-rimmed, they were dry as he scrambled toward the village, bent on completing his important errand with haste.

"Now, Amicia." The cold glint in Galen's eyes was warning of his displeasure over her foolhardy determination to follow him into what might well have been mortal peril. Courage in the face of danger was admirable, but ignoring prudent caution and seeking it out was another thing entirely. He reached out to wrap a strong hand about the back of her neck and gently but firmly urged her to retrace their trail.

⇜§ *Chapter 9* §⇝

Amicia's indignation burned. Galen was herding her along the return path like some erring lamb, and she resented it! Her resentment was deepened by the amusement of his two companions. Although unspoken, 'twas something she could feel. Her shoulders were stiff in rejection of the gentle yet inescapable grasp he had on her neck, and her step became a decided stomp.

Long before they reached the pool at the waterfall's base, Galen's anger had evaporated but not his determination that Amicia learn the folly of her wild ways. Carl and Walter returned to the cave while Galen kept Amicia moving through the forest. Switching his hold from her neck to her hand enabled him both to lead the way on this track newly blazed by his recent answer to the horn's call and to hold branches aside, easing her way. The thought of the bird doubtless now done to perfection was a sharp reminder of a hunger unfilled by the meal he'd missed. Without conscious intent his pace quickened under the promise of tender meat at journey's end. 'Twas a meal he'd share with the headstrong maid after she'd been convinced of the error in ill-considered actions. When the flavorsome aroma of roast pheasant wafted to them on a faint breeze, Galen lengthened his stride, hastening ever faster toward its source, unaware that to keep pace with the man clasping her hand Amicia was forced from a trot into a run.

Their path came to an unpleasant end, same as the one he'd unknowingly led her down earlier. Galen's headlong momentum abruptly ceased at the sound of the baron's vicious growl. With stealthy caution he pressed deeper into woodland shadows. Although the spongy ground beneath absorbed the sound of footfalls, he felt Amicia close at his back and his frustration with her propensity for rushing heedlessly into hazardous situations increased. He wished that for once she'd cower back like any other woman would. At the small clearing's edge he carefully parted the broad leaves of an oak to peer at an ominous scene while Amicia peeked from behind his broad back.

"A dullard I know you to be, Randolf, but I'd not thought you so much a fool as to poach my game." The still-mounted Gilfrey brought the switch he'd harvested from a nearby sapling down on the serf's meaty shoulders—once, and again, and again.

To prevent a dangerous and useless groan of anguish, Amicia bit her lip and curled her fingers so tight into the strong arm she'd wrapped them about that imprints would be left. At last the groan Amicia held back came from Randolf's lips as he fell to his knees beneath the sneering baron's stinging lashes.

"'Tis only a taste of the price you'll pay for taking what is mine when you thought me too preoccupied by other matters to notice your crime."

"'Tweren't me who caught the bird and set it to roast—" Randolf's plea of innocence broke on a groan of pain as again the switch came slashing down, leaving a red line of blood oozing through his whip-torn shirt.

"You lie and for your lies I'll make you an example,

a warning of the vengeance to be wreaked upon the head of any who dares abuse my property."

While the baron poured his invective over Randolf's hapless head, Galen evaluated the situation. Clearly all but one of the baron's men had gone ahead to stable their horses. The sole guardsman who remained, like his master, was of advancing age and looked to be an unworthy foe. Then again, looks could deceive. Galen would not make the mistake of underestimating his opponents, and opponents they were for he could not allow the guiltless man to pay a further price for the "crime" that was his.

"In the castle courtyard before all, I'll see your thieving hands sundered from your body and the bloody stumps seared with red hot metal." Gilfrey worked himself into a rage and spit its venom forth in fiery threats. "And your lying tongue, too, will part company with you. Then I'll have you dumped in the back streets of London where you'll spend what's left of your life dependent on the charity of others, begging in the streets, and sleeping in gutters."

Tears poured down Amicia's cheeks, tears of regret too late to have meaning. She had done this to Randolf; she had made him bring her to the mainland; she had run off, leaving him to chase after and stumble into hopeless danger. Randolf—that simple man of endless patience and unswerving loyalty— would pay dearly for her wayward actions. Unjust, unfair. Helpless against the Dark Lord's bitter rage, Amicia clenched her eyes shut and pressed her burning cheeks into the back of Galen's unyielding shoulder. Never again could she meet Orva's eyes. Never could she explain how her thoughtless deed had cost the older woman the well-being of her son.

When Gilfrey's aging knight dismounted and uncoiled a length of stout rope of a certainty intended to wrap the hunted Wolf's Head in captivity, Galen thrust Amicia into a clump of tangled undergrowth and leaped into the glade. Pushing the unsuspecting baron from his saddle and following through with a powerful fist on the startled knight's jaw, Galen took control of the scene. The knight fell senseless to the ground even as Galen slapped the rumps of both steeds. They bolted, dashing riderless into the woodland. Gilfrey, aching legs already swollen and suffering from days spent in the saddle, found it difficult to rise. His rough descent had ended with his body in an awkward heap, and trying to get his feet beneath him made drawing his sword an impossible task. His curses grew colorful indeed when Galen calmly bent to rip the weapon from his hands and throw it into the brush on the clearing's far side.

"My friend." Galen smiled at Randolf. "If you'll pull the sleeping one over here next to this foul-mouthed toad, we'll bind them up together." Galen laughed in amusement at the vicious man's impotent ire at having been foiled by the outlaw yet again.

Randolf, recovering from the shock of his unexpected rescue by a stranger, rolled to his feet and bent to the task given him.

Galen bound the baron's wrists behind his back, fastening them to those behind his knight's back. Then he wound the rope many times about their chests before laying them on their sides and running the rope down between their legs to the ankles he soon had likewise trussed. All the while the baron grew ever more inventive with his litany of curses.

"You are such a sweet-tongued swine that almost I regret the need for a gag. Still, 'tis only prudent to end the outpouring of your words else you may find there are no more left to speak." Taking one end of the baron's velvet cloak between powerful hands, with a mighty jerk Galen ripped free a strip of rich cloth which he then wrapped about the snarling man's face, reducing the steady flow of abuse to a muffled and useless rumble. "Moreover, for your own safety I've done the deed," Galen solemnly assured the man bristling with thwarted animosity. "By your repeated blasphemy I fear you may earn a lightning bolt from the heavens."

After the shock of her abrupt journey into amazingly soft greenery, Amicia had scrambled to her knees without wasted thought on her close proximity to the thorny clutches of a neighboring berry thicket. From her grass-padded haven she'd watched the incredible scene, and with difficulty restrained herself from cheering the daring man who'd succeeded waylaying Sir Oswald's defense and in giving the Dark Lord the chastisement she'd so oft dreamed of delivering. When Galen motioned Randolf to the place from whence he himself had leaped, she jumped to her feet and stood waiting.

Galen was much aware of the need to avoid speaking her name or allowing her voice to be heard within hearing distance of Gilfrey. The moment he stepped into the wood, he wordlessly indicated to Amicia his intent to retreat to their only safe repose—the waterfall-hidden cave.

Though surprised to see his young mistress join them, Randolf instinctively knew the imperative need for silence and held his tongue. In the lead, Galen feared leaving a path too easily tracked by the men who would eventually come to find their missing lord. Thus they took a route different from the one by which he and Amicia had arrived. Zigzagging back and forth and betimes retracing their steps to lay false trails to nowhere, at last they came to the stream's edge.

Following Galen's example, Randolf and his lady stepped into the gently flowing water. They continued this untraceable path until Amicia's ankles ached with the cold and her shoes were assuredly in such hopeless shape she wondered how she'd ever explain them to Lady Anne. Listening to the ripple of water about their feet, Amicia smiled grimly. Such mundane matters were unimportant after the threat they'd so

recently defeated. Her smile warmed to pleasure—
she'd happily disappear from Castle Dungeld and
spend her life here in the greenwood with Galen, like
Lady Marian with Robin Hood.

Slowly awareness of a growing roar seeped into
Amicia's dream-filled mind. The waterfall was near.
"Galen." She whispered although the likelihood of
others near enough to hear was remote. "I fear if I
don't leave the water soon, my feet will be too numb
to safely descend the wall."

Galen glanced back, silver-green eyes dropping to
thin kidskin slippers on small submerged feet. With
such costly footwear how in the name of all that was
holy did she expect to pass herself off as a common
serving maid?

Amicia followed the path of his gaze and cringed.
After escaping Kelda, in her haste to join Randolf
she'd forgotten to change into her sturdy and unre-
markable shoes. No wonder her feet were so cold!

"Oh, no!" She sought to put all her initial regret
into the words. "I forgot to change out of the shoes the
lady gave my sister—you remember, my sister Melly
who is maid to the heiress?" The innocent smile she
gave Galen suffered a momentary flicker when
Randolf's gasp came from behind.

To hide his amusement with the less than effective
liar near caught, Galen returned his attention to the
stream while waving her to the shore.

As Amicia stepped from the icy flow to the moss-
slick bank, she bent a hard glare on Randolf, wordlessly warning him against gainsaying her words.

Randolf had no notion of her reason but knew he'd
trouble enough without the possibility of alienating
his saviors. Shrugging, he nodded his acceptance of
her silent command.

For the short distance remaining the two men
continued amidst the shallow water edging the stream
while Amicia walked carefully over treacherous moss,
listening to her shoes squish and hoping the excess

water would be gone before she need lower herself over the cliff's edge.

"I'll go down first," Galen announced when they stood at the brink of a sharp drop. Randolf's eyes widened and he took an instinctive step back from a deed the stranger clearly meant for them all to do.

"Randolf, don't be afraid," Amicia quickly comforted. "I've climbed down many times, and if a mere girl can safely descend, surely a man as strong as you has no reason to fear. There's a stairway of sorts carved into the stone—firm holds for fingers and toes. And you've only to go halfway to where a ledge will take even your full weight."

Randolf was not convinced. After all, this tiny creature had no more weight than a thistle's fluff and possessed more daring than near any man he knew. Thus, that she deemed it safe was no reassurance. Still, he'd never be able to name himself a man if he cowered back from an action she plainly meant to perform.

Through narrowed green eyes Galen watched the exchange between these two, obviously of long acquaintance, and in their talk he saw precisely what had brought the hulking giant to a roasting bird. Clearly it was Randolf who'd brought Amicia to the mainland, and it was the quicksilver maid who'd slipped free of the giant's watchful eye to find him. By her determination to come to him, then, Randolf had been left to track her path in the slow and methodical way he demonstrated in his every action from dragging an unconscious knight to the uncomplaining trip over what he'd doubtless found to be an oddly winding path. Aye, Amicia had led Randolf into a danger that had near ruined his life. But, Galen grimly reminded himself, he was not blameless, for this foolish journey would not have come about if it hadn't been for her desire to be with him and his earlier promise to meet her.

Stepping forward and gazing over the brink, Galen

spoke in a calm and confidence-inspiring voice. "Randolf, come near and watch as I make the downward trip."

Randolf found courage in the yet unknown stranger's steady words and obeyed. The man was as tall though not as heavy as he. Seeing the stranger lower himself over the edge and carefully seek each hold, unmistakable once recognized for what they were, Randolf's anxiety faded into determination. He never feared the long climb down the steep and oft swaying stairs at the castle's back, and this was little different.

Amicia held her breath while Randolf lowered his huge form over the cliff face. Already today she'd been the cause of one hazardous event in Randolf's placid life and wordlessly pleaded with all the saints whose names her desperate mind could dredge up to see her gentle giant safe to the end of this one.

At last Randolf stood on the narrow ledge beside Galen and Amicia's teeth released a greatly abused lower lip before she tucked her skirts under her belt without thought to modesty.

Seeing Amicia lift the hem of her gown, Galen knew what would follow. This was neither the time nor the circumstances under which to lay himself open to temptations that would distract. Besides, he preferred not to share the delicious view with another. Touching Randolf's thick shoulder to call his attention, Galen tipped his head to the side in silent command for the giant to follow.

By the time Amicia, descending with the speed of long and recent practice, reached the solid ledge, her companions were stepping under falling water and into the cavern behind.

Hearing a scuffing sound at the cave's mouth, Carl's gaze turned in that direction while a kneeling Walter looked up from the small black pot of simmering stew suspended over the firepit from a tripod formed of stripped green branches.

"Strange happenings," Galen growled, lifting his hands palm-out before him to hold back questions he was not ready to answer.

Neither of the cave's occupants spoke but Carl's expressive brows lifted, and when the girl stepped in behind the men, they rose amazingly high. Strange happenings indeed! The irritated man who'd gone to see a maid on the homeward path had returned with not only the maid but a hulking stranger as well!

"Randolf, this is Carl." Galen waved toward the curious man leaning against the cave wall, honing stone in one hand and dagger in the other. Both hands occupied, Carl nodded in welcome.

"And our young cook is called Walter." Galen gave a teasing smile to the sandy-haired adolescent who scrambled to his feet and offered the newcomer his arm in greeting.

From but a step within the dim cave Amicia saw the hesitant question in the eyes Randolf returned to the speaker, and she provided the last but all important name. "Galen is the man who saved you from the baron's fury."

Recognizing his omission, Galen looked toward the girl with a smile of thanks. She stood silhouetted against the sun-glittering crystal backdrop of falling water while firelight from in front turned her tawny hair to golden honey and deepened the velvet of her eyes. His heart turned over in his chest, and as if drawn by a power beyond his considerable will, he moved to her side.

"I fear our rescue has ended in the raising of a hue and cry that will keep the baron's men combing the forest until nightfall is fully upon us." Galen's murmur was too soft for others to hear its words clearly. "Thus, 'twould be unwise for you to leave before the moon rides high."

Far from easing Galen's frustration with her rash behavior, their adventure had increased his determination to see it tempered. Yet, he didn't fool himself that he was less than pleased by the reasoning which gave excuse for her to stay with him until low tide released the causeway for her crossing. Doubtless the giant had brought her by boat, but no matter her personal bravery, there was no possibility of her having the strength to row against the incoming sea's buffeting waves to safe harbor. Indeed, the men who'd already gone to stable their horses when he and Amicia had come upon the baron had surely found the boat Randolf used and arranged for the craft's return to the isle.

Amicia's warm relief glowed in her smile. She was thankful that she needn't pretend a return to the village and then hide with questionable success from the troops sent by the Dark Lord to scour every part, every fragment of the woodlands. Moreover, 'twas a wonderful excuse to linger with the man whose every action, from the restoring of a wrongfully taken donation to the aid of serfs and the saving of Randolf, had earned her respect, planting and nourishing a tender love that wound its roots ever deeper into her heart. Although Kelda, Lady Anne, and her castle friends would worry about the fate of one who'd disappeared without a word, she'd not waste precious moments fretting over what she could not change. Harder to dismiss was the thought of Orva's alarm when returning guardsmen reported her son's wrong-doing, subsequent escape, and flight from deadly pursuers.

Galen gallantly offered his arm; and, with equal formality, Amicia lightly rested small fingers atop, allowing him to lead her toward the blanket spread out on one side of the cheery fire.

Stepping out beneath the falling river transformed by moonlight to liquid silver, Amicia preceded Galen from the cave. Once beyond its sparkling curtain, feeling Galen's warmth close behind, she paused to carefully turn and speak words the water's roar would assure unheard by those still within the dark cavern.

"Must I go back to my parents?" she asked. Since their return to the hideaway, they'd sat together beside the fire in a contentment interrupted only by the tasty meal a surprisingly inventive Walter had prepared. The realization of how short-lived must be their time together had added a piquant desperation to those moments of near silence when eyes had spoken of longings and emotions that words couldn't—not in the company of others, mayhap not even in solitude.

The face lifted to Galen was moon-pale but even that orb so practiced at robbing the earth of color was unable to steal the golden highlights twined through thick honey tresses.

"You know 'tis not possible, leastways not now." He'd not take the precious gift offered by this well-born maid—'twould be dishonor to her good name and a blemish on his own. Still, it was near too much for him to resist. As a result, his jaw went hard and when he spoke his voice was gruffer than intended. "I've important tasks to be done and cannot afford the distraction you would be." The moment he'd fulfilled his charge, he meant to return as the great lord he was and honorably court this fair and, by his hard-won restraint, unsullied maiden.

Amicia mentally flinched at this reminder of the trouble she'd already caused. Although 'twas a selfish and unworthy thought, her eyes went dark with pain at finding herself of less import than the villagers. "Then I must be gone."

Galen saw the shadow of unhappiness pass over the pure loveliness of her features, as if a cloud had crossed before the moon. His frustration with the problems created by their hidden identities grew. "I'll escort you." The clipped words were gritted out between teeth clenched to hold back a denial of the rejection she obviously believed intended. It was better, safer for her to think it true and until the quest was complete stay clear of the danger that stalked him.

"There is no need." Amicia refused to let fall the burning tears gathering behind her lowered lashes. That she'd read more into the moments shared in the false intimacy of low-burning flamelight seemed painfully evident. "As you said, you've important tasks ahead."

Galen opened his lips but the headstrong girl forestalled his words as she rushed to speak again. "Truly, there is no need, and the villagers desperate for your help likely are already gathering. And we both know that the Dark Lord's men fear to be abroad in the forest after twilight fades into night." Not pausing to weigh her words, Amicia hit out with an insult she instinctively knew would be a blow. "As for other threats, surely the baron's extensive searches prove there are no unsavory brigands lurking about—save you and your men."

Galen didn't flinch. His face froze, and he went stiff with the will demanded to keep from telling her precisely who he was. Her impulsive behavior and tongue that spoke without thought had early convinced him that such a confession was something with which he dare not trust her. He questioned her ability to keep it a secret, no matter her good intentions, and in a temper, as now, it might be dangerous in truth.

As if it were an injury open to view, Amicia felt she could see the wound she'd dealt him and took a short step forward to lay her hand against his chest. "I didn't mean—" Unable to find adequate words of apology, her voice trailed off. In desperation she repeated, "I didn't."

Galen met her pleading gaze with an ever deepening sense of frustration. Did he need it, here was proof that she was too quick to speak imprudently, proof he must not share with her his full name and heritage.

That he could not only increased his impatience to see an end of the chore whose goal he'd yet to learn. All his irritation with the lack of progress gleamed like silver frost in the eyes narrowed on the dainty fingers touching him.

"Oh—" The glare on her hand felt like the brush of an icy breeze meant to freeze hope. Beneath his apparent rejection of her romantic dreams, worse, of her love and utterly oblivious to her precarious footing on a narrow ledge above a sharp drop, Amicia jerked her hand away and stepped back.

"You fool!" Galen growled, wrapping strong arms about the reckless maid and cradling her tight to his chest while he leaned back against the cliff's solid rock wall. "You sweet, sweet fool." As he buried his face in a soft cloud of lustrous hair, his voice came to her ears like a low and distant thunder. "Our time will come. I swear it on my honor." He twined his fingers in tawny silk and gently pulled her head back until he could gaze down into melting honey eyes. "And I am a man of honor."

"I never doubted it," Amicia instantly responded. "Never, never—" Her fervent reassurances were lost beneath the short, tantalizing kisses Galen rained on cheeks and eyelids, brushed against the corners of her mouth, and pressed into the sensitive hollows beneath her ears. All a tempting delight but utterly unsatisfying.

Amicia rose on her toes to wrap her arms about his neck, bury her fingers in cool strands of black, and tug his mouth to hers. Yet still his open mouth only bit softly at hers, tongue entering and withdrawing in teasing strokes like a bee after honey, tasting the nectar while his breath came fast and ragged. With a small, wild cry she instinctively aligned her soft curves against the heated contours of his powerful body, and his iron restraint shattered. His hands swept down her back to lift and crush her nearer. Together they fell into blazing hunger, feeling, breathing, tasting each other in a fever of need.

The loud splash of some large piece of stream-borne debris tumbling into the pond below suddenly returned Galen to awareness of where they stood. He lifted his head and let it rest against the cold wall at his back, welcoming cool spray to temper the raging fire in his veins. Gently holding the trembling maid close, again and again he stroked slow comfort from the vulnerable neck beneath masses of tangled locks to near the bottom of her spine. His submission to passion's lure had been a witless deed, but a delicious folly. Realizing that his fingers were growing too bold and less a solace than an incitement to more, he forced them to go still on her waist.

Opening his eyes to the mystery of moonlight, Galen spoke with quiet conviction. "The time and place are purely wrong, but soon the night will be ours and all through the hours of dark we'll build fires that blaze hotter than the sun and taste sweeter than moonlight."

Allowing Galen to move her safe to the side, Amicia looked up into crystal light eyes wherein she saw both the fire and the sweetness and believed his promise with her whole heart. The smile Galen gave in response to her open trust was tinged with regret for the web of lies he'd have to see carefully unraveled else it might strangle any emotion she felt for him. He brushed her cheek with the back of his hand before motioning her on toward the upward climb. "I'll accompany you a part of the way."

"Nay." Her soft denial was full of unspoken love as she returned his caress, running a fingertip down the crease his smile laid beside his mouth. "The hour you named in summoning the villagers is fast approaching, and I would that you get your task quickly done to be back in the cave before dawn and the baron arrive—keep safe until our time comes." With a tender smile, she rose on tiptoe again, pulling his face down to lightly brush her lips across his before moving to the carved stone ladder.

Mayhap she was right, Galen silently agreed as he watched her tuck the skirt under her belt and begin to climb, although for more reason than even the promise he'd given the folk of Brayston. He dare not accompany her above for once on firm ground he'd no faith that his control was equal to the great temptation—fully claiming the prize he wanted more than ever any other and before she learned of deceits that might forever hold them separate.

Only after Amicia had reached the cliff top and begun to navigate the forest path did fears assail her confidence in their future. Oh, she'd no doubt he meant his words—to a village girl, but would he dare the near universal vengeance that assuredly would befall a common man making off with a maid well-born? She wished she could tell him how little she desired a noble-bred man who would wed her only for the fiefdom she'd bring her husband. By her hidden identity her heart was trapped, prevented from confessing her heritage and convincing him that he was a man far more valuable to her than either her inheritance or the name and title of any other.

Each step away from her love seemed only to bring additional misgivings and further weaken the new, fragile link between them. *Linger too long,* she reminded herself, *and the rising tide will steal your only path for a safe return and leave you stranded in the woodland for a furious Dark Lord to find.* The caution intended to lend haste to her feet failed entirely. It seemed a very fine excuse for returning to the cave, yet a moment's thought mocked her impulsive scheme. How could she explain such reasoning to the Wolf's Head who believed she lived in the village? Quickening her pace, with a grimace of wry self-disgust, she shook her head in firm rejection of what she longed to do but clearly could not. Couldn't not only because of the difficulties born of her hidden identity but also because by giving over to her selfish desire she'd fail a friend brought to woe by her actions. For Randolf's sake she owed Orva reassurances of her son's good care.

Amidst the moonlit path an exposed root lay clearly revealed, but troubled brown eyes saw nothing of the danger. Amicia stumbled over it, nearly fell, and was forced to give more attention to her progress. Roused from bleak thoughts (though they lingered in the back of her mind like an ominous cloud laying a shadow across her bright happiness in Galen's promise), she glanced about and was surprised to find herself already at the point where woodland greenery thinned to open on the shore.

Trudging across the rock-strewn beach, Amicia studied the waves barely receded enough to risk a crossing, still jostling against the causeway's sides and occasionally splashing over the narrow span. She lifted her gown's hem and glanced down at her feet with wry amusement. Leastways, she could do no further damage to slippers already abominably abused by earlier adventures and her stroll through the stream.

Losing no time in making the crossing, she hurried up the steep, winding path with all the haste allowed by muscles wearied by the adventures of an over-long day. So stealthily did she move through the dark stable that not a single horse nickered at her passing. As she slipped inside the castle proper, the creaking of the door was the only sound and one so faint it caused no interruption in the soft sobbing nearby.

Amicia stepped behind the curtain of homespun that lent a rare privacy to the small alcove built into the thick wall of the corridor between outgoing door and stairway to the kitchen. Here on her straw pallet a large woman sat, hunched against cold stone.

"Orva," Amicia gently whispered.

Face buried in shaking hands, the one called clearly hadn't heard. Amicia moved forward, dropped to her

140

knees, and wrapped her slender arms about heaving shoulders to pull the older woman near.

"Orva," Amicia murmured, "Randolf is fine—fed and sleeping safe, protected by a mighty warrior who saved him from the baron's unjust condemnation."

Deep in an ocean of misery, Orva hardly noted the small creature's attempts to wrap her stout frame in comfort, until the sound of her son's name broke through. She pulled back and looked into the maid's solemn gaze, searching for hope. The desolation on a face previously ever-smiling struck Amicia anew with a painful awareness of the unhappiness brought by her selfish use of Randolf's generous nature. Guilt burned —like the fires of hell where the priests said the wicked would pay for their evil deeds?

"He is not mortal injured?" Orva asked, her desperation to believe plain in imploring, red-rimmed eyes.

Amicia took the two plump hands lifted to her in supplication and soothed, "He was whipped but the baron's strength is not so great as to render more damage than will soon mend." She had no guarantee that she spoke the truth but fervently prayed she'd not lied.

With the younger woman intent on her need to comfort and the older clutching at the tenuous lifeline of hope tossed into the sea of despair threatening to drown her, neither noticed Anne's presence. She stood as a silent observer in the gap left open between humble curtain's edge and wall when Amicia rushed to a hurting mother.

Fear drove Orva to further questions before the first answer had faded. "What will he, a serf, do when he cannot return yet cannot live elsewhere? How will he eat without truly breaking forest laws?"

Gently squeezing the anxiety-clenched hands still in her grasp, Amicia rallied her flagging spirits and with a confidence she hoped was justified claimed, "You need have no fear. The same man who rescued Randolf will see to his needs." Seeing that her attempt at solace had merely confused, she explained. "The Wolf's Head whom the baron, as diligently as he has tried, has failed to find is the man who holds Randolf safe."

In this undeniably admiring talk of the outlaw Anne heard confirmation of the truth behind Kelda's worried fears. After the disaster of Amicia's absence from the evening as well as the noontide meal, and fearing for her friend's safety, Kelda had admitted they'd both crossed the outlaw's path. Hands twisting together, she'd confessed the tales Amicia told of a stunningly handsome Wolf's Head.

"I don't know how Randolf can've come to such folly when only did he go, as so oft he does, to ensure that feed be evenly distributed betwixt isle and shoreline stables." Without understanding of the facts, Orva plainly feared that the baron's condemnations were true. "The baron says by running Randolf's admitted of poaching, of thievery, and has earned an outlaw's brand."

In the simple woman's face Amicia saw painful doubts and couldn't allow the mother to doubt the honesty of her son when it was all a result of her own wrongdoing.

"If I hadn't cajoled him into taking me with him to the mainland; if I hadn't broken a promise to him and slipped away while he faithfully completed his task, he'd never have stumbled upon the roasting bird. 'Tis my fault the baron has condemned him for poaching and pronounced him an outlaw for escaping a hideous punishment. 'Tis my fault, and I'll never absolve myself of the blame."

The open-hearted cook forgave and drew Amicia into her well-padded embrace. While the gentle comfort earlier given was returned to the weeping girl, Anne pondered the confession. If truly Amicia had learned a lesson, though a ghastly price for its learning was paid by others, she hoped some small good might come of this dreadful day's work.

"In truth, 'tis a shame upon you that an innocent man pays dearly for your thoughtless deed."

The two on the straw pallet broke apart and turned toward the unexpected witness to their sorrow and guilt.

"Only do I hope," Anne continued, taking a short step into the alcove and gazing with a reproach tempered by pity into eyes of deep brown, "that you'll think of the consequences before taking rash actions."

"She'll not have another chance to commit 'thoughtless deeds,'" jeered a voice full of spite.

Lady Anne whirled to face the speaker then fell back, nearly stumbling over a mattress on the floor and too close in the confined space.

Gilfrey's sneer deepened, spreading wide the thin lips out of proportion with a face turned fleshy by self-indulgence. He'd arrived just in time to hear Anne's scolding and enjoyed the way both she and the cook cowered from him. That Amicia straightened and tilted her chin defiantly merely made his next words only taste the more satisfying on his tongue.

"By week's end she'll be wed to one of my choosing, one who will bridle and break her of wild ways. Until that day, while a guardsman stands at my lady-wife's door to ensure her privacy continues, night and day Mag will be within an arm's length of this untamed creature." He disdainfully waved toward Amicia.

Until he spoke the crone's name, Amicia had not allowed her gaze to break from his glare. And then she gave only a cursory glance to the wizened hag who peered from behind her master's back. The Dark Lord's minion, bent and face so lined with age her features were near indistinguishable—save piercing eyes of no color—was near as black-souled as he.

Though her heart had dropped to her toes, she lifted her eyes to again meet his, unflinching. No doubt he meant to see her laboring beneath the crushing weight of an onerous marriage to some old and disgusting man as cruel as he. Worst of all, a man Gilfrey had certainly urged to carry her off to some bleak and distant domain, putting an end to the golden dream of the shared future Galen had promised. For a brief moment her lashes dropped under the pain of what seemed an undeniable fact—she would never see Galen again!

❧ Chapter 10 ❧

Your quiet defiance of the usurper proves you to be a courageous people, loyal to one another for the common good." Powerful form outlined by the pale light from above, Galen stood on the loaded wagon's seat in the center of a clearing crowded with people. The words he spoke were clear and easily heard in the stillness of the night hour midway betwixt sunset and dawning. "Take heart, the absence I propose will be temporary, although mayhap long enough for Baron Gilfrey to chafe under the dearth of men to harvest the crops that feed him."

Not so much as the faint sound of a single twig snapping under a restive foot broke the apprehensive hush of women clinging to their men and children to their skirts. The pleasant notion of the lord punished in even a small way by their actions lessened but did not overcome their fears. Under Edgar's urgings they'd packed their few prize possessions and the goods of survival into the wagon before coming to this gathering, yet not all were convinced of the need nor committed to the journey.

"What choice have we?" Edgar demanded, stepping to the front and turning to face his fellows. "Would you meekly wait like sheep for slaughter to watch as the baron, seeking to force us to his brutal will, burns one home after another? Or would you turn to skulking ways, ferret out the answer our foe demands, and betray the one who has proven himself friend. Betray this man who risked his life to save from the baron's injustice a common man like as are we all." He motioned toward the hulking serf standing between the outlaw's two supporters. "Betray the man who filled our empty bellies and now offers us hope?"

"More than hope," Galen called out above a growing murmur. "I give you my oath on the Holy Cross that you need be gone only a short while before your true lord comes to drive Gilfrey from the lands he stole by murder and deceit."

This announcement of such a one as they'd never heard cast a spell of utter silence over the glade. Indeed, how could it be? Baron Conal had only one wife and with her only one child and that a daughter. Did he mean a man who meant to claim the heiress and seize her dowry? Or son of bastard line? In either case hardly a strong claim, but certainly any other would be better than their vindictive lord. Heads began to nod and whispered agreement grew to an audible approval.

"But where can we, as serfs, go without being hunted to ground?" The questioner was a woman whose plain face had been lent the beauty of character by the bright intelligence in her gaze. "Any noble lord would be honor bound to return us to the baron's savage punishment." She stepped to Edgar's side and bravely met the stranger's eyes, mysterious and penetrating.

"Do you know of a man called Willikin of the Weald?" Already the name of the famous warrior was widely recognized and revered. 'Twas said he held the dense forest of the Weald so firmly in his control that the invading French trembled at the name and dared not risk entering his forests' fearful depths.

"Will is my friend," Galen calmly stated, pride in his older cousin swelling with the respect for the mighty knight which he saw on the faces of these people. Despite his nine-year seniority, Will was friend as well as cousin—they shared the same grand-father. "Carl, my supporter, is ready to lead you to temporary safety in the Weald. But, on my honor— and you must trust that it is something I possess and hold most dear—I swear you'll return to a just lord intent on seeing you and your homes restored to peace and prosperity."

"Because I do trust you, I and mine will gladly go with hope for a better future." Edgar, left arm about the woman at his side (clearly his wife) held out his right arm in demonstration of his faith in the outlaw's promise.

Galen jumped to ground cushioned by crushed foliage and, standing on a level with the brave man, wrapped his hand about the extended arm just below the elbow, joining their forearms in mutual respect.

"I go, too," a young voice piped.

Galen gazed down into Davie's earnest face. Re-specting the youngster's sincerity, with a serious smile he offered his arm next to the boy. "You earlier proved your bravery, and I salute your courage in giving your backing to my plan."

Davie joined his small arm with the iron-thewed limb of the other and grinned with pride for the praise of this man smart enough to outwit the wicked baron at every turn and strong enough to save a serf from an unfair punishment.

Galen glanced up at a sky brightening with the first pale shimmer that precedes the dawning and warned. "Best be that those who go set forth without delay. Soon the baron will begin the hunt anew."

The woman at Edgar's side went pale. That the law called a vicious retribution down upon any bound to the land who attempted freedom was far too well

147

known to take so serious a step lightly. Yet, she squared sturdy shoulders, resolved not to shrink from the challenge.

Edgar looked slowly from one of his fellow villagers to another. Gray-streaked hair brushed his shoulders as he nodded his understanding of their wordless communication. Turning back, he solemnly met Galen's eyes straight on. "We all go."

Much relieved that none would remain behind, increasing the danger to both themselves and their departing friends, Galen motioned Carl to climb into the cart's seat and take command of the ox yoked to pull its heavy weight. As the people lined up behind the destrier tied at the cart's rear, he saw the fears beneath their grimly determined faces and gave one more promise. "I will lead the baron on such a merry chase that he'll not have time to discover you gone until it's too late to fetch you back."

Quickly coming to believe Galen as near to infallible as a mortal man could be, the people's tension momentarily eased into grins, but Carl gave him a worried look and silent plea to take care. Although Galen nodded, his one-sided, sardonic smile lent the scowling Carl no comfort.

The group began to move, yet Randolf held back. In gratitude he earnestly pumped the arm of his savior of the day past before falling into step at the end of the small band of travelers.

Galen watched them disappear into thick forests before motioning Walter to help him mask their outgoing path through forest wall. Once done, they mounted and rode out to perform the dangerous promised deed.

Staring fixedly into a candle's flickering flame, Amicia seethed. The thought of what the Dark Lord intended to impose upon her was surely as foul as the odor of the taper's tallow. Beneath the emotionless mask she'd worn since the moment he'd delivered his announcement burned a resentment that had grown so fierce in its fire that she was indifferent to the unwavering eyes of her keeper. Here in the window-less chamber long shared with Kelda was Mag, huddled in the gloom of one corner, impervious to the chill of the stone wall at her back and the discomfort of the prickly rushes covering the floor.

Without natural light to mark the progress of time, Amicia had no way to know whether 'twas still night or if late afternoon had fallen by the time she came to a decision. Her stepfather had the lawful right to choose what greedy man claimed her inheritance through the marriage bond, but before she allowed him the choice of to whom she gave her innocence she'd walk willingly into the fires of hell. The bold decision to thwart Gilfrey at least in this thawed the cold horror which despite the heat of her anger had slowed her nimble mind until near frozen to a halt. Horror cold, but temper hot.

Noting that the candle was now almost reduced to a puddle of tallow, she wondered if 'twas the heat of her temper that had melted the taper or if truly that much time had passed. Aware of the steady gaze on her back, she focused on the first step to her goal, the need to find a way free of the crone. Only then could she escape the castle's confines and cross to the mainland. But how?

In the next instant, as if in answer to an unspoken prayer, the heavy door opened, scraping across plank flooring.

Unsure of her welcome from the friend she'd betrayed, Kelda hesitantly peered in, eyes dark with guilty repentance. Although she'd promised Farrold to do all possible to see the outlaw captured, only worry and good intentions had prompted the confession given her mother of the relationship between the man and Amicia.

Kelda's arrival bolstered Amicia's hopes for escape, and she gave the other girl a bright, pleased smile.

Apparently Kelda had been hustled from this chamber in the midst of the night for it had been empty when Mag led her here. Surely, despite the emotional oath to Farrold, Kelda would lend aid to any strategy her life-long friend devised.

Seeing Amicia's open response, Kelda realized she'd yet to learn even that the story of her relationship with the outlaw was known let alone that 'twas her friend who had tattled secret tales. She wanted to confess, have it said, and seek forgiveness—but not in front of Mag. Returning Amicia's greeting with a weak smile, Kelda stepped into the room and sank down beside her. Blue eyes skittered away from brown.

Desperately searching for innocuous words to share, she found only a inane comment. "Looks as though you'll need a new taper soon."

"Aye." Amicia barely registered Kelda's odd tension as she gave a quick glance to the flame grown weak and flickering above the pool of tallow dangerously near to extinguishing its feeble light.

Kelda jumped to her feet again. "Then I'll fetch you a new one." She was pleased to have some little chore she could do for her friend, a start on the atonement she owed.

Roused from hours of dark thoughts, Amicia discovered an emptiness in her stomach. Knowing any plan—and she'd no doubt she'd find one—would require strength, she said, "A candle I would appreciate but a meal even more. It's been a long night and I'm fair starving."

Kelda's jaw dropped. "Night? The day is close to done. Does this mean you've not eaten since last night?"

"Truth be known," Amicia shrugged, "not since twilight was falling yester eve." Memory of the magnetic man with whom she'd shared that repast while velvet coils of attraction wrapped them into their own silent world warmed brown eyes to golden honey.

"'Tis near that time on a new day." Kelda's voice was heavy with disgust that no one had thought to provide Amicia with a meal, but then she hadn't done so herself—an unforgivable omission, but one that wasn't so very difficult to understand. The whole castle was in chaos under the white-hot fury of a baron on the rampage to see an outlaw in "a living hell" for trussing him like a hunter's prize and leaving him for his men to find—a shame few lords could bear. Each time he roared another threat of the retaliations to be wreaked upon the Wolf's Head and all who supported him, Orva near went hysterical. What were too kindly named meals were inedible.

Amicia's brow creased in consideration of Kelda's words. The approach of twilight meant she'd less time to plot an escape than she'd thought. As she acknowledged that fact an idea flashed into her mind. She spoke quickly, halting her friend at the door.

"Kelda, I've a thirst even greater than my hunger." She rose and stepped between the older girl and the shadows where bided their silent observer. "Could you bring to me some of your mother's special sweet wine? Its silky magic would be the very thing to soothe a dry throat."

Startled blue eyes went wide and for a dangerously long moment silence reigned. "Yes, of course." Kelda's voice was a tight squeak but she soon recovered to add, "I should've thought of it myself. 'Tis the very thing and, though mother hoards the precious brew, I don't doubt she'll willingly share it with you."

Kelda solemnly nodded into Amicia's broad grin. They understood each other well. Anne, serving as castle chatelaine in the withdrawn Lady Sybil's stead, had long ago learned the uses and blending of medicinal herbs. In particular the importance of the one that, when joined with sweet wine, lent a gentle but not easily interrupted slumber. A fine decoction most useful for those too pain-filled to find easy rest—and for one whose sleep would release another from captivity. Anxious to prove herself still a worthy conspirator, if only to herself, Kelda hurried away to fulfill her charge.

As the door closed, Amicia settled again on her pallet. She drew her knees up, let her forehead rest atop them and her hair slide forward, providing a tawny silk curtain between Mag and her excitement-blushed cheeks and satisfied smile. Restraining her anticipation to hold motionless while awaiting her friend's return was a difficult chore. It seemed like a lifetime had passed but, judging by Kelda's haste-quickened breathing, it could not have been so very long before the door opened once more and a young serf carrying a heavily laden tray preceded Kelda into the room.

"You are fortunate indeed. For a night and now near full day, the inhabitants of Castle Dungeld have been cursed with dreadful meals. Yet, when I asked Orva to make up a tray for you who'd not eaten since the past eve, she rushed about and with her own talented hands provided this." Kelda nodded at the serf's burden. "Leaving me with only the task of protecting it from the thieving hands of the hungry masses as we brought it to you."

The young boy who settled the heaping platter on a trunk at the bed's foot gave it such a look of longing before he left as to give credence to Kelda's claim.

"'Tis wondrous what Orva can do with brined fish. And there's a salad of purslayne, rosemary, and other such greens, as well as a healthy measure of yester morn's wheaten bread and a jug of milk." Kelda motioned so innocently toward the tray with one hand that Amicia didn't think to notice that the other was still tucked at her back.

The amusement rightfully earned by Kelda's foolery did nothing to lessen Amicia's dismay. Believing that the planned reprieve was now lost, smothering vines of disappointment wrapped about her chest and tightened until she could draw only shallow breaths. To hide her emotions, she lifted the fresh candle laid between the two mugs on one side of the tray, lit it, then blew out and removed the stub of the old. She held the blunt end of the new to the pool on the candlestick's base until it hardened enough to hold of its own.

Kelda had meant to banter with her down-hearted friend, but seeing golden sparks of hope fade to deep brown ashes, she repented.

"And to compliment the final dish of cheese and fresh berries, as promised, I've brought a bottle of my mother's sweet fruit wine."

Amicia's glance flew up to the flagon Kelda had produced from behind her back, but her grimace of irritation with her friend's poorly timed jest faded into an affectionate smile.

"Bringing these treats to you has doubtless made me late for what will have to pass for my own evening meal, and I must hurry or risk a scolding for my tardiness."

As Kelda rushed away Amicia scooted on the end of the bed to be nearer the over-burdened tray.

"Mag," Amicia began hoping her anxiety-filled voice sounded more normal and offhand than she feared. "I can nowise eat all of this vast repast and don't doubt but that you are as hungry as I. So, come, share it with me."

Clearly Mag viewed with suspicion this invitation from one ever hostile. Nonetheless, her need of food outweighed caution and she sidled slowly nearer until she crouched on the far side of the chest, just opposite her hostess. Amicia ate with her customary, long-ingrained manners while the hag snatched at the food as if she were still the child born a beggar in city gutters presented with a feast and fearful of its sudden withdrawal. Amicia strived not to show her distaste for dirty, claw-like hands, one prying meat from bones, the other grabbing hunks of bread, and both stuffing her mouth until her cheeks bulged and juices dripped down the sharp chin jutting out from folds of wrinkled skin.

Pouring frothy milk into one of the two crockery mugs on the tray, Amicia politely offered it to the old woman. Mag drew back as sharply as if 'twere poison. Amicia carefully controlled the grin tugging at the corners of her lips. She couldn't have planned a better opening to her own design.

"Then, please, have some of Lady Anne's very special wine." The invitation was issued in a carefully neutral tone, and Amicia waved absently to the flagon with one hand while the other carefully lifted a golden crust to her lips.

Eyes again sharp with suspicion, Mag studied the girl apparently occupied with easing her hunger. What was one wee sip of wine—or even more. There weren't a man in the castle what could out-drink nor hold his liquor so well as her. Asides, how oft was the likes 'o her gifted with wine the sort what the well-born drank. She snatched up the flagon and boldly poured a right full mug o' the stuff and gulped it down in one long draw.

Unable to control her surprise, Amicia's eyes widened. The hag had emptied the mug and filled it again in less time than it took for her to take a single sip of milk.

Mag was gleefully amused by the maid's surprise. Amicia was an insipid creature, no matter her wild ways, if'n she couldn't do justice to such silky but surely impotent stuff as this wine. Why she, Mag, much preferred the hearty fires of honest ale to this weak wine what could hardly warm the belly let alone endanger a clear mind. And to prove it she polished off another full mug in little more'n a gulp.

Before Amicia had finished one mug of milk, Mag

had emptied the entire flagon of wine and her eyelids, already near lost beneath heavy folds of flesh, seemed to remain open only with great difficulty. Amicia carefully set her mug down to watch as Mag lost the battle and flopped back, lost to the world of the waking until at least this time two days hence. Amicia hadn't expected the crazy creature to drink the whole, and for her gluttony she'd pay, first, with missing days and then doubtless with the brunt of Baron Gilfrey's ire. Too late now to consider what she could have or should have done to prevent such events, Amicia lost no time in scrambling to her feet and peering out from a door cracked open. Through the arrow slit at the end of the short hall she saw the darkening of a sky filled with clouds—rapidly darkening, but not quickly enough.

She forced patience on her impatient soul and moved back to the pallet, mentally plotting her course from this point on through the stolen night. There'd be a price to pay, but a payment only for her and she'd willingly submit to the Dark Lord's anger if first she could rescue from his hold the gift that was truly her own to give and claim the promised night of fire and sweetness from the man who'd sworn to give it to her.

Mag's heavy breathing had fallen into a monotony of deep snores before Amicia rose, took her dark cloak from the peg and eased the door slowly open. First peering down the corridor one way and then the other, she slipped out and pulled the heavy planks closed behind her so carefully the iron latch didn't even click. She quietly padded to the stairwell and descended so slowly her footfalls made no sound.

From the foot of the stairs, Amicia passed unnoticed through the hallway and by the busy kitchen, then down to where she'd been discovered the evening before. At last she exited the tower. The causeway betwixt isle and mainland would not be tide-freed until near the morning light (and by then she must be ready to make the return journey). Thus, she'd little choice but to duck through the close confines of the rear tunnel and cautiously navigate the narrow path to the back of the castle and the steep wooden stairway to the dock.

Gloomy day had faded into a night wherein hazy clouds drifted across the face of a partial moon, one moment stealing its pale light from the earth and the next allowing teasing moonbeams to dance across rolling waves and lend a glow that left the horizon a sharp silhouette. Staring down into the darkness obscuring the bottom steps and even the dock from her view, her knees shook. *You are brave.* The scolding she gave her fears did little good. Her courageous front was no more than a mask such as mummers often wore to hide realities behind—useful for fooling others but a worthless ploy when turned on herself. Moreover, with no one to pretend for, it was harder to maintain the image of bravery. *No time to turn craven now,* she berated herself. *You can't take action to impress another with your courage, but how much better to accept a risk for the reward of Galen's embrace!* Refusing to think of the dangers, she began descending the steps and was very soon at their bottom. To forestall further fears, she untied the same small boat Randolf had always taken to the mainland and stepped inside. Her heart rose to her throat as the vessel rocked precariously under her feet. She sat down, determinedly lifted the oars to maneuver away from the dock, and pointed the prow toward shore.

It was very hard work even with the tide's flow aiding her journey. When at last the hull scraped bottom, she lost no time in scrambling out, burying feet and hem in the water. She dragged the boat as far up the shore as she could and moved quickly into the shield of dense woodland, soaked shoes squishing with each step and wet feet picking up dust that turned to mud as she climbed.

Upon reaching the stream's edge, never for a moment considering the possibility of a human observer, she sank down on its moss-softened bank. She pulled off the soft leather slippers she'd again forgotten to exchange for more practical shoes and rinsed them in its flow. Next, into the solace of cool liquid she plunged feet aching from a climb that should have been undertaken in nothing less than stout boots. Then, anxious to be as fresh and attractive as possible when she found Galen, Amicia wasted no time on false modesty in the anonymity of a dark forest. Throwing off her cloak, she released the plain ring and pin brooch that held the front of her simple homespun daygown closed at the throat.

Watching from a thicket very near the stream where he'd been on guard since twilight deepened to night, Galen knew he'd waited too long to reveal his presence. Alert to the sounds of someone moving through the forest, he'd carefully peered through dense greenery only to be shocked when the well-born maid stepped into the glade. Curiosity for the purpose of her wild adventure warred with a strong desire to paddle a sense of caution into her—except that were he to touch her he doubted that he could prevent the physical guidance from taking a far more satisfying turn.

First rinsing a sea-soaked hem in cool water, Amicia used the damp cloth to rub refreshment across flesh rowing and haste had left overwarm. But these efforts, restricted to an area revealed by opened neckline, provided only minimal relief. She struggled to loosen the dress's front lacings and pull her arms free of its raglan sleeves. Shrugging out of the loose bodice, she let the unwanted material fall to her waist, leaving her skin free to the brush of water-cooled cloth and the caress of a welcome breeze.

Galen's eyes widened. He should move away. No, the rustling would draw her attention. Self-contempt curled his lips at the pleasure this excuse gave, and he firmly commanded himself to look away—but could not.

Dipping the hem back into the stream, without bothering to wring it out, she lifted it again. Her head fell back, allowing her thick, tawny mane to cascade down her back while from beneath heavy lashes she gazed into a mysterious sky where parting clouds allowed the moon to peek down. Her lips parted on a sigh as the soaked cloth held high above dripped refreshing water.

Saints! Galen silently gasped, unable to look away from the trickle of liquid leaving a gleaming trail as it slowly traced a path down the elegant line of her throat to disappear into the deep valley between luscious breasts. His mouth went dry. With her eyes half-closed, lips open on a soft sound of pleasure, and delicious body arched toward the moon, it looked as if she were some virgin sacrifice to ancient woodland gods, as if she were offering herself up to a longed-for lover. A groan welled from his depths at the thought of being that lover, of tracing the water's path with fingertips and mouth.

The undeniably human sound shocked Amicia. Clutching to her breasts the material once rumpled at her waist, she struggled to stand only to discover that feet numbed and wet from the stream were unable to find sure footing on the moss-slippery bank. She fell back, landing hard on her derriere and banging her head.

"Oh, love." Galen rushed to the fallen girl. "Are you all right?" He swept her into his arms, settling back with her across his lap while he absently rubbed the portion of her anatomy that had taken the initial blow.

With the first touch Amicia had recognized her consoler and happily relaxed in his embrace, snuggling closer to bury her face into the crook between his shoulder and throat. Reveling in the nearness she'd come seeking and found unexpectedly soon, she closed her eyes, purposely sinking into the welcome realm of unthinking sensations. Nuzzling against firm skin that seemed to take fire beneath the touch, she surrendered to temptation and let her tongue venture out to taste the expanse beneath her lips.

At the tantalizing touch, the blood in Galen's veins caught fire and the hand once stroking comfort over tawny locks twisted in the silk at the back of her neck to gently pull her head back until he could claim the teasing mouth with his own. Nibbling at its contours, he silently nudged it open, wordlessly urging her to repeat teasing strokes. When she answered the call, he captured her tongue's tentative motions and taught her the depth of what she'd evoked.

Hungry for the contact, Amicia twisted to press fully against his warm, strong chest while a tiny, inarticulate sound welled up from her core at this delicious play, sweet and devastatingly hot. The sound forced upon Galen an unwelcome awareness of what was happening—all too enjoyable but utterly wrong. He muttered something faintly violent, eyes clenched shut. Too clearly he could feel the burning temptation of full breasts—bare and branding their seductive imprint against his broad chest so that now he would never be free of the feel of them there. He wanted more than anything ever before in his life to rid himself of the shirt that was the only barrier between him and her succulent flesh. Even as he sought to drive back the almost ungovernable compulsion, he realized that in his hand he cupped firm round flesh. Nay, he squeezed and stroked in far, far too intimate a caress. He should stop. He should—but— His fingers rhythmically squeezed and rubbed as if the mind that controlled their action was separate from that which scraped together enough breath to scold.

"You shouldn't be here in the forest at night! Don't

you know the dangers?" His voice was rough, and even his passion-befuddled brain recognized that the naive girl who'd known only his embrace had no way to know the depths of this danger and his irrational exasperation was more for his own wavering self-command. Still, any female should have sense enough not to travel a night-dark forest let alone to strip and lure a man with temptations near beyond bearing.

Lost in a smoky haze of pleasure as his urgent touch stroked over her flesh, Amicia's eyes drifted shut. A burning hunger was building, a hunger she didn't understand yet had no doubt he could satisfy. She ignored his question and instead gave him a whispered plea.

"You promised me a night of fire and sweetness." Desire-weighted lashes lifted just enough for her to gaze into his eyes as she brushed curious fingers back and forth across his lips before lifting her face and laying her petal-soft mouth against his ear. "You gave an oath." Her beguiling voice held the same irresistible enticements as a siren's call. "You are a man of honor and on that honor I've come to demand that it be fulfilled."

Shocked by her words, Galen drew back. To go further, to surrender to even a small portion of the delight demanded by the words whose full meaning this naive maid's could nowise understand, was to lose control. Black lashes lifted—a deed immediately proven foolhardy. He found himself gazing down into slumberous eyes until, unable to prevent it, his attention recklessly dropped to the passion-bright lips lifted and begging for the return of his. Worst of all, he fell prey to an overwhelming urge and visually traced an elegant throat down to perfect globes full and coral tipped.

"Galen." His name came out an aching sigh; and, beneath the green fire in a gaze that felt like a physical caress, Amicia arched her back. Galen's tenuous grasp on the last faint measure of restraint fast slipping into oblivion, he bit back a ragged growl as his hands moved to her waist with an honorable but weakening intent to push her away.

Refusing to allow him success in his half-hearted rejection, Amicia twined her arms about his neck and again slid her fingers into thick black strands. She clung to him, desperate for the anguished pleasure to continue, and pressed closer against him until his mouth came down to cover her raised lips. Eagerly, she yielded to the insistent possession of that deepening kiss.

Under the sensual onslaught of wild, untutored responses, Galen slowly fell back until he lay on a cushion of crushed grass with the small tempting form full atop his hard contours. She wanted the fire he'd promised, the fire that had long since set the blood in his veins to steaming. This delicate creature had dangerously fanned the flames to shatter his good intentions, and he meant her to pay with an insatiable hunger as deep as his own. Taking her shoulders in a firm, gentle grasp he pushed her away, and with his great strength held her a short distance above his prone body.

Amicia moaned at the loss, uselessly struggling against the hold until the unexpected touch of his mouth brushing lightly across her breast stole breath and the will to move. Suspended in unfamiliar, aching sensations, her eyes closed and every feeling centered on the teasing caresses doing impossibly exciting things to her. Too far under his potent spell for the rational thought to which in any case she'd long since closed her mind, her fingers speared into his cool hair and pulled the tormenting mouth closer until at last he settled his kiss on the aching peak.

Suddenly, Galen rolled over to reverse their positions and raise on one arm. Crystal green held melting honey-brown in unbroken thrall while with his free hand he swept her already loosened garments from her. "I've gone hungry for you too long." His low words were a liquid fire that washed over her as he ripped open the laces of his tunic and stripped it off in near a single motion.

Aching with delicious pleasures she'd never dreamed existed, Amicia's starving gaze feasted on the magnificence of his bare chest—a powerful expanse of bronzed muscles partially covered by the arrow of dark hair which spread across its width and drew her eyes down over a flat, firm belly to where chausses were tied at his narrow hips. His face went taut and he shuddered at the intensity of her gaze. Very little more of this delicious maid's innocent wiles could he bear.

Galen stretched out at her side and for long moments his hands and lips stroked hot pleasure over her willing body. She melted against him, burning with unimaginable heat and wordlessly begging for surcease. But only when the flames of her passion had her body twisting in fiery need did he strip off his remaining garments and, with hands braced amidst the tawny silk beside her shoulders, rise above her once again. Slowly he lowered himself over her, letting her feel the tantalizingly gentle rasp of wiry curls across soft flesh. The tremors of helpless response sweeping through Amicia brought a sensual curve to his mouth.

Sinking into the blaze of a devastating desire that would not be denied, Amicia reached for the goal withheld from her, determined to draw him down to lie with her amidst the ravenous flames. She smoothed her hands in fascination over the wide expanse of his torso, reveled in the clenching of the powerful muscles beneath her touch. Still Galen held his grip on the last vestiges of control—until she arched up to mold her soft flesh to the warm strength of his and writhe against him with shattering intimacy in the age-old manner that instinct taught as effectively as experience. He came down, crushing her yielding body beneath his full weight. She welcomed the power of his form, gloried in the closeness. It was a torment sweeter than mulled wine and hotter than wildfire, yet not nearly enough. Merely did it stoke the flames of desire to awesome heights. She yearned to be nearer, wanted more, and wrapped her arms about his wide shoulders, urgently running her palms over the hard contours of his back and up to lock about his neck. Her nails dug into the smooth flesh beneath as she instinctively twisted against him again, exciting, enticing.

Drowning in forbidden pleasure, Galen's hands swept down skin like hot satin to tilt her hips into his and ease the joining their feverish need demanded. Into his open mouth he took her short gasp of pain, holding motionless until it was she who moved against him. Only then did he show her the purpose for the actions she'd so recently learned to incite him with, rocking them both higher and ever higher on the searing delight at the blue-white extremity of flame. Trembling at the height of need, Amicia feared being consumed by the blaze of her own hunger. Her sobs pleaded for release until with Galen's harsh growl the conflagration burst into glittering sparks of mindless ecstasy.

After long moments that seemed to stretch without end, Galen rolled to his back and drew Amicia into the shelter of his arms while he stroked gentle ease over the trembling maid, smoothed the tangled silk of tawny hair, and pressed tender kisses to the top of her head. He marveled over the fact that the realities of this magical creature far surpassed even his sensual dreams, wildly passionate yet full of honeyed sweetness.

Floating through blissful lassitude, Amicia savored the feel of crisp curls and hard muscle beneath her hand and nestled against the heat she now knew could blaze into incredible pleasure. Slowly the heart beneath her touch eased its heavy thumping while Galen's breathing deepened into the sleep of satisfaction. Still she lingered at his side, savoring the last moments of the precious fire and sweet pleasure he'd promised—so soon to be forever lost to her.

If only this night would go on endlessly. If only her fervent wishes could give as much reality to this dream as similar wishes had given her outlaw, this man in her arms. If only— Refusing to give in to the gentle beckoning of satisfaction's sleep, she remained wakeful, pulling her cloak over them both, and cradling to herself these last fleeting moments of ill-fated happiness.

Inevitably a creeping glimmer lightened the eastern sky from indigo blue to deep gray, and Amicia was forced to accept the undeniable approach of a new day. No longer could she put off her return when even now the causeway was likely near lost to the sea. Cautiously she eased from the embrace of her dream hero turned fiery lover, surprised that the inner cries of despair so loud in her heart did not waken him. She donned her gown but tucked her cloak gently about him as protection against the chill harshness before the dawn. It was of no use to her—wool no matter how thick lacked the power to warm a heart turned stone cold by the loss of him.

Following the old trail through the yet nightshadowed forest that she and Kelda had blazed long ago, all too soon she arrived at the shoreline. The rising tide already threatened the causeway's safety. Still, she meant to follow it back to the castle, leaving the boat on the shore for another to fetch—she was certain that in her state of lassitude she hadn't the strength to row back to the isle. Only under effort of will did she force herself to begin. As if each footfall added weight, every step seemed harder to take. For the first time in many years, Amicia failed to find courage to meet a foe full on. And against predawn's cloud-filled sky the castle-isle looming ahead was that. 'Twas a symbol of the inevitable fate awaiting her—a prison where neither happiness nor dreams were allowed. Throughout the ever slower crossing, her unseeing gaze rose no higher than the pathway directly ahead, a pathway washed by rising waves.

"At last the willful wanderer returns." The acid in Gilfrey's jeering words was meant to burn.

Met by the Dark Lord yet again, Amicia dully acknowledged. But, so lost in her own misery was she that for once she failed to respond with her usual rebellious fire. Indeed, she didn't even bother to lift her gaze to his surely scornful stare.

"I wanted to be certain your spouse understood how much you are in need of an iron fist to crush your wild, wanton ways." Gilfrey's sneer deepened in cruel enjoyment when the insolent girl stiffened although still she did not look up. "So, I've brought him to see your return afore the dawning—tousled and clearly bedded by another—no longer a prize to any honorable man."

Unashamed of her actions and wanting her proposed mate to know it so, Amicia's defiance flared and her head snapped proudly up. Her mouth dropped in surprise. The Dark Lord stood directly in front of her, but with him stood two more—her mother and *Farrold!*

"At midmorn of not this day but the next, in the castle's chapel, you'll wed my son." Baron Gilfrey near crowed the announcement. Cruel satisfaction for this culmination of all his long years of planned vengeance reverberated in each word as he added, "And by the children he gets on you my bloodline will hold Wryborne ever more." Even his fury with the outlaw paled into insignificance beneath his pleasure in this scheme. 'Twas his ultimate triumph over Conal, the man who he blamed for once robbing him of a position he'd thought to hold a lifetime, and for subjecting him to bitter humiliation.

Refusing to let Gilfrey see the shock she felt, Amicia tilted her chin and slowly turned emotionless eyes to examine the two at his side. While sorrow twined with defeat in Lady Sybil's face, a shamefaced Farrold fairly oozed with misery.

⊷§ *Chapter 11* ⧉⊶

Lady Sybil is in no danger," Abbot Pieter promptly announced to the tall man filling the door of his austere chamber. "Leastways no more than she's been in since the day Baron Conal died." He waved Galen toward the stools waiting by the table where coins had been piled while last they'd talked. "'Tis another for whom she fears."

Galen ducked beneath the door's low frame and moved to the same stool he'd occupied during his previous visit. The abbot's words, although unexpected, did not surprise him. In truth, he should've realized earlier that his pious foster mother would never complain of ill-treatment nor ask for aid to protect herself—only for the safety and happiness of another beloved was she likely to seek help. That thought brought him up short. He swung around to question more harshly than the abbot had reason to expect.

"Who? Who is it that she fears for?"

To Galen it seemed that the aging man took an inordinately long time settling on his chair. In reality the priest was assimilating the realization that his news had already upset Galen, either with disappointment for a quest lost before it had begun or irritation for its waste of his time. He drew a deep breath and succinctly gave the explanation the other man impatiently awaited.

"When I visited the castle yester eve, Lady Sybil told me of the plan Lord Gilfrey concocted to secure the fiefdom of Wryborne for his life and beyond. He means to see her daughter wedded with his illegitimate son."

"Married to his bastard son?" Honed by disgust, Galen's voice was blade sharp. The mere suggestion that another man would claim the sweet maid as he so recently had, and not once but always, was more than Galen could easily endure. He clamped his mouth shut to hold back the growl of refusal clawing at his throat. After awakening in the forest alone, but warmly tucked about by her cloak, he'd come directly here praying for news of a danger that could be quickly foiled, a feat that would free him to go to Castle Dungeld as his true self and publicly claim Amicia as his own.

Pieter nodded confirmation to clipped words, and the white hair encircling his shiny pate glowed in the light of the candle necessary on a cloudy day's early morn. But, lost in his own bleak thoughts on the matter, he failed to rightly interpret the frozen expression on the younger man's face. "Lady Sybil is devastated by the threatened alliance. She says that one woman sacrificed to Gilfrey's greed is penance enough to expiate her wrong in deserting holy orders to selfishly claim a decade of worldly happiness."

"What rot!" The instant the words left his mouth Galen realized to whom he spoke, a man who might very well be offended by his opinion. "My pardon, Abbot Pieter, but surely God would not punish so blameless a woman yet allow filth like Gilfrey to go unscathed."

Over lips pressed firmly together to restrain an ill-timed grin for Galen's initial reaction, the abbot's eyes twinkled. Here was proof that the boy raised by a father who abhorred "pretty lies excused as tact" and urged plain speaking in all things still lived 'neath the exterior of this grown man. Once Pieter had mastered his amusement, he responded to Galen's explanation.

"I agree that Lady Sybil is blameless and do not believe the difficulties of her life are punishment from Him. Yet, the Lord works His will in uncounted ways, and He may well be using this wrong to some good by calling her again to His service. As to the last, you've not seen Lord Gilfrey else you would know he has not gone unscathed but rather is sick in body and spirit. He knows his days on this earth are drawing to a close and his eternal destination unpleasant. Doubtless 'tis why he's so desperate to see some part of himself live on, to be the forefather of a great earthly dynasty of power and wealth."

Studying hands palm flat and pressed so firmly on the table that fingertips were white, Galen chose not to tell of his confrontation with the baron over a roasted pheasant. But, aye, he'd seen the man's pain in striving to rise, yet felt no pity for him—either then or now—and returned their talk to the subject of utmost import to him. "Did you tell Lady Sybil I'd arrived and of my willingness to do whatever she bids?"

The abbot gave a sad smile and repeated the formal thanks Sybil had bade him relay. "She appreciates your coming and willingness to lend aid. Too, she prays that you will go safe on your return journey and begs that you give her fondest greetings to your parents."

"She expects me to return to Tarrant without even making some attempt to intervene?" Galen jumped to his feet, torn between horror at the thought of meekly allowing Amicia to wed another and indignation at the affront to the pride of an honorable man who'd come to serve.

"Galen." The abbot called to the broad back of the man pacing restively toward the door, and continued in soothing tones. "She has no doubt of your abilities.

After all, you are your father's son." When his visitor
turned, Pieter saw dark brows drawn into a fierce
frown and, having no idea that the lady's daughter was
known to him, simply assumed he'd taken Sybil's
words for an insult, however unintended. "But she, as
I, sees little you can do at so late an hour."

Crystal light eyes had narrowed into dangerously
gleaming slits. "Is the hour so late?"

"Indeed, yes!" The abbot grimaced and his face
settled into glum lines as he explained his reasoning.
"First, Lady Sybil told me that the rite was planned
for the morrow. Then, as I made to depart, the baron
joined us in her chamber and demanded I perform the
ceremony at midmorn one day hence."

Behind his impassive face, Galen's thoughts
whirled. There was an answer, a simple answer, but
one fraught with the pitfalls of deceit surrounding
hidden identities already in place.

"Only one action can effectively prevent Gilfrey
from forcing the maid to wed his son on the morrow—" Galen moved back to the table with slow
deliberation and sat down facing his host. "I will wed
Amicia today."

The abbot was stunned. Meeting the penetrating
power of a steady silver-green gaze, for the moment he
could do no more than gasp.

Although inside the ranks of the baronage marriage
bonds were oft entered into with strangers for the sake
of a dowry or family alliance, he argued, "You can't—
you don't know her—she doesn't know you."

Stress had robbed Pieter of the ability to string
phrases together in sentences. "You're here—she's in
the castle on a nearly inviolate isle." Recognizing the
disorder of his words, he paused and tried to organize
his thoughts into a sensible response to Galen's proposed action. He leaned forward while in his earnest
words and solemn tone he made clear his concern for
the misplaced honor of a young man planning to
accept a responsibility that would linger a lifetime.

"You can't take so permanent a step simply to aid a lady in need or to defeat a foe."

Intending to answer the abbot's objections one by one, Galen calmly said, "You are wrong in thinking Amicia and I are unknown to each other."

The abbot sat back, staring down at the foot he absently tapped on the rush-strewn floor, a frown of concentration furrowing his brow while he tried to remember if he'd ever mentioned the maid's name to Galen. Nay, he was certain he had not. Therefore, in truth the two had met. But then, it had been unworthy to doubt Galen's honesty.

Galen waited until the other man again looked up to meet his gaze before continuing. "We met in the forest, where she mistook me for some romantic outlaw of the greenwood—a hero like Robin Hood. Assuming the guise of a village girl, Amicia came to me again and again." Galen looked straight into the priest's widened eyes. "I do not excuse my actions by pretending to have been fooled when, by her resemblance to her father, I knew who she was the first day I saw her." It was the truth, if not all. "But, for the sake of our mysterious quest I deemed it best to hold my own identity as hidden—at least until we learned the reason for our summons."

Preoccupied with the questions of how Amicia had happened upon strange men in the forest and who had allowed her to return more than once, Pieter failed to see the major hurdle placed in their path by false identities. Instead, he absently continued his first line of argument. That it was, under the circumstances, a foolish objection proved him not actually attending his own words.

"In the few days you've been here I cannot believe you've formed such an attachment to the maid that you would forego the approval of her parents and your own." White hair gleamed as he shook his head, honestly puzzled over the whole of this odd relationship.

"Father Pieter, you know that Lord Conal would have approved of a match between his daughter and the heir of his dearest friend." Galen put a tight rein on his impatience with the priest, who'd been abruptly dumped into the middle of an unsuspected muddle. "Lady Sybil, too, would approve even without the certainty that the action will save her daughter from Gilfrey's hold." The thought of Conal's just ire if he knew the events of last eve further battered Galen's guilty conscience and firmed his determination to claim the willful maid. His smile turned wry. "As for my parents, they'll be happy I've settled at last."

Still, the abbot was uncomfortable with the furtive nature of the deed, worried for this man who would undoubtedly become the object of Gilfrey's murderous rage. He was certain to act on the reality that by killing Galen, he could yet attain his planned goal.

Galen saw the abbot's continuing unease and without hesitation wielded the one weapon he knew a priest could not refute. "When a nobleman takes the innocence of a well-born maiden, what is the price of his deed?"

Pieter abruptly straightened. "You claimed Amicia's maidenhead?" He asked, honestly horrified.

"Only hours past," Galen declared with more pride than contrition. "And I stand more than ready to pay the price by wedding the maid I wronged."

This put a whole new complexion on the situation and the abbot turned all his energies from arguments to assistance, even giving naught but a passing acknowledgment to the news later imparted of a Brayston emptied by the villagers' flight.

"It won't happen. It simply won't happen." Kelda murmured again and again, patting slender shoulders that still heaved after an hour of drenching tears. "I tell you," she repeated to the friend stretched out face down on the curtained bed, "Farrold loves me as I love him." All the while as she spoke, niggling doubts assailed Kelda's confidence in her beloved. She tried to smother them beneath the strength of her emotions. True, Farrold wasn't a strong person and given to bowing under his father's will, but he wouldn't risk their happiness. He wouldn't! As much to reassure herself as Amicia, she firmly stated, "We plan to marry, and nowise will he go along with the Dark Lord's wretched plan."

Face buried against a tear-damp pillow, in the gloom of her memory Amicia could too clearly see the image of Farrold standing beside Gilfrey, morose but cowed, to accept Kelda's reassurances. Yet the other girl would never easily accept a denial of her claim. Indeed, likely she'd deem any argument against it an insult of her love. Kelda would have to hear the news from Farrold's own lips to believe.

Amicia rolled over, scrubbing her palms across wet lashes. To her mind tears were a shameful sign of weakness. Unfortunately, they could seep through even a small crack in the barrier of her bravado. And this morn's disaster, so close upon a night of such delight, had sundered the wall completely, allowing a flood to pour out. Pushing black clouds of despair back, Amicia sat up and scooted off the bed.

"Let's find Farrold." Amicia held out her hand to the friend suddenly cringing away as if she'd offered a poisonous adder. "Come, we'll see what he means to do about this match between us." She issued the challenge gently, heart crying as much for the pain it would bring Kelda as for the pain it had already brought to her. Yet, there was nothing to be gained in hiding from truths that would have to be met in the end. Surely, 'twas better to have done with the deed and face the grief than to linger in the dread of its unavoidable coming.

Recognizing Amicia's willingness to confront a possibility that would affect her as adversely, Kelda rose and took the outstretched hand, bracing herself to bravely meet the truth she feared.

Kelda knew that with Mag asleep, Gilfrey had ordered her mother to stand guard over Amicia. But, taking pity on two grieving girls, she'd left them to their private mourning and inadvertently provided the freedom for them to leave their chamber unobserved.

Knowing, too, that Farrold would be standing guard atop the castle wall, Kelda led the way down the dimly lit corridor and up the narrow stone stairway. She'd even pushed open the heavy door at the top before her courage faltered. Pausing a step within the shadows, she left Amicia to step into the daylight beyond.

"Farrold," Amicia called to the back of the figure on the perimeter's far side. Unmoving, he seemed not to have heard, and she wrapped her arms about her midriff, wishing she'd thought to wear her cloak. Summer it might be but when clouds hid the sun, the air was chill. In the next instant she remembered with whom and when she'd left her cloak and immediately became convinced that it was the death of her dreams that made her cold.

"Farrold." Kelda had bolstered her courage to advance far enough onto the fearful wall to add her call to her friend's. She didn't like this dangerous walkway and wanted to venture no further.

Looking out over the endless expanse of sea, then down at the wild waves breaking over the forbidding rocks below, Farrold had failed to hear Amicia's call, but with ears heart-attuned, he easily heard Kelda's voice above the sound of crashing waves. He turned with a smile for her. It quickly faded when he found two girls waiting. Feet dragging with dread for the reason of their visit, he began making his way toward them.

The small glimmer of hope Kelda had maintained was extinguished by Farrold's slow approach and inability to meet her eyes. "You will marry Amicia even though you love me," she flatly stated as soon as Farrold stood within hearing distance. "Neither you

174

nor she wants it so, but you will do it to please your father." A frustrated anger added fire to her tone, and uncaring of the walkway's great height she jerked away from the comforting hand Amicia tried to lay on her shoulder.

"I love you, Kelda, and would wed you if I could. But how can a penniless, *bastard* knight who alone has no hope of a future worthy of you defy the sire who holds the key to it all?" Farrold's voice ached with regret while pain roughened his throat with unshed tears.

Having no answer to give, a despairing Kelda threw herself against the unyielding crenellated wall and laid her burning cheek against the cold stone ledge in one of its dips.

Farrold immediately went to Kelda and wrapped his arms about her. "Don't cry, Kelda." He buried his face in the curve between her neck and shoulder. "Please don't cry." That he had not followed his own advice neither bothered to acknowledge.

Feeling like some prying old biddy peeping in on lovers unaware, Amicia slipped away. Silently entering the stairway's shadows, in self-mockery she recalled her fear for Kelda's ability to cope with the ghastly truth of Farrold's intent. Leastwise Kelda had the comfort of the man she loved—more than Amicia could claim.

She stopped, one foot poised a scant distance above the next step down. Why couldn't she? All in the castle thought her still closeted in her chamber and sobbing her sorrows out to Kelda. Aye, there was no reason why she shouldn't go to the man she loved. The causeway might be too far under sea, but the boats were always at the isle's back and untended. Apparently no one had yet discovered the missing boat, or anyway hadn't tied it with her forest visit, probably because she'd returned via the causeway. If they had, she'd have a guardsman detailed to watch her door even while the tide was high. It was a perfect plan.

Who would suspect that she'd depart in such a manner? The oars were difficult work, but not impossible, and anything was better than remaining here.

Kelda's love could find no answer to their dilemma, but she'd infinite faith that her Galen would. The hero of a minstrel's song always saved his lady-fair. Hadn't King Arthur always protected his Guinevere, just as Robin Hood saved Lady Marian from any dastardly deeds that threatened?

With renewed spirit, Amicia nearly skipped down the remaining steps to the level of her own chamber. Once inside she rolled a horsehair brush, a pretty jewelled dagger in its leather scabbard, and a favorite broach into the folds of her second homespun gown. Lifting the bundle, she quietly crept down the corridor, then the stairway, and past the kitchens where again the many were too busy to note the passing of one.

⇜§ *Chapter 12* ߷⇝

A wave broke over Amicia's head, drenching her. It was not the first one to do so. The task had looked so easy when Randolf smoothly rowed the boat to shore, and although it had been tiring last night she hadn't had this much trouble. Another wave swept over her, and she gasped for breath. She'd been rowing for what seemed like hours and had made little progress. Indeed, she'd come only halfway round the island from the docks at the back. Very soon she came to realize that she was no longer making any forward progress yet she feared to go back, certain the mighty sea, far more powerful than she'd bargained for, would smash her against the jagged rocks at the base of the isle. Almost she wished Farrold and Kelda weren't so preoccupied that the ramparts were virtually unguarded and the sea unwatched.

The muscles of her arms and shoulders trembled with the effort to simply maintain her position, and she'd stopped trying to see the coastline through the never-ending mountains of briny water by the time another small craft came parallel with hers. The second boat was headed in the opposite direction, but thankfully the two cowled figures inside took pity on her plight.

"Stop flailing your oars about."

Amicia let her arms go slack, never questioning the order given by a blessedly familiar voice.

"Now bring the oars inside the boat." Galen's tone was harsh with worry for her safety and anger for her foolish action. Plainly the impetuous maid had set out on the open sea in a tiny craft, intent on traveling against the tide by physical strength alone.

After Galen's boat had drawn alongside and she'd been plucked from her craft by his strong arms, Amicia cuddled in their hold and looked up into silver-green eyes undimmed by the shadows of a monk's hood. Physically exhausted and emotionally drained, she'd no thought to question what had put him in clerical robes and on the sea. She only knew that he'd saved her life. And if he'd saved her life, surely he'd save her from other threats as well.

"What were you doing, going out on the sea alone?" Galen gruffly demanded.

"Coming to you," Amicia said simply, impervious to the chill in his tone. Although clouds remained to darken the sky overhead, for her the sun shone.

While Amicia gazed adoringly at her savior and Galen struggled to tame the anger raised by his fears for her, a monk called Ulfric secured the empty boat to the back of the one now riding dangerously low in the water. Bringing this stranger along on his daily trip to Castle Dungeld had not been his idea (in truth, he thought it too risky) but he was obedient to his abbot's commands. Picking up the oars again, he headed their small flotilla toward the docks at the isle's back. 'Twas a far more sensible task to travel with the tide than against it, and he very soon had them resting against the pier. Carefully he climbed from boat to wooden walkway. Then, unsure what his passengers intended, he looked to the still seated man with a question in his eyes.

Galen met the dour monk's gaze. "We'll wait here while you conduct your business in the castle. By the time you've gathered the day's alms and come back, surely the tide will have turned, and we can ride its currents to the shore."

Folding his hands together beneath his chin, the monk silently nodded his acceptance and moved to climb the rickety wooden stairway with all the slow deliberation in his nature.

Once the monk was beyond hearing distance, Amicia plucked at the rough brown homespun Galen wore. Both fear and weariness driven into the forgotten past by the warmth of his arms, she grinned up at him with a teasing light in her eyes. "Your religious garb eases the way for a confession I must make to you, Galen."

A great relief swept over Galen when he recognized what she surely meant to say. Yet, anxious to do nothing that would hinder her intent, he held his face impassive and allowed brows lifted in question to be his only response. Amicia's telling of her true name and heritage would ease the way for him to speak of his own. He'd earlier decided he couldn't bear to wed the maid with these secrets between them. It would be too great a burden on his truthful heart and unnecessary now that the goal of his quest was not only known but would be resolved by this deed. Even had he promised Abbot Pieter to take this boulder from their path of future happiness. Moreover, with this one removed he'd greater confidence that he could safely skirt the one remaining—the one that was not his to reveal.

Amicia felt the arms about her unaccountably tense, and she feared a face gone suddenly expressionless masked the first vestiges of condemnation—a possibility that weakened her facade of confidence. Before it further eroded she rushed on to bravely announce, "I am not who or what you think I am." To avoid the sight that raised her doubts, she stared determinedly at the upright tree trunk that served as a piling for the dock where they were moored. When she

179

told him of her noble blood would he, a man of more honor than most, think himself unworthy and send her back up the stairs to the castle too near? In the next instant she perversely wished she could've come to him dressed in silks and jewels, or leastwise clean of sticky seawater. Anything but looking like the pitiful drowned creature she doubtless resembled at the moment.

Galen saw her spirits droop and hastened to bring the subject into the light of honesty before she could retreat with it into the shielding gloom of continued deceit. "Are you so sure?" Flying in the face of his long training to caution, he didn't pause to consider the wisdom of being first to speak the facts she'd feared to reveal. What could it matter when soon they'd both stand free. "I believe you to be the daughter of Baron Conal and Lady Sybil of Castle Dungeld."

Galen's gladness in a battle half won added such warm textures to his tone that Amicia returned her eyes to him and looked into a smile of blinding warmth that near melted her bones. Yet, although happy to find him anything but shocked by the truth, she was determined to say her piece before he could say something to forestall the words and gave no thought to the source of his knowledge or reason for happiness.

"'Tis who I am," she agreed, curling her fingers into the cloth across his chest in fervent appeal as she added more. "But I beg you to believe that I've only distaste for all well-born lords, so greedy for more and ever more that they'd do any villainy, swear any false oath to secure what they covet." Privately, Amicia only half believed her sweeping denunciation but, hopefully, it would accomplish her goal in assuring Galen that she'd be happy with him even though he was not her social equal.

"I am the heiress to the castle above and the whole of the Wryborne fiefdom, and therein lies my problem." Thus embarked on her real reason for seeking Galen out, Amicia rushed to tell the whole. "You see, for the sake of my inheritance my stepfather—Baron Gilfrey—means to see me wed against my will to his son, although Farrold wants me for wife no more than I want him for husband."

Galen paid little attention to her statement of facts he already knew. A new problem occupied his thoughts, and he cursed himself for having admitted his knowledge of her identity before she spoke of it. Now if he told her who he was she'd likely think him merely a cunning hunter misrepresenting himself to secure his prey. The fact that he had more than enough wealth of his own would make no difference if she believed him greedy for more. That she did not now nor ever had possessed the Wryborne inheritance, he couldn't prove without breaking an oath held for a lifetime. Trapped by promises which, if betrayed, might cost another's life, he'd no choice but to continue the pretense and pray that she'd not learn the truth until after the need for secrecy came to its natural end. Regretfully accepting that the path must remain blocked by the boulder of deceit laid there by circumstances beyond his control, Galen turned his thoughts to what Amicia was saying.

"So," Amicia couldn't help but be aware of the cold withdrawal smothering his earlier warmth and brought her hands down to twist together in her lap. She continued only under sheer determination to see the matter through. "When you saved me from being smashed against the rocks, it gave me greater hope that you'd free me of the baron's mortal threat to my future and happiness." Amicia held her breath in anxiety over Galen's response, and in the time before he spoke her hands went numb under the strength of their joined grip.

"Even the man you call the Dark Lord cannot force a woman already wed to marry again." While waiting for Amicia to acknowledge his meaning, Galen studied the maid he'd just suggested should become his wife. A sea drenching had not lessened her beauty. Bountiful tresses tamed by crashing waves, the pure lines of her small face and elegant throat were more plainly revealed, and her widely spaced eyes, gone a doe brown as soft as velvet, dominated the whole. He'd no regret for the choice but deeply rued the circumstances surrounding the deed.

Amicia hesitated. If the frost in his crystal eyes was a true indication, he found the prospect of their joined future bleak. Still, this giving of the very answer she'd hoped he would suggest couldn't fail to bring her pleasure. Surely, his doubts were merely for her ability to be happy sharing the kind of uncertain life he led, and she would prove them wrong. With him she could live anywhere. She refused to let doubts fog the clarity of a wonderful future, a dream come true. But then, of late, every one of her dreams had become reality—a hero brought to life the greatest of all. Completely forgetting her bedraggled appearance, she wrapped her arms around his neck and gave him a kiss that returned the passion he had so recently taught her.

As in the hours of the past night, Galen surrendered to Amicia's wiles. He willed them to block the problems looming ahead, for the moment, and returned her fervent caresses with interest. The chill of cloudy day warmed to the blazing heat of a mid-summer while in the fire of their embrace they lost track of time and place and counted both well lost.

The sound of a throat being cleared failed to interrupt the self-involved couple, so Ulfric resorted to dropping his bag of donations from the castle kitchen into the boat. Filled with the alms Gilfrey gave only because he knew that right-raised lords would do so, the bag containing uneaten foodstuff from the past day's meals was heavy and landed so abruptly it wildly rocked the small craft.

While Galen's one arm instinctively wrapped tighter about Amicia, as if it were humanly possible to hold her any closer, he reached out with the other to grasp the dock and steady the boat. His gaze moved from the brown homespun hem at eye level up to the bland face of the returning monk. Though he suspected the hint of a gratified smile played about the corners of a mouth held in firm keeping with a meek expression, he couldn't be certain.

"Welcome back. As you see, the tide is indeed going shoreward once more. I propose that you take this boat while I row the maid to the mainland in the one she was forced to abandon."

Ulfric was relieved by the stranger's sensible suggestion. He'd feared that the pack, added to the weight of three people, would see his boat on the bottom long before they reached the coastline. This good opinion of the man's wits went far in smoothing sensibilities ruffled by the scene he'd interrupted. He thought the young woman whom he'd seen only from the back of her sea-drenched hair plainly too loose with her morals, yet went so far as to give her a hand in rising from the man's lap to the dock. Only when she stood beside him and for the first time he looked her full in the face did he realize who she was.

Whatever else was wrong or right, Ulfric was certain any action that included the heiress was dangerous, and he wanted out of it with all possible speed. The instant Galen stepped from the boat, Ulfric fairly tumbled in and immediately shoved away from the dock, anxious to leave the others as far behind as he could manage.

Amicia stared in consternation at the back of the clearly fleeing man. Had the kisses she'd shared with Galen so deeply offended the pious man that he felt the need to run away? Her own thought shocked her, and a bright blush stained her cheeks when she mentally replayed the scene as viewed through his eyes. Only a fortnight past she'd have thought any unwed woman who willingly sat on a man's lap and kissed him to be a woman of lost virtue. And was that not precisely what she was?

Rightly reading the emotions chasing across Amicia's face, Galen reached out to gently shake her. "You have no reason for shame. What we did today is natural for any man and woman soon to be wed."

Amicia looked into silver-green eyes but couldn't maintain their penetrating stare. Today might be excused, but not the previous night when she'd come to him brazenly.

"'Tis a shame to me that by my lack of restraint last night happened, yet I refuse to rue it and would that you do not either."

How could the shame be his when it was she who'd sought him out solely for the purpose of giving her virtue to him? She couldn't find the words to speak of it, and in any event they couldn't have passed the lump in her throat. Likely he was marrying her solely to save her from the thing she dreaded, a decision too certainly reinforced by his guilt over their night of passion. She shook her head and pulled away to step into the waiting boat, overcome by the likelihood that he bore for her no share of the love she felt for him. The fact that he'd given not a hint of his emotions when offering to wed her stole a measure of happiness from the day that should have been the most joyous of her life.

Knowing there was little more he could say, Galen settled in the boat behind Amicia. Not words but action would put an end to her concerns, and he took up the oars to begin steadily propelling the craft toward the shore and abbey where they'd be wed.

By the time they were nearing the pebble-strewn beach, Amicia's natural spirit had reasserted itself. The best thing she could do, she firmly advised herself, was to accept his lifestyle as her own. By proving herself a worthy mate, even if she didn't have his love now, in the years to come she'd earn it from him.

As their boat's hull scraped across the small rocks half buried in the sand lining shallow water, they could see their monk-companion of earlier rapidly disappearing down a heavily wooded path branching off to the left. It was a fairly flat track that, though circuitous, was the easier route to the Abbey of St. Jude. The only other way there involved a steep trip up the hillside, around the waterfall, and through the village. 'Twas a much more arduous path but Amicia prayed Galen would choose it. Then, hopefully, he'd allow her to stop at the cave and freshen her sea-bedraggled appearance. After all, this was her wedding day and though 'twouldn't bring the grand and opulent ceremony other well-born brides expected, it was the only one she'd ever have or want.

First bending to free the tightly rolled bundle wedged in the prow of the small boat which Galen had dragged well up the beach, Amicia turned and lifted brown eyes softened to an aching tenderness to the strong man who silently waited.

When Galen met her gaze, Amicia glanced pointedly from the monk's path to the hillside climb. Clearly his bride preferred not to follow the other man. A slow smile warmed his cold expression with an odd mixture of cynicism and awe. *His bride*—how strange it was that, despite his long dread of the wedded state and the difficulties that surrounded this rite, he was satisfied with the prospect of their joined futures. Gallantly he motioned in the direction she wanted to go and rued only that this was such a very small gift for the heir to an earldom to give his well-born bride on the day of their marriage.

For Amicia the afternoon from that point on passed in a rosy blur. Allowed a time of privacy in the cave, she quickly rinsed the sticky sea residue from her hair and body with handfuls of the fresh water falling at its mouth. Then she donned the second gown which, rolled with brush and dagger inside and stowed in the boat's prow, though only her forest green homespun, had remained remarkably dry.

Upon climbing back to the top of the cliff, she found both Galen and his young companion waiting. Walter handed her a chaplet of late-blooming lilies and when she kissed his cheek in thanks, he blushed a shade that emphasized the ruddy highlights in his hair. As they passed by the strangely quiet Brayston, Galen explained the villagers' flight to safety in the Weald with his friend, Williken. That the famous knight of the forest was Galen's friend reinforced her belief in him as an honorable outlaw.

She'd neither understood nor cared to question the look of warning Galen gave the abbot when asking him to perform the simple ceremony for Galen Fitz William and his bride, Amicia, or the priest's momentary frown of censure.

Walter and Ulfric, already knowing something of their relationship, witnessed the short rite, and at its conclusion they all shared a simple meal. Only as he and Amicia stood at the door prepared to depart did Galen turn back and address their host one time more.

"You will go to the castle at the appointed hour on the morrow and tell Lord Gilfrey that his stepdaughter is already wed."

"I will keep my promise. Will you keep yours?" The abbot's steady gaze near drilled holes in the man who'd promised to confess his true identity to the prospective bride but clearly had not.

As if struck, Galen straightened and folded his arms across his chest, bracing against the possibility of another blow. Did Abbot Pieter mean to force the issue here and now? Pray God not! Galen wanted time to convince Amicia of his feelings for her so that she would know without doubt that it was her own sweet self he sought, not the inheritance she thought she possessed.

Her gaze having seldom moved far from Galen since he'd become her husband, Amicia saw and was amazed by the look of guilty discomfort that flashed over his face. Other than his claimed shame for their night of pleasure, she'd never seen him aught but self-assured and certain of the rightness in his way. Strangely, she found it endearing that he, too, was prey to doubts on some level—what level hardly mattered. She tucked her hand into the crook of his arm and squeezed.

"Nightfall looms, let's be off to our destination before the dark is upon us." Feigning apprehension, she gave a convincing shiver that only she need know was born of anticipation, not alarm.

One corner of Galen's lips lifted in a sardonic smile. As if, after last night, he'd ever believe she was afraid of traveling through the dark or the consequences it might bring. Nonetheless, he was more than willing to accede to her wishes. As he deftly worked the simple rope and iron latch to open the door, he gave the abbot a challenging stare that dared him to hinder their leavetaking.

Abbot Pieter merely bade the couple a gentle farewell. But after closing the door behind them, he wearily leaned back against it, eyes closed in a fervent prayer to see the new-wedded pair safely over a future path littered with falsehoods. Long moments later the sound of awkwardly shuffled feet brought him free of his preoccupation with the follies of youth. His guest for the night, Walter, waited to be shown his bed, and he pushed away from the door, motioning the boy to follow.

At near the same point on the abbey's outgoing cart path where Carl and Galen had once stopped the baron's tax collector, the new-wedded couple walked. The silence between them was so filled with considerations of what massive changes the actions of the past afternoon would make in their lives that neither noticed its length. Although they each saw the future as bright and full of hope, their views were widely different. The difference lay in the fact that one saw the future within the framework of reality while the other saw its reflection on the shiny surface of a bubble, a dream ever in danger of bursting.

She was supremely happy, Amicia told herself. Her fantasy had come true. She would spend her life in the forest with her romantic outlaw, defender of justice for the poor and misused. To be with Galen was worth any price. That, leastwise, was a truth she meant to the bottom of her soul. It was only that after spending two nights on the ground, its appeal was just the tiniest bit tarnished. Surely such delights as they'd shared the night past could be only enhanced by the comforts of a real bed—with warm covers, soft pillows, and drapes to keep the cold at bay?

Amicia frowned, irritated with herself for allowing any selfish thought to mar this beautiful event. And anyway, what did it matter where now they slept? She was an heiress. Even if they couldn't live in Castle Dungeld until Gilfrey was gone, someday they would. Would they? Would he? Could she expect a man whose life was in the forest to follow her into the structured world where laws and wicked men ruled? Nay, she would not change him, not one little bit! If learning to sleep on a slab of granite and to cook over an open firepit (she hadn't more than a faint idea how) were the price for her love, then it was small indeed! Nonetheless, if ever he chose the easier life, she assuredly wouldn't object.

By unspoken mutual consent they cut from the cart path through the forest diagonally and presently stood on the moss-softened edge of the pool. Galen glanced down and saw the lingering frown whose shadow had stolen the gold from brown eyes. Again, he cursed the circumstances that forced him to live a lie with her.

He'd no doubt but that Amicia was worried about the problems surrounding their marriage, yet he dare not reassure her that he had them well in hand even while time moved inexorably on toward their final resolution. Such explanations would involve the telling of secrets he'd sworn to keep. Worse still, he was certain that she rightfully questioned a lifetime shared with a Wolf's Head in the forest. The urge to talk with her about their future at Castle Tarrant once matters here were settled was powerful. He wanted to tell her about the days of warmth with family and friends, the nights of far warmer love that awaited them there. On the verge of speaking despite his sensible decision to stay silent until all could be explained, the words were forced back in his throat by Amicia's awed gasp.

He followed her enthralled gaze up to a magical sight. In the western sky the clouds of day had parted to allow the rays of a setting sun to beam their rich colors over the waterfall's sprayed droplets. It looked as if a rainbow had been shattered and its shards flung up to dance in the air.

"I thank you for the gift of filling the remaining days of my life with this unparalleled beauty! Never, never in all the great palaces could the grandeur of something like this be found." Amicia turned and threw her arms around Galen's neck, tugging his head down to whisper in his ear. "Far rather had I to spend my life with you in nature's green palace than with some greedy lord inside the restraining gloom of stone walls." The fervency of her declaration was aimed as much at convincing herself as Galen.

Automatically wrapping his arms about Amicia, Galen took her speech for fact and wondered sourly how she'd feel about nature's palace when cold winter stripped it of color and turned it to ice. She leaned back in his hold to give him a dazzling smile that he returned, although his was more than a little strained. Her speech merely reinforced his dark fears concerning the complicated twists of the path he must navigate in coming days—support her misbeliefs for now, then rip them from her hands without leaving her feeling a victim of deceit and thievery.

Overtaken by the joy in her right to stand thusly with Galen, Amicia saw nothing of his quandary. She was free in the eyes of church and man to touch as she would, and she would touch this man who was more than she'd ever dreamed. Slowly her hands stroked over the breadth of his shoulders, then down his strong arms and back up his chest. When the muscles tightened beneath their touch, she reveled in newly learned power and bent her head to nestle tawny silk beneath his chin while hugging herself tightly against him and whispering what she couldn't when meeting his penetrating gaze full on.

"Take me to the cave and show me again passion's fire and sweetness."

Galen's ill temper melted and even the reason for it was burned away 'neath the fire her words lit in his blood. Tangling his fingers through the honey-silk curls at the back of her head, he gently tugged to lift her face to his questing lips. He kissed closed eyelids, cheeks, and the corners of her mouth before giving a quietly teasing answer.

"Alas, I am unable to carry you either up the stream of falling water or down the cliff's face."

"Nay." Amicia impishly met his gaze, and the laughter that rose to dance on the air sparkled near as bright as the gold again in her eyes. "I can find my own way. In truth—" Thick lashes swept down. "I wager that I can be there before you. But—" She peeked at him flirtatiously. "If I win, you must pay whatever forfeit I demand."

Without pausing to see if he'd accepted her challenge, Amicia pulled from his arms, scrambled up the hillside path, and let herself down over the sunset-bathed cliff. By the time his large silhouette appeared against the opening's rose-glittering backdrop of falling water, she was sitting atop the blanket at the fire's edge.

"I win." Her grin was infectious. "And I claim the prize."

Looking down at the mercurial water sprite, arms wrapped about the updrawn knees her chin rested atop, Galen could near believe her a lovely child. Yet, the golden flame burning in brown eyes proved her no longer a child. He soothed his prick of guilt for being the cause of that truth with the balm of his honest dealings in making her his wife. Honest? What honesty in making her the wife of an outlaw? No matter that it was untrue, she thought it so which only deepened his wrong.

Amicia saw Galen's expression darken and wondered what she'd done to irritate him. Had the fact that he'd lost the race to a woman bruised his male pride? She'd not thought him so lacking in confidence that such a thing could bother him, but—

"I'm sure I only won because I gave no fair warning. Rather, I issued the challenge and departed before you'd clearly understood. 'Tis a certain truth that you are far faster than I will ever be."

Her words broke Galen's preoccupation. When he realized that she thought him upset with her for reaching the cave first, his head tilted back and the ends of his black mane brushed his shoulders while he freely laughed.

"Nay, sweeting, I didn't even try to catch you. Why would I when I'm certain I had rather pay the forfeit than win the game."

As his knowing gaze stroked over her with the sensual power of a physical caress, Amicia's cheeks burned, and she nibbled her lower lip nervous of what she'd claimed as her prize. Still, she didn't look away.

Galen studied the sweet beauty from the honey of her hair to the tender silken skin that in memory he saw beneath the rasp of homespun. She'd taken the lead in their relationship from the first, impetuously seeking him out when he thought it unwise, even offering, nay, seducing *him* to take her virtue when he, as an honorable man, would not seek it. Now, she belonged to him. Although she might rue it when she learned his true identity, he was justified in taking the reins to guide their path both in this coming together and in their future.

The light of determination that burned silver in green eyes merely increased Amicia's excitement. Her steady gaze did not falter as he loosed the neck lacing of his tunic and pulled the fine green cloth over his head, ruffling his dark hair and once more revealing to her the stunning sight of his hard male chest. Breath halted in her throat as muscles rippled and whorls of dark hair gleamed with the faint reflected light of the glowing coals while he jerked boots from his feet. Only after he'd unwound the cross-garters holding cloth tight to strong calves and untied the fastening of his chausses did her courage falter and her attention drop to his growing pile of clothes. All her earlier bravado fell, vanquished by the doubts of limited experience which held her motionless.

Taking pity on her unexpected shy modesty, Galen left the pants loose about his waist and legs while he knelt beside her. Cupping her cheeks in his hands, he lifted her face and bent to brush the tantalizing flame of his kiss lightly across her lips until they opened, seeking the source of the fire. He accepted the gift and returned it with a restrained ferocity that poured oil on the smoldering embers between them. She arched up into his arms, all inhibitions lost in the searing smoke of desire as she rose on her knees to bring her body into alignment with his. Welcoming the feel of her melting against him, his hands swept down the arch of her back to cup her derriere and pull her tight to his urgent need. Far from frightening her with his action, she moaned and twisted against him, plainly impatient with the barrier of her skirts and even his loose chausses.

Galen lifted his face, seeking cooler air to damp down the fire while cursing himself for moving too fast. He was determined to regain control, elsewise the pleasure would cease too quickly. In the hours of the past night she'd pushed him too far beyond the point of rationality to be certain that she was as far lost as he before the end came. Then she'd been gone before he awoke. Tonight he meant to see her as deep into the consuming fires of passion as he, and at the last to plumb the depths of the blaze together.

"Slow, sweeting, slow," he murmured, voice a gentle growl. "The flame that's long in building burns hotter, lingers longer."

Though he'd moved a handsbreadth away, his deep whisper stroked across Amicia's senses like rough velvet and a tremor passed over her from head to toe.

Galen reveled in the awareness that he was the source of those delicious reactions and that now she belonged to him, giving him the right to ensure that they were his and his alone. He was the victor, the baron and his son the losers.

Holding her captive by the power of his penetrating crystal gaze alone, Galen trailed one finger down her throat to nudge the laces at its base. She bit her lip but couldn't look away from the man intensely studying her while deftly untying and loosening the neckline of her gown. For once Galen was thankful that Amicia wore this simple one-piece gown rather than the several layers a maid of her position ought to wear. He curled his fingers around the curve between shoulder and throat, a tense smile lifting one side of his mouth when with his thumbs he found a pulse madly pounding in the dip at the center. Slowly he slid his hands under the cloth and deliberately moved them out over her shoulders, brushing the gown free to slip a distance down her arms. He traced the cloth's fall and outlined its resting spot from upper arms across the swell of her curves.

The gown had come to rest only a fraction above the tips of Amicia's breasts, and her thick lashes drifted down, closing her eyes in an aching anticipation. His hands did not move. Amicia drew a deep breath and held it waiting endless moments of growing tension for him to ease the unwanted material away. When instead he took his hands away, her breath came out on a sigh of frustration. It was enough to dislodge the last barrier. Brown eyes flew open while her hands instinctively flew up to shield the bounty thus revealed.

Galen reached out, capturing her hands and holding them away while a green-fire gaze seared over skin like honey mellowed with the ivory of cream. One taste and he was lost. He'd proven that last night. Yet, it was a delectable feast he hadn't possessed the will to forgo then nor to postpone now.

Amicia closed her eyes against the intensity of his gaze, unable to withstand its power and still maintain the strength to keep from begging him to bring an end to this burning anguish, nay, to make its heat flare higher. With hands still lightly shackled by his and held out on each side, behind lowered lashes she was lost in a dark cavern of depthless longing. When Galen gently laid his lips over one peach tip, flames burst in the black void, and she cried out at the unexpected pleasure, arching toward the sweet torment.

Already shaken by the sight of silken curves that had haunted his dreams from the first and the fresh taste of the rich feast, Galen was stunned anew by her ardent response. Wanting to wrap his arms around her waist, he loosed her hands. They immediately twined into his hair seeking to hold his mouth where it gave such wicked delight, but he pulled back. An anguished protest escaped her tight throat, and Galen was pleased by this further proof of her uncontrolled need. Yet, when she sought to press aching curves into the strength of his bare chest, he held her a whisper from him, only close enough to feel wiry curls rasping across sensitive tips, eliciting from her a sharp shiver of delight.

Carefully leaning forward and urging her back, he lowered her to the blanket Walter kept so neatly spread out by the fire. His eyes laid a trail of fire across a passion-flushed cheek to reclaim hers in a devastating kiss. She yielded eagerly to his demanding mouth and to the burning caress of his hands stroking downward, brushing her garments aside, completely freeing her body to his possession.

He pulled away but only far enough to allow a small distance between them. Reservations long since fallen to ashes, Amicia tested the feel of firm muscle and smooth skin, rubbing her fingers over the burning flesh of his strong back and broad shoulders, tangling them into the wiry curls that had so recently tormented her. A caldron of potent need boiled on the fires of passion, and nothing existed by the feel of him, all heat and iron-thews.

While with her caresses she praised his form, Galen let his fingertips lightly trace from the base of her throat through the valley between her breasts and down to explore the tiny indentation of her navel. Their tantalizing journey was too much for Amicia to calmly withstand. Her head arched back and her arms slid around his torso. Caught unprepared, Galen came down over her. Heedless of his goal for restraint, he gloried in the feel of her bare flesh crushed to his unyielding body, softness matched to hard, a universal miracle. And when she helplessly writhed against him in the same intimate rhythm they'd danced to the night before, he knew the time had come. Pulling from clinging arms, he smiled through desire-tight lips at her moan of loss and ruthlessly kicked useless, unwanted cloth from his legs. He shifted to lie full atop her slender length. She cried out with the pleasure of his full weight, as hot and strong as iron fresh from the forgers' fire. Tonight he had no need to lift her to the joining, she met him eagerly in the deed.

Braced above her, Galen's eyes burned down with a steady green flame, heating hers to molten honey as he began a slow rocking that drove them deeper and ever deeper into the fires of pleasure. Amicia arched to meet each thrust and tugged at the thick black mane framing his passion-tense face, yet she could not force him to speed their dance's primitive rhythm to the destination agonizingly beyond reach. When she thought she could not survive another moment of the building heat and would be consumed by its hungry flames, he growled, "Now, together into passion's blaze!"

Into the pyre they fell, drowning in burning depths of pleasure until the need was filled and overflowed in a sensual lassitude that carried them through the tender corridor of satiety and into the sleep of satisfaction.

❧ *Chapter 13* ❧

I prayed, beseeching divine aid to see my child saved from the same humiliation I have suffered at Gilfrey's hand, but help arrived too late." In despair, the frail woman still abed let her head fall forward into cupped hands while the weak light of an early, cloudy morn wended through the cracks in the window's shutters to glow like a blessing on pale hair. Now that Gilfrey's wretched intent was known throughout the castle, and likely across the fiefdom, Anne had been allowed to come to Sybil and hear the lengths to which the lady had gone in an attempt to see it prevented.

Anne, aching with her friend's pain, stood in the opening offered by one looped-back panel of the bedcurtain and laid a comforting hand atop the bowed head. "Young Galen has returned to Wryborne?" She simply wanted to ease Sybil's way and asked the question more to draw the hurting woman's thoughts from her woe than in honest curiosity.

Sybil lifted her face and gave Anne a gentle smile of appreciation for the attempted ploy. Still, she answered. "He has returned, but Abbot Pieter says he's now a man full-grown. Only did he recognize Galen for his distinctive silver-green eyes and the fact that he has matured into the image of his father, Earl Garrick. You remember the earl who visited here many times before my Conal was taken."

Anne berated herself for the poor choice in distractions which had merely ended with a reminder of painful wounds from the past. "Mayhap, then," she went on with determined brightness, "the man Galen now will find some path to circumvent this disaster that would leave both our daughters with a lifetime of unhappiness."

The last part of Anne's statement proved a better distraction than her first attempt. Sybil leaned back against her pillows and gazed questioningly into Anne's face.

"Oh, aye, my daughter deems herself in love with the boy your daughter is doomed to wed." Anne shook her head in mock disgust for the strange coils the young had found themselves caught in. In truth, she sorrowed for the unhappiness of all three.

"Farrold?" Sybil was amazed by the mere possibility. Yet, almost instantly, she felt a stab of remorse. Never, she realized had she thought of him as person, only as the agent of Gilfrey's wicked plan.

"Jasper has been working with Farrold for near a fortnight and says he seems a harmless sort, gentle-natured and eager to please. Unfortunately, the boy is forced by the circumstances of his birth to please his father first of all—a fact Kelda finds difficult to understand."

Acknowledging her former view a prejudiced one and ever anxious to see the good in others, Sybil willingly accepted Anne's assessment. That the boy had found himself as foully trapped in Sir Gilfrey's toils as had her daughter she could easily believe.

"In my endeavors to see the marriage forestalled I've failed indeed." Sybil sighed, heart so heavy it felt like a cold, black stone weighting her spirit down. "Three young lives ruined by one wicked man."

"Wait." Anne immediately rejected Sybil's acceptance of defeat. "Don't so hastily discount what you've already done. Galen may yet be able to do something." As she remembered the boy, he'd had an uncommonly quick mind.

Despite her own gloom, Sybil smiled fondly at her loyal friend; and, rather than further upsetting Anne with her woe, she allowed her lashes to drop wearily, bringing a close to the discussion that could have no better end.

Anne recognized the action for what it was and patted the fragile hand lying limp on the bedcover. Letting the drape fall, she left the woman to mourn in the privacy of her darkened bed. Soon enough Sybil would have to rise and prepare for the ceremony she dreaded to attend.

When Anne stepped into the corridor and closed the chamber door behind her, her eyes widened at the strangely matched twosome awaiting.

"She—" Kelda's single word held a wealth of disgust, "insists on coming into the chamber to see Amicia. But, mama, Amicia is asleep at last, and I refuse to let her be awakened so soon. There's plenty of time before the ceremony is to begin."

Anne heard the anger in Kelda's voice, also the thread of fear that doubtless Mag heard as clearly. Some reason there was for not seeing Amicia, and vague possibilities stirred anxious fears in her.

"The baron says as I gotta sit with her in sight 'til the wedding begins." Mag's wheedling words were respectful enough but the hard glint of her colorless eyes negated any positive effect. "By her actions, she's already brought me trouble enough, and I daren't risk more."

"A guardsman has been sitting outside their chamber door since the tide went out aforenoon yesterday. What wizard's trick can either you or the baron fear—that Amicia has sprouted wings and flown through the solid stone walls of their chamber?" Into the words Anne put every scrap of disbelief she could muster, despite her own apprehensions. In reality, the true wizard's trick lay in the old crone's recuperative powers. A whole flagon of her special sweet wine should have kept Mag deeply asleep until tonight at the least.

"If all is well," a voice dripping with acid spoke from the stairwell shadows, "why need you to so earnestly protect Amicia's privacy from even a glimpse by another?"

Gilfrey leaned heavily on his dual canes, put one foot on the landing, and hoisted a stiff leg up behind him. Days of fruitless riding in search of the outlaw had aggravated the swelling and worsened his already black temper. Even the long-planned and anticipated final act of vengeance so close to fruition seemed threatened, and he'd do anything to assure its smooth accomplishment.

"She's suffered enough at your hands. Is it not sufficient that you mean to ruin her life? Need you force upon her the further humiliation of having one bearing her no affection attend preparations for the wretched deed?"

The fiery disgust in Anne's denunciation went far in soothing Gilfrey's likely unwarranted fears. It was true that since the tide went out the day past, revealing the causeway path to the mainland, Oswald had stood watch outside Amicia's chamber. Having been equally as demeaned by the outlaw's hand as he himself—trussed like an animal and left for those in his charge to find—Oswald had diligently fulfilled the charge to insure Amicia remain. He surely would've caught the maid had even one of her toes crossed the threshold.

"Have you seen her this morn?" Gilfrey's smile, nearer to a sneer, held more satisfaction with her distress than concern.

Anne drew a deep breath and nodded a lie she would do penance for later, while at the same time praying for a right conclusion to this entire predicament.

"Then, dear woman," his words were an intended insult, "I will hold you accountable rather than Mag if Amicia fails to appear when she should—and my anger is a thing you may rightly tremble before." With that cold warning and the aid of two canes, he stumped past Anne to enter the chamber door she had so recently closed.

As Anne turned to her daughter, Mag faded into the dark of the stairwell but her cackle echoed hollowly against its enclosing stone.

"Will my defense of you and Amicia lay me exposed to the baron's ire?" Anne quietly asked of her horrified daughter.

"Oh, mama, mama—" Kelda stepped forward, wrapped her arms about her mother, and laid her cheek on the older woman's shoulder while tears silently flowed. "She's gone—" Kelda pulled back and drew a shaky breath. "Been gone since I came down from hearing the worst from Farrold yester morn."

As if Kelda were the one in peril and in need of reassurance, Anne ignored her own thumping heart and distress over worst fears realized to carefully lead her daughter down one flight of stairs and into the girls' cheerless room. When the door had closed them into the tiny chamber lighted by the poor efforts of a single tallow candle and Kelda sat disconsolate on the bed, tears streaming down her cheeks, Anne stepped back to face her.

"Then the last time you saw Amicia was on the ramparts when you and she sought Farrold out to confirm his intent for the proposed match?" Anne knew of this visit from a talk she and Kelda had shared the night past. The same talk wherein Kelda had confessed her painful love of the trapped Farrold. But Kelda hadn't mentioned whether, as all in the castle assumed, Amicia was truly in their chamber, refusing both company and meals and crying out her pain. And, despite Anne's knowledge of earlier escapades, occupied with her daughter's doomed love, she hadn't thought to ask.

"I said nothing earlier because I thought she'd come back." Looking into her mother's disbelieving gaze, Kelda plaintively added, "She always has before."

Surprise lifted Anne's brows and shifted the burden of apprehension from one threat to another. Worse and worse. Although Kelda had spoken of Amicia's forest visits with the Wolf's Head before, Anne was truly horrified to learn that not only had her lady's innocent daughter gone into the wild to meet some less than reputable man but apparently alone and at night!

"All she talks about is that wretched outlaw!" Kelda continued. "His silver-green eyes and midnight black hair." Once having confessed the secret of night exploits that she'd promised to keep, there was little reason to stop. "I told you, she thinks he's a real-life Robin Hood, a romantic hero in the flesh. She says he used the coins he took from the tax collector to buy grain for the villagers and that it's he who saved Randolf from the baron's ire, and—"

Kelda's words abruptly broke off when her mother sat down heavily beside her, as if all the strength had suddenly gone from her legs.

Anne gave her head a sharp shake to free it of the scattered debris of unimportant details already heard in castle gossip and Amicia's words to Orva.

"Amicia was gone *all* night." The quiet statement of an actual event effectively hid Anne's grave fears for a maid's virtue and a nobleman's honor. She had witnessed a late night return herself, but to be certain there was no mistake, she asked a direct question. "Are you saying Amicia has spent nights in the forest before?"

Hands twisting tight together, Kelda nodded. Dark disasters and revelations of wretched secrets were piling up on her head too fast for her to see any glimmer of hope through them. "Away from the castle but not in the forest."

"If not in the forest, then where?" Anne was calm, her initial urge to panic smothered by the melding of two facts she should've put together earlier.

"In a hidden place, a haven where she is safe." To Kelda it seemed important that leastways the secret of Amicia's cave be kept, if for no other reason than that the thought of two girls climbing down a sheer rock wall would only trouble her mother the more.

"You think she's there now?" Anne asked so matter of factly that she might have been questioning a fact as mundane as whether a guest preferred his wine mulled.

As if light of day had burst through the bleak clouds of her despair, Kelda turned to her mother, eyes wide. "I'll go fetch Amicia whether she wills it or no." Kelda jumped to her feet, determination sparkling in dark blue eyes.

Anne reached out to clasp a hand around the girl's wrist, restraining her from a precipitous dash for the door. "You'll be prevented from leaving alone."

Kelda's shoulders sagged in unhappy recognition of this truth.

"But—" Anne offered an alternative to circumvent the baron's will. "With your father at your side mayhap an excuse can be found. Gathering fresh blooms for the ceremony?" She suspected Gilfrey might be gratified by the notion of two less than friends doing something to enhance his son's wedding.

Kelda looked down and her mother's steady gaze cooled her flustered thoughts, allowing her to view the problem with a measure of objectivity. She would lead her father to the waterfall cave and together they'd bring Amicia back in time to save her mother from the Dark Lord's vengeance. That it would mean a further betrayal of Amicia's trust and break the bond between the girls was of no import when laid next to the right in preventing her mother's punishment for a wrong not hers.

Once Kelda gave her agreement, of necessity events progressed quickly. There was no time to be lost when the ceremony was such a short time distant. It seemed to Kelda that even before she could draw a deep breath, her mother had given her father a very brief version of the problem at hand (only that Amicia was hiding in the forest and must be secretly fetched or the baron would punish her instead.)

The flower-gathering excuse opened the fortress's front gates for them to pass through unchallenged. They crossed the barely revealed causeway before the cloud-shielded sun had cleared the horizon, much aware that while Gilfrey might have questioned the truth of their excuse, he deemed the return of his stepdaughter worth the price of allowing himself to be fooled.

Kelda led the way up the hillside path and through the meadow, but as she parted the foliage to bare the secret trail toward the waterfall, she could feel her father's unspoken reproach heavy on her back. Whether he was angrier with her or Amicia mattered little when he was so clearly upset with them both. Unused to his disapproval in the first instance, the fact that he'd gone to such lengths to befriend Farrold made it all the harder to bear. Last night even had he urged her mother not to think poorly of their daughter's feelings for the boy.

"What are you doing?" Jasper asked aghast.

Lost in her gloom over his displeasure, for once Kelda had approached the cliff and lowered herself over the edge without a thought to its dangers. She paused, bent arms and chin still resting on the level. Filled with an unexpected feeling of accomplishment, she quietly explained. "There are steps, of a sort, and a ledge half way down." Giving him a bright smile, she disappeared.

Jasper was amazed at his daughter's daring. Sweet Mary's Tears! Kelda avoided looking out from the arrow slits in the castle's stairwell and generally refused to walk the ramparts for fear of the sheer drops they involved. He'd never seen any sign of a courage to meet such terrors in her before—except when she forced herself to follow the adventurous Amicia's lead. But then, it was Amicia they'd come to retrieve. Peering over the edge, he watched until she reached the ledge and waved him down. He wasn't certain whether to be more proud of her for overcoming a fear or fearful for her future safety were she to consistently take such risks.

He glanced warily from the water falling dangerously near to the narrow footholds barely visible in the wall, but lowered his much larger body without hesitation to travel the same route his timid daughter had braved.

When they stood together on the narrow ledge, Kelda immediately led the way straight toward the falling water, and this time her father followed the seemingly deadly path without question.

"God's Blood!" Jasper growled the moment his horrified eyes had adjusted enough to the dark interior to take in the damning view of two unclad bodies, asleep but intimately entwined. "Stand and meet my blade you blackhearted toad. I demand your life for the dishonor of a pure maiden!"

From the total relaxation of sated sleep to utterly wakeful warrior, a nude Galen leaped from his soft pillow against Amicia's breasts to meet the furious man who stood in the cave entrance, sword drawn and threatening. He silently cursed himself for having allowed private joys to distract him, even this once, from seeing his own sword within arm's reach.

Eyes blinking against the abrupt end to pleasing dreams, Amicia sat up, disoriented. In less than a moment she saw the deadly intent in the disastrous scene and jerked the crude blanket around herself as she struggled to stand and put the barrier of her own body between Galen and Sir Jasper.

"Nay!" With tawny hair tangled and eyes flashing gold, Amicia was the picture of a lioness defending her cub. "Galen and I are wed," she stated, proudly tilting her chin.

"Galen?" Jasper's sword tip wavered, and he took a short step forward peering at the dark face near lost in the shadows above the maid's fire-honeyed curls. "Galen, it *is you!*"

Having jerked on his loose chausses, from behind Amicia, Galen extended his arm toward the advancing man. "Sir Jasper, I'm glad to see you are well and as dedicated to the upholding of honor as you always were."

While Galen spoke, he wrapped his free arm around the front of Amicia's shoulders, as if to further secure the precarious garment in danger of slipping to again reveal more of her than he cared to share with another man, even an old friend.

"And I'm happy just to see you once more," Jasper responded, then stopped, "though not precisely this way—" His voice trailed away uncomfortably, and he gestured aimlessly at the two caught unprepared. Trying to make sense of this remarkable event, he questioned, "But—a marriage? And to Conal's daughter?" He shook a head muddled with facts that did not match at any turning, yet one thought wiggled its way to the top. "He'd be pleased, you know, his daughter and the heir of his dearest friend. Nay, Conal would be thrilled! And your father, Earl Garrick, is he pleased?"

Galen felt Amicia, already tensed under her attempt to fathom the acquaintance between the two men, go stiff with sudden comprehension. No doubt she now saw him as a wealthy lord so intent on adding to his riches that he would live a lie, if only long enough to claim her inheritance. Galen's eyes clenched shut in frustration, prevented by an oath of honor from explaining how very wrong she was in her false assumptions.

When Jasper caught a fleeting glimpse of the distress on the younger man's face before the dark head bent regretfully over a tawny one below, he knew he'd spoken out of turn. Jasper's attention, too, dropped to the new bride.

Amicia felt as if she'd been returned to childhood, watching her precious crystal unicorn splintering into a myriad of useless pale green shards. Galen had done the same, had taken her dreams and carelessly destroyed them. Although he'd admitted he knew who she was before she told him, doubtless because she'd also told him of her wish to marry no lord anxious for her inheritance, he'd tricked her into thinking him someone else. Nay, not just someone else, but the very person she'd dreamed of meeting—it was a calculated cruelty worse than torture.

"Sweeting," Galen whispered in her ear, voice rough with emotion, "you must believe me, nothing is as you think."

Amicia pulled sharply away, glaring at him in disgust. Only she knew that the emotion was as much a response to her own weak reaction to his nearness, to his voice, as it was to the wrong he'd done her. "I think you wed me for my inheritance. Now by law you have it, but you will never again have me." She tried to ignore the undeniable truth that her declaration brought more pain than satisfaction.

Jasper looked in confusion from Amicia to Galen. "What— But haven't you told—"

Black hair whipped about Galen's head as he gave a sharp negative shake and met the older knight's gaze with a pointed silver warning in his green eyes.

"I don't pretend to know of what you speak." Kelda anxiously broke into the conversation she deemed a waste of precious time, and turned her back on the man who, in the heat of their discussion, the others had apparently forgot was still standing half-clad.

That he was stunningly attractive did not make it right; and that, rather than being who he'd claimed, he was apparently noble born did not excuse his lack of modesty—not before a maiden—herself, even if Amicia was one no more. "But, father, I do know we've no time to waste on sorting it out. We've got to take Amicia and hasten back to the isle."

Frustration over the unforeseen confrontation deepened Galen's irritation with the speaker's pointed action, plainly meant to show him that his semi-clothed state offended her. From the description of castle inhabitants Amicia had given during one of the night's moments of calm, he recognized the girl as Amicia's friend Kelda. But, while he wouldn't choose to walk unclad before others, neither would he cringe in shame where there was no shame. Nonetheless, he bent and rifled through the clothes kicked aside until he found his tunic and while Kelda continued her plea deftly slipped it on.

"We must hurry! They'll all be gathering in the chapel by now."

"Be calm, Kelda," Amicia soothed, holding her blanket wrap up with one hand and with the other reaching out to squeeze the tension-twisted fingers of her friend. "The abbot will simply tell the Dark Lord that I've wed another, making my return a needless folly."

"Oh, no! That will be the end of us all." Kelda's wail was sincere and full of anguish. "You don't understand. I didn't know where you were and pretended you were in our chamber, prostrate with grief for the deed to come. Gilfrey sent Mag to see and be certain. Then, to protect us both, my mother confirmed your presence in our chamber this morn, and the baron swore that he'll punish her if you fail to appear for the ceremony."

Amicia bent and scooped up her clothes, motioning Kelda to follow her into the shadows at the cave's back. "Hold this blanket up while I dress behind, and we'll return to the castle before the abbot speaks. I've nothing now to hold me here." Eyes like hurtful bruises met pale green glittering with irritation and frustration.

Galen acknowledged the right in one of his father's favorite maxims. Lies spun more lies until like a spider's web they wrapped about a man, held him helpless and only truth could set him free. But in this instance, the instrument of freedom he could not wield.

❧ *Chapter 14* ❧

Dare Amicia tarry much longer," Gilfrey snarled, eyes drilling like poisoned arrows into Anne, "and I'll claim the forfeit from you." He advanced menacingly on the woman he was certain had lied to him, the woman seeking to cover an attempt to rob him of his moment of triumph, his victory in what had become an obsessive goal—the permanent securement of Wryborne to his own *male* heirs—not Conal's daughter alone!

Anne faltered back a step, only to have a slender arm wrap about her in support.

"If Anne says Amicia will come, then come she will." Sybil's soothing voice was not enough to calm the savage wrath boiling within her husband. "There is time, even Abbot Pieter has yet to appear."

Near certain that Sir Jasper and his daughter had gone out to insure Anne's safety by seeing her promise come true, Gilfrey turned his spite to taunting this second woman. "And when Amicia arrives what a pleasure it will be for you to watch as your friend, the abbot, binds your daughter to my son by God's law and man's." Impervious to the cringing boy at his side, a cruel laugh of satisfaction rasped from

Gilfrey's throat at sight of the pain momentarily flashing across the ice of Sybil's pious facade. Scoring even so minor a victory over the bloodless woman he'd married provided a flicker of pleasure to the mood already blackened by news of a mysteriously vacant village.

Sybil schooled her features into serenity and turned her attention to a study of their surroundings. It was an unhappy task that lent no comfort. The offspring she and Conal had so long anticipated should have been wed in a grand cathedral amidst flowers, light, and a multitude of well-wishers, should have been wed to a suitable mate who would bring a lifetime of happiness. Instead, the man who was source of near two decades of misery would have the rite furtively performed in a bleak chapel long unused, smelling of must, and lit only by a trio of tapers. Letting her lashes fall, Sybil prayed for the strength to see the deed through without breaking down in tears, and also for guidance in giving her daughter what little comfort could be found.

Gilfrey watched his wife's quiet acceptance and saw when she retreated into prayer—how like her. That she'd sought its shield yet again further infuriated him and, unaware of the action, a growl welled up in his throat.

Anne's own fears faded beneath her concern for the gentle creature who'd withstood the baron's bad temper for years. Sybil's long-suffering endurance shamed Anne for the weakness of spirit she'd shown, and she straightened to lay her arm protectively about the smaller woman's slender shoulders, returning the baron's cold glare with one of her own.

The tension in the chapel was increasing, like a leather cord stretched taut and near to snapping with the backlash of a whip, and Farrold was caught in its midst. He'd pay near any price to be anywhere but here, yet he hadn't the courage to refuse his sire's demand. Which, he acknowledged, made him the lowest of worms. It was with deep relief that he heard the echoing sound of someone climbing the stone stairway. Surely the arrival of another, any other, would release the ever-tightening strain before it broke into violence of one sort or another.

"You are all here then," the abbot wheezed as he stepped into the chamber. He was not as young as he'd been when this chapel on the fortress's highest level was his domain, decades past, and he paused to catch his breath from the climb.

"Nay, we are *not* all here," Gilfrey responded with barely controlled anger. "The bride has yet to appear." He sent another scalding glance in Anne's direction. "Thus, to save her friend from my retribution."

Eyes hastily lifted heavenward, Pieter crossed himself and softly intoned, "Holy Father, I pray mercy and strength." Carefully folding his hands, drawing a deep breath, and affixing a painfully tight smile to his lips, he looked to the baron and spoke words he knew would be unwelcome. "I fear, my lord, that Amicia will not be—"

Letting the priest get no further, Gilfrey roared, "You are a part of this treachery, too?"

To the baron's surprise and greater ire, Pieter's mouth relaxed into the gentle smile lent by his complete faith in higher powers. With renewed peace he quietly answered, "There is no treachery in my delivery of a message entrusted to me."

In the furor none of the people already in the chapel noticed the arrival of three more. Even before Amicia heard the abbot's words, one look at her stepfather's temper-contorted face had warned her that she'd arrived near too late.

"You are justified in accusing no one of treachery save me," she boldly announced, advancing with steady purpose to within two paces of Gilfrey. "Although I've Sir Jasper and Kelda to thank," she made the word of gratitude sound an insult, "for bringing me back to you, 'twas I who slipped away—without the help of any other." She hoped her proudly stated disclaimer would be enough to keep the Dark Lord from punishing the others for her misdeeds. Yet, she was realistic enough to know that if she failed to divert his attention, he'd see them pay. "I outwitted you all and slipped away to wed the man of my choice, not yours."

If Gilfrey was fooled by her attitude of disdain for the others, he was the only one. However, she had succeeded, leastways momentarily, in shifting his attention from the others' wrongs.

"Wed to another, hah! Do you take me for such a simpleton that I would accept your flimsy foolery?" Aye, the maid had run away, but she'd returned and returned alone. His relief in seeing her gave him a feeling of invincibility, and he gleefully ridiculed her attempt at resisting his will. "What man do you know who would risk my ire by marrying you?" He'd caught her sneaking back after a night in some man's arms, true. But, while one might dare taking his pleasure with the plainly wanton girl, he was certain that he held all of Wryborne in such fear that neither worldly man nor priest would risk his wrath by seeing her wed without his blessing. She was here and now nothing could prevent the fulfillment of his plan! "One of my guards?" He continued with the mockery of disdain. "Or, mayhap, one of the village peasants who've so opportunely disappeared?"

The abbot kept his expression completely devoid of emotion, but he took joy in deflating the baron's belief in the impossibility of Amicia's claim. "Nay, it was not one of your men nor one of the serfs whom she wed in the abbey chapel last eve."

Impervious to the pains the action sent shooting down his legs, Gilfrey whirled toward the abbot, red rage instantly mottling his pitted face. *"You* performed the ceremony that saw her wed to another! Treachery, treachery—" Fists clenched, he leaped at the offender. Before he could land a blow, he was restrained by the arm his son wrapped around his throat from behind.

"Not a priest, not a priest—" The plea Farrold gasped into his father's ear seemed to restore a measure of control to the man.

After a moment of aching silence, Gilfrey shook himself free from Farrold's loosened hold and gave no notice when Kelda stepped forward to twine her arm through the boy's. The baron advanced to stand motionless a handsbreadth before the abbot, and his cold control was more threatening than the hot fury of his earlier physical attack.

"You've wed Amicia to another man, despite the prior commitment you knew full well existed?" The question he delivered bore the same smooth texture as poison.

Amicia hadn't thought even the Dark Lord was so lost to reason as to attack a priest, nay, an abbot. Shock held her immobile until the boy she'd thought too weak to stand against his father had put an end to it. But now she reached for her stepfather's arm, attempting to return the focus of his ire to herself. "It was none if the abbot's doing, but mine, only mine."

Gilfrey shook the distraction from his arm with enough force to send Amicia sprawling on the floor while he continued his condemnation of the abbot without pause. "'Tis a wrong you will now correct, good father, by seeing that she is granted an annulment on those grounds." It was not a request but a command plainly backed by force. "If you do not, I will take charges of your wrongdoing to the king—he has no love of Rome and no fear of wreaking judgment upon the heads of its lackeys."

Abbot Pieter was not so easily intimidated by the

judgments of men, and as Anne bent to help the fallen girl he calmly responded to the baron's groundless demands. "A prior commitment involves the consent of two parties. While, as father of the groom, your intent was clear, the approval of the bride's mother was never given. Therefore, no prior commitment existed, and there is no just basis for an annulment." With a bland smile he looked straight into the baron's growing wrath to add, "Moreover, 'tis a judgment no king has the authority to either grant or deny."

Sybil had watched her husband's vitriolic attack on a blameless priest with forced calm, had restrained the urge to go to her abused child—all to be certain she'd not miss what she strained to hear. Now even her patience had reached its end. It was plain that without a direct question, the one fact most important would be lost in the thunder of Gilfrey's outrage. Quietly she stepped to the priest's side and laid her hand on his arm.

Her touch was soft but instantly drew the abbot's attention. He looked down into the lovely face of a woman whose fortitude of spirit had been sorely tested for years. He was now as always willing to lend whatever solace lay in his power.

"To whom is Amicia wed?" The question was so simple, so self-evident, so important that while Amicia gasped in renewed anguish for the accurate response the other listeners were amazed that securing its answer had been overlooked.

"Lady Amicia of Wryborne is the wife of Galen Fitz William, heir to the earldom of Tarrant." The abbot watched quiet joy warm Sybil's usually serene face with an inner glow and felt he'd been repaid a hundredfold for any trouble his action might bring. It had been a long time coming, but at last the stormy tide had turned and events were flowing toward the shore of peace for this gentle lady.

A growl of rage broke from Gilfrey. It couldn't be, it

couldn't! He himself had delivered the physical blow sundering the friendship between Wryborne and Tarrant—his lifelong foes. Wryborne was dead but now one of Tarrant blood had risen to steal victory from him—again as once before, so very long ago.

"He can't be here, he's never been here!" The baron's voice rumbled from his depths.

"Are you so sure?" Sybil asked, the quiet words so great a contrast to her husband's bluster that it took a moment for the others to comprehend. Their eyes widened in surprise, Amicia the most surprised of all. What had her mother to do with Galen's presence? Indeed, ever bound within castle walls, how could she know he was here?

"What do you mean?" Gilfrey turned on Sybil. "Is it you I have to blame? Did my pious wife scheme behind my back to arrange this marriage?" His description of her was delivered with a sneer of disgust.

"Nay," Sybil denied, a slow smile growing. "But had I thought such a wonderful answer possible, I would have."

"If not by your mother's hand, then how did you meet?" Gilfrey demanded, lashing out to fasten a hand about Amicia's arm and drag her closer.

"I met an outlaw in the forest and fell in love with him," Amicia defiantly answered, calling on all her fine bravado as she met the baron's gaze with tilted chin, refusing to acknowledge the punishing tightness of his grip.

"The heir to Tarrant is an outlaw?" Gilfrey angrily shook the girl in his hold as if to do so would loose a sensible answer from her reluctant tongue.

"So it would seem." The response came through teeth gritted against the jarring motion, but even could she, Amicia would say no more.

Gilfrey ceased his bruising action and glared down into the girl's unblinking eyes for a long moment before pushing her from him like a useless bone

216

stripped of meat, although retaining his grasp on her. He wouldn't allow it, he wouldn't. Dragging his unrepentant stepdaughter behind, he strode to the chapel door and bellowed for his guardsmen.

Thrusting Amicia into the hold of one of the first two to arrive, he gave an implacable order. "Put this devil's spawn in her chamber and stand guard outside the door while you," he swung around to face the second man, "fetch Mag and tell her to never let more than an arm's length separate them."

Though far from gentle, the guardsman's hands were not as rough as the baron's and Amicia went with him willingly enough. Whatever else had gone wrong this day (and it seemed almost everything had) she comforted herself that leastwise she'd succeeded in diverting the Dark Lord's fury, drawing his retribution upon herself. What the baron chose to do with her mattered little now that her dreams had been betrayed by the one who'd made them real. Live in her chamber or in the dungeon—what difference did it make?

In the chapel, Amicia's one solacing thought was proven in error. Other guardsmen arrived by the time the first two and their charge had departed.

Gilfrey pointed at the abbot and hissed, "Take that wretched priest and lock him in the dungeon until he decides to see things my way."

Pieter's face was as white as his hair, yet when the guardsmen briskly escorted him past the baron he looked straight into furious eyes and firmly stated, "Even be it that I spend all my remaining days in your cage, I'll not do your bidding."

Gilfrey stood in the doorway and watched until the abbot and his gaolers had disappeared into the stairwell gloom before glancing back into the chamber behind. Five pairs of condemning eyes were trained on him. Sir Jasper was grim, Anne and Kelda disgusted, Farrold horrified, and his wife distressed.

Their attitudes were more than Gilfrey was willing to deal with after the confrontation just concluded. Calling a vicious curse upon their heads, he turned and, despite the agony in his legs aggravated by the morn's activities, he stomped down the steps.

While descending a path as dark as his emotions, Gilfrey melded his determination to successfully wrest Wryborne from the sole ownership of Lord Conal's heir by supplanting his own with a resolve to put an end to Tarrant's male line as well. One goal would serve the other. 'Twas a fact that pleased him greatly and laid a cold smile on his thin lips.

Once the sound of Gilfrey's descending footfalls striking stone had faded into silence, through weakly wavering candlelight the five who remained in the chapel looked from one to another.

"Right, then," Sir Jasper nodded to the two older women whose expressions he read as clearly as the tracks of a hunted animal. "I'll go back to Galen and report what's happened. Most like he came from Tarrant with a plan that'll defeat the shadows of fear the baron strives to see us cower beneath. Indeed, enough years have passed that surely it is time for—"

Anne sent her husband a sudden look of such strength that it pushed further words back into his throat. Apparently, Jasper acknowledged, she deemed it right that the secret still be kept. But soon, surely soon?

Sybil saw the strange exchange between the couple but matters of far more import spread over their lives, a darkness deeper than mere shadows. She wanted no time wasted on else but forcing it into defeat before the illumination of victory's advance.

"Go and talk with Galen," Sybil urged. After all, he had come in answer to her plea and had already defeated the baron's wicked plan. She would willingly put her faith in the gallant man to see the evil

218

darkness fully driven out. "Tell him I am most grateful for his action and will pray that it brings only happiness and good fortune to them both."

Jasper smiled at the earnest woman who he doubted able to recognize the possibility of a wrong in the foster son she'd known. Yet, after pondering Amicia's reaction to Galen's true identity, he was at a loss to understand what had passed between the young couple. But he meant to find out! He turned to go only to be halted by the much younger man who stepped into his path.

"Please, Sir Jasper," Farrold set out to plead his case, "let me come with you." He'd stood up to his father once and survived. He couldn't bear to now step back under the man's smothering shroud. "I want to see my sire's plans foiled every bit as much as you. My future with Kelda depends upon it, and I'd deeply appreciate the chance to prove my worth to both you and her."

Jasper gave the other a long, considering stare. Farrold stood unflinching, meeting his eyes without hesitation. At last he smiled.

"Aye, son, 'tis time you made your own decisions, fought your own battles." Jasper offered his arm. When Farrold extended his, the two were joined with hands wrapped around the other's arm below the elbow and forearms bound together in a gesture of honor. Kelda beamed.

"Come." In camaraderie Jasper threw his arm about the younger man's shoulders. "We'll go by boat if the causeway is sea-covered."

"Farrold, wait." Kelda spoke for the first time in near the whole of the time since she'd arrived.

Jasper's arm fell away as Farrold immediately turned toward the maid he meant to wed.

"You've already proven your bravery to me, and I'm sorry I doubted you." Suddenly overcome with shyness, she stared at the ground beneath his feet.

"You were the one who stopped the baron from a wicked assault. I'm proud of you!" She moved forward and, despite their audience, threw her arms around her beloved's neck to give him a resounding kiss. "I know our future is together, and I know that we'll be happy in it."

☜§ *Chapter 15* ࢦ☞

So few?" Galen could easily believe that Baron
Gilfrey had sent the greater share of his guardsmen to
aid in King John's struggle against rebellious barons
and French invaders. However, Sir Jasper's account of
the extent to which the garrison had been stripped was
incredible. Only a complement of such meager proportions as to be no real protection were left to guard
Castle Dungeld, and in the news Galen heard not only
the way to free a priest but the way to free himself of a
dragging encumbrance to his peace with Amicia. The
time was ripe to liberate a long-held secret and lift the
hovering clouds of a usurper's oppression from
Wryborne.

"Walter, I'd as lief not lose your aid before Carl
returns, but 'tis of utmost import that a message be
carried to my parents and their charge."

Walter had been leaning back against the cave's wall
and straightened, an argument tumbling from his lips.
"But you need someone here with you, someone to
share the watch."

"Therefore," Galen cut off his squire's words, "you
must return to Tarrant with all good speed, tell them
of my marriage, of the people's oppression, and—
most importantly—of the castle garrison's severe

limitations." Turning to face Sir Jasper, Galen added, "Doubtless my father and the one you've not seen in a great many years will arrive within the week."

Jasper's stern face broke into a broad smile. "I'm relieved. As isolated as we've been, Anne and I had worried—even natural accidents occur and illness takes so many afore their time."

For the first time Galen realized that from the moment Jasper had delivered a bundle to Tarrant's lord and lady, the pair who'd managed its transport had had no news.

"My pardon, Sir Jasper." Galen laid a hand on the other man's shoulder, sorry that the mysteries surrounding his return to Wryborne had prevented him from earlier seeking out the man who'd risked much. "My family and I have kept the secret so close and for so long that I failed to think of two others who'd a share in it and might long for confirmation of the right in their actions." Returning the knight's smile, he gave the shoulder a squeeze. "But, I'm certain you'll be pleased by the result. It's as if one we all loved had returned to us."

While the two men spoke in riddles, Farrold watched the one called Walter scramble amongst shadows at the back of the cave, gathering his things for the trip. Farrold came to a decision. Bolstering his courage, he stepped from relative obscurity near the cave entrance to interrupt the odd conversation.

"I was fostered at Salisbury and have spent the time since earning my spurs in its service—all told a goodly number of years." It was an awkward beginning, and he cleared his throat nervously as the other three turned startled faces toward him.

"Salisbury?" Restraining his irritation at the poorly timed and meaningless interruption, Galen gave a polite response meant to end the subject. "It borders my lands. Indeed, my mother, too, was raised within its walls." Galen looked back to the knight who'd brought the strange young man here.

Farrold nodded; and, although he'd near lost the men's attention, continued speaking before he lost his courage. "I tell you this so you'll know I can make my way to Tarrant Castle as easily as your friend." He paused, gulped, and added, "And I would appreciate the opportunity to have a part in your works."

Galen had been surprised when Sir Jasper introduced his companion as the baron's son. Immediately he'd recognized that then this must be Amicia's intended bridegroom. Yet, Amicia had said the boy no more wanted to wed her than she him. So, that the elder knight trusted Farrold had been enough. Enough, that was, to accept him as visitor to the hidden cave, but not enough to explain his exceptional offer. There was no need to verbally ask. Dark brows arched inquiringly above penetrating crystal eyes were sufficient.

Farrold squared his shoulders; and, when he spoke, his voice held more firmness than he'd yet shown. "It was I who my father sought to wed with Amicia." He felt sure Sir Jasper had specifically left that point out of his introduction to the overpowering inhabitant of this cave. "The scheme was no more to my liking than hers." Suddenly he realized that Amicia's intimidating husband might think his words an insult and hurried to explain. "I am in love with another," he glanced at the knight who'd brought him, standing close and grim. "'Tis Kelda, Sir Jasper's daughter, whom I wish to wed."

"And to further that goal you would sunder your loyalties to your sire?" Galen asked, uncertain whether to congratulate the boy on good taste in distancing himself from the spiteful man or condemn him for betraying his own father.

Farrold recognized the bad light this cast upon him but refused to cower before its truth and bravely answered the questioner. "Would you honor a sire like mine? For near all of my eighteen years I've obeyed his wishes, but the time has come when it would surely be a greater dishonor to obey than to defy. Again I say, surely, the circumstances dictate that 'tis right for me to give more care to the preservation of my own honor."

Despite the lie Galen himself had been forced to live of recent times, Farrold's honesty did more to earn his acceptance than anything else the youth could have said or done.

"Then, come, sit down." Galen put his hand on Farrold's back and urged him toward an upended round of firewood conveniently placed beside the ring of stones. "Let me outline for you the details Walter already knows so that you may provide my family with all the knowledge they'll need."

Once Galen had given Farrold a point-by-point list of facts to carry to Tarrant and the boy had departed, Galen again faced a patiently waiting knight.

"Now that the final scene of this pageant has been set into motion," Sir Jasper quietly said, "tell me how you came to know the daughter of Wryborne when never since her birth has there been contact between Tarrant and Wryborne?"

Galen acknowledged that the knight who'd been caught in the web of falsehoods their relationships had spun deserved an explanation. However, he'd prefer complete privacy for the telling. He looked to the squire gone motionless, back turned as he bent over the belongings he'd been restoring to order at the back of the cave, but ears doubtless straining to hear.

"Walter, the wood pile is dwindling, and we may not have time to replenish it later. So, pray, fetch enough to see us through the night."

Walter took an inordinately long time gathering up the rope and blanket they'd formed into a tote-cradle for the careful lowering to the cave of adequate stores of firewood. But his hope of satisfying his own growing curiosity by hearing even a little of the explanation was doomed to disappointment.

Galen stood at the cave entrance and watched until

Walter had scrambled up the cliff wall. Only then did he drop heavily to the firewood round where Farrold had earlier sat. With fingers interlaced and hands dangling between his wide-braced knees, he told Sir Jasper of the well-born maid, pretending to be a peasant, who'd chosen to think of a stranger as a romantic outlaw. Too, he told of the stranger trapped by a quest's uncertain goal and oath-sworn secret into hiding the truth from her.

"I've been caught by the tangle of my own lies, yet I'm unable to use the truth to prove my innocence," he concluded. "Amicia believes I've tricked her into marriage for the sake of an inheritance that is not hers, and I cannot tell her the wrong in her thinking. Worse yet, she fell in love with an outlaw only to find he didn't exist. 'Tis a web of deceit, and I'm trapped in its midst."

Even though Galen's words were very nearly a repeat of Amicia's statement to her stepfather, Jasper refuted the argument. "Galen, you are yourself and Amicia is who she is. Truly, no matter what clothes you dress yourselves in, you are still the same beneath. Given a short while of quiet reflection, Amicia cannot fail to see that as clearly as do I." Jasper desperately wanted to ease the hurt of the man in whom he still saw the honest lad he'd loved for his unfaltering support of honorable ways. "If she loves you, she'll trust you." He only hoped his comforting words were true. "Soon, boy, soon." Too likely their best hope lay in the fast passage of time.

"Soon the truth will out," Galen agreed, hands now unthinkingly clenched. He'd have no share of the happy ending awaiting the people of Wryborne if Amicia could not be made to understand, and he bitterly spoke his fear aloud. "But what part can trust play in a love based on lies?"

Amicia had no trust in him, and a relationship, whether knight to liege-lord or wife to husband, could not thrive without trust at its base. Certain that no good would come from dwelling on the matter until it shoved more immediate problems aside, Galen shifted the subject to one that must be addressed without delay. "Whatever the outcome of the bond, the priest who formed it deserves to pay no forfeit for its doing."

Sir Jasper's deep sigh proved him not so willing to give up the argument, yet he acknowledged the greater importance of seeing the priest free and bit his tongue into silence.

"I have a plan," Galen announced, rising to gaze down at his old friend with a grim smile. "How many will Gilfrey take from other duties to act as guards on the dungeon level?"

"Guards are never posted there. The cage is barred and locked so there's no need." As a glimmer of understanding began to burn inside, Jasper looked into silver-green eyes. "'Tis a strategy that assumes the prisoner to be a stranger, unaware of the fortress's last-hope defenses. Any such captive who won free of bars and locks would have to pass through the great hall to reach the outgoing door. Then, even if he could slip unnoticed through that broad, open space, he'd have to cross a busy courtyard and descend a narrow path, unshielded from arrows near certain to be loosed by the guard on the ramparts. Most daunting of all, he'd have to time his escape to match the tides—a difficult chore for one bound in the dark of a dungeon with no way to measure time." Certain he now clearly saw the younger man's fine plan, Jasper stood to meet his accomplice on a level.

"Excellent reasons," Galen stated with a cold laugh, "to use neither the front approach nor the causeway, but rather to use the postern door and the docks at castle back. At what time do you take the watch on the ramparts overlooking the sea?"

Jasper grinned his approval. Galen and Walter could easily slip inside the castle and, with justified assurance that not one among the peasants working in the kitchens would raise an alarm to see a priest held, carry Abbot Pieter away, leaving the baron none the wiser.

"Amicia—"

Amicia sat straight up in response to the gentle call. When the guardsmen had deposited her in the windowless prison of her chamber, she'd retreated to this curtained bed, her last haven. Although Mag sat somewhere on the far side of tapestried drapes, she'd been left in the cool, dark privacy to wallow in her misery. She'd thought mayhap Kelda would come, even Anne, but years since had given up hope for her mother's comfort.

Sybil parted the enclosing folds and stepped inside to perch on the edge of the bed where her daughter sat, eyes red-rimmed and cheeks still wet.

"I came to tell you how happy I am for you, how proud of the fine marriage you've made. You were very brave to defy Gilfrey as you did, succeeding where I failed." It was not quite the truth as Galen had appeared in answer to her call, but God would surely forgive her this trespass in the name of motherly concern.

A flood of fresh tears was Amicia's response to her mother's congratulations on a deed that had gone so wrong, proven so far from what she'd dreamed. Yet, Amicia couldn't explain that she had married for love only to find she'd been wed for greed. Not to her mother.

Sybil wisely chose to ignore the renewed rainfall. "I thought a great deal of the godson who became my foster son and am well pleased that he is now my son by even stronger ties."

"Godson? Foster son?" As upset as she was, Amicia couldn't help but seek further knowledge of the man who was now her husband.

"Oh, aye. Surely you knew that Garrick and Nessa, the Earl of Tarrant and his lady, were our closest friends—your father's and mine. What more natural but that we should stand as godparents to their heir, and when the time came take him to foster in our home?"

Fortunately, Amicia was required to do no more than shake her head while tears retreated. By the time she was old enough for serious discussions, her mother had withdrawn so far into the realms of piety that their rare visits seldom covered more than religious training or mundane daily events and had never touched on the years gone by. Moreover, in her talks with Sir Jasper and Lady Anne, if ever she inquired further into the past than her real father's character they'd shifted the subject. Not wanting to force them into reliving memories they plainly found painful, she had retreated from the questions.

"Galen was a fine boy," Lady Sybil continued. "Although at times painfully honest—a habit which even at that young age had already been ingrained in him by a father who despises any untruth."

"Then the man I wed cannot be the same Galen of whom you speak." Amicia flared and immediately wished she had not, for now she'd doubtless be called to explain.

"Why do you say that?" Sybil asked, fulfilling Amicia's unhappy expectations.

Even in the curtained bed's dimness, her mother's hair glowed about her head like a halo. How could Amicia possibly lie to her? But, why should she when 'twas lies that had left her floundering in this quagmire. Although she intended to speak and speak the truth, somehow she couldn't force a single word beyond the uncomfortable lump growing in her throat.

"Could it be that you thought Galen was a man such as Robin Hood and were upset to learn your assumption was wrong?"

Amicia was shocked by her mother's perception and stared into the lovely face too serene to be real.

Sybil's ability to wipe all emotion away with the cool breeze of complete tranquility was a talent Amicia had often admired and wished to emulate. Now she found it only depressing, for it had never been so far beyond her ability to attain.

"This morn, though the abbot explained precisely who you'd married, you told us that you'd fallen in love with an outlaw," Sybil quietly explained. "And when I heard you say that, I thought of the minstrel who recently sang for us the tales of the common folk's hero, the outlaw of the greenwood."

"Aye, I thought the man I met in the forest, wearing no armor and carrying no knightly badge or noble standard, was an outlaw." Amicia's confirmation was softly spoken but her chin tilted and bitterness crept into her voice as she tried to make her mother understand the source of her pain. "That was my mistake, but his was in knowing what I believed yet never telling me I was wrong, never telling me who he truly is."

"He told you his name was something other than Galen?" Sybil lifted her brows in mock amazement.

Amicia shook her head, while holding brown eyes wide to keep brimming wetness contained.

"And when you wed, did the abbot not make you the wife of Galen Fitz William?" Sybil was careful to allow no tinge of disapproval to touch her words as she probed for a confession that would take them one step closer to reality.

"Aye." Amicia saw the trap that had been gently laid for her and resented it. "I married Galen Fitz William, but I did not know I had wed the heir of Tarrant." She spat the statement out as if it tasted bad on her tongue. But, though her anger grew, it was the anger of hurt, and tears again dripped down flushed cheeks. Even did she try with limited success to close her mind to the realization that Galen had never once claimed to be an outlaw. It was she who in the first instance had illogically convinced herself it was true and in the second unquestioningly accepted Carl's agreement.

"Oh, my baby." Sybil relented in her attempt to make Amicia see reason and leaned forward to cradle the child she'd seldom held in her arms for fear Gilfrey would see her love of the child and wield it as a weapon of punishment—harming them both. Praying for divine guidance in her quest, Sybil held the younger woman close until the wracking sobs lessened their intensity and wet cheeks dried. Then, once again, Sybil tried to help her daughter see the unfairness of her actions, but by another, gentler route.

"You claim to have fallen in love with an outlaw. If 'tis true, that outlaw must have done something to win your love."

Although suspicious at first, Amicia wanted her mother to know her emotions ran deeper than mere childish dreams. She told her how Galen had retrieved coins stolen from the abbey and used them to care for the people. She talked with pride about his saving of Randolf from the baron's cruel punishment, of his care for a lad whose home had been burned, and the answer he'd provided the villagers caught in the threat of Gilfrey's revenge. Implicit in her every word was Galen's consistent concern and tender dealings with her herself.

Sybil smiled. "The man who did these things sounds a man of honor, a man to be respected, to be trusted."

Amicia's pain in what she viewed as Galen's betrayal was lost amidst the emotion in her description of the hero she loved. She nodded agreement with her mother's words, proud that the other saw the same things in these actions that she had seen and thus would understand her feelings for an outlaw.

"You must realize—" Sybil said quietly, taking her daughter's hands again, "Galen is the man who did those things. Whether he calls himself an outlaw or lord makes no difference. If you love the man, then you love him whatever lands either he or you might possess. You think he wed you for your inheritance, but it seems to me that 'tis you and not Galen who has allowed the possession of material goods to stand between you. Moreover, because I knew Galen the child, I am certain the man can be little different. If Galen told or leastways let you believe in falsehoods, then he has a good reason. You've got to give him your trust—without trust love cannot survive."

Amicia leaned back to study her mother through narrowed eyes. How could this woman who'd retreated far from earthly matters, from a daughter, know even that much of love?

Sybil's smile was very real as she squeezed her daughter's hands. "It was in the Abbey of St. Margaret's where I was raised that I learned with love comes trust. Again, I assure you that one cannot survive without the other. If you love God, then you put your trust in Him. And, if you truly love a mortal male, then you must give your trust to him. I loved your father, and because I trusted him I'd have done whatever he asked of me."

Today was the first time her mother had ever spoken to Amicia of the man who was her father. Even as a child she'd wondered how such an odd-matched couple—a postulant nun and worldly lord—had come together. And as she grew up she'd doubted that she could've been born of love. A doubt that had seemed confirmed by the distance ever between mother and daughter.

Sybil saw the disbelief in Amicia's eyes and sadly stated, "'Struth, I loved your father deeply and if he'd told me to jump from the ramparts, I would have done so without question. Sometimes love demands we give blind trust and endure pain. I lost my beloved Conal but still I love God and trust Him to hold you safe, even though it must be at the price of a mother's anguished separation from her child." To Amicia's slowly shaking head, Sybil sadly explained, "Only to prevent another from using my love for you as a weapon have I held you separate from me."

It was clear to Sybil that new facts and ideas were falling too fast on the young woman already overwhelmed by a storm of events all in one day's time for her to immediately sort through them all. She gave her daughter only one more piece of advice. "'Tis time to grow up, leave childhood fantasies behind. I promise you that reality can be far more rewarding."

Having taken the matter as far as she could, Sybil hoped that leaving her daughter in quiet solitude would finish the task. Leaning forward, she laid a gentle kiss on the girl's overwarm cheek before backing from the bed and closing the curtains behind her. As she departed the chamber as well, she was careful to give no notice to the malevolent stare of the old crone crouched at the foot of the bed.

·§ *Chapter 16* §·

Alone again in the bed's comforting darkness, Amicia's earlier anger with Galen for his betrayal and self-pity for the pain rendered by the shattering of a fragile fantasy gave way to serious consideration of all that her mother had said. And with the unexpected but warm support of a mother's love declared at last, she put aside selfish thoughts of her own hurts to consider Galen's position. He'd never claimed to be anything but what he was—Galen Fitz William, the man who'd worked for the people, who'd treated young Davie's fears so gently, who'd saved Randolf from harm. Her mother had spoken the truth. No matter whether the heir of an earldom or an outlaw, Galen was the same, and it was Galen she loved. 'Twould be the act of a foolish child to reject the very real man for the sake of a useless illusion, a hero of no substance.

"Amicia."

For all it seemed so real, Amicia was certain the soft sound of her name on Galen's tongue was merely a reflection of her thoughts.

"Amicia!" Still little more than a loud whisper, the sound of her name came more urgently.

It *was* real and its source was Galen! He was looking for her. Fighting the restraining folds of skirts and bedcover, Amicia scrambled to her knees, answering, "I'm here, Galen, here."

In the stairway arch at the end of the hallway, Galen paused, straining to hear an answer to his call. Coming here had not been a wise choice. Yet, whatever the price, he had to see and talk with Amicia. And he'd taken the precaution of first fulfilling every task that could be done before the force from Tarrant arrived, even waiting until Walter had had time to safely row himself and Abbot Pieter more than halfway to the mainland's shore.

Having thrown the bed curtain wide, Amicia was about to descend from the bed when the chamber door flew open. "Galen, I'm here."

Silver-green eyes instantly settled on the figure revealed in the parting between two panels of tapestried cloth. Raised on her knees with masses of gold-streaked hair tumbling about narrow shoulders and lush figure, Amicia held inviting arms out to him while love softened her eyes to warm honey. Oblivious to the hunched figure that scurried past him as he strode from the doorway to the bed, he answered the look he'd come hoping to win.

Caught up in his strong arms, Amicia wasted no time in questioning the miracle of his sudden appearing. This, this was reality and worth far more than the shifting mists of a dream.

"Amicia, you must believe me," Galen's voice was a rough velvet whisper in her ear. "I love you and of my own choice would have done nothing to trick you." Explanations did not come easily to Galen. As an honest man, he'd seldom had need to attempt them. But now another's understanding was more important than ever before, and he must try. With hands on her shoulders he held her in a grip harsher than he knew as he leaned away and tried again. "I meant not to act on my feelings until I could come to you honestly as the earl's son I am and court you as the daughter of Wryborne. Then matters went awry and to save you from Gilfrey's scheme I had no choice but to take the actions I did." Frustration knotted his jaw when he reached this point only to realize that the situation had not changed. "Worse yet," he gritted out, "I still cannot tell you the reasoning behind my actions. But trust me, please trust me when I say that it will all come right in the end."

"Hush," Amicia soothed, tender fingertips reaching up to brush away the lines of stress creasing his firm cheeks before twining through cool strands of black. "I do trust you, and I'll not ask for the explanation I know you'll give when freed to do so."

Galen's answering slow smile was a thing of such power that, as in times before, Amicia melted against him. Inwardly, Galen near burst with pride to find that Jasper had been right. Amicia had given him her trust, and her trust made the coming struggle easier to face. "We've a bright future on the horizon, I swear it," he murmured, his faith in its soon coming increased by the rightness in their embrace.

As Galen kissed her with overwhelming tenderness, Amicia felt her soul rise to meet his. Truly, she marveled, here was proof that childish dreams were as useless as the shards of broken crystal her unicorn had become. In their place was a far finer reality of flesh and blood, a future certain to surpass ethereal fantasies.

All at once a horrifying certainty occurred to her. The future she envisioned could exist only so long as her all too mortal hero. Struggling to hold herself back from Galen, she gazed up at him with alarm darkening her eyes to pools of fear.

"You must go. Run," she urged. "Run from this place before my stepfather finds you here. He means to see our marriage annulled and I yet wed to his son."

"Nay, Farrold will wed his love, just as I have wed mine." At peace now that they'd come into harmony,

Galen smiled down into her earnest face. For this he had taken the risk, and it was worth any price he might be called to pay—a price surely limited by the events he'd already set in motion.

Fear strummed an urgent tune on the fine strands of Amicia's nerves. Galen showed remarkably little sign of taking his danger seriously. Had he been this frustrated with her when she'd ignored his cautions, she wondered, even as she tried again to convince him of the importance of taking care. "It's because I love you that I could not bear to have you taken from me, so please, please go now!"

In her declaration of love made not to an outlaw but the man he truly was Galen found a treasure of the greatest value and couldn't resist one last kiss. One last kiss to keep between them until they were re-united for the final scene—at the end of three days, a sennight, or longer? That uncertainty added fervency to the kiss. Lost to their surroundings, to dangers too near, the kiss blazed with a heat that made the cold spiteful words that interrupted all the more hurtful.

"How considerate of you to save me the trouble of coming for you, Wolf's Head." Gilfrey was jubilant with the unexpected gift fate had given him.

Breath caught painfully in Amicia's throat. Across Galen's broad shoulder her eyes flew to the beefy man blocking her chamber's door, blocking the only means of escape. What a wretched end to so beautiful a moment of love revealed and returned.

Galen's face had gone to carved ice, and frost coated the narrowed gaze he turned to level on the intruder. Without shifting his attention from his foe, he gently but deliberately pushed Amicia back into the bed's shadows before moving to stand facing Gilfrey, a living shield between the maid and her stepfather.

"'Tis a fair exchange—an outlaw for a priest and village of near useless serfs." Gilfrey near chortled his satisfaction. "In truth, you'd no need to steal the serfs of Brayston. I'd have given them to you willingly enough. After all, there are other villages on Wryborne and far too many serfs claiming a portion of my wealth to be fed."

Still Galen did not speak, and Gilfrey found himself shifting uncomfortably beneath the odd power in an unblinking stare of pale green. Although he wouldn't admit it, he wasn't certain he could prevent the man should he choose to leave.

"Guards!" The baron took immediate steps to prevent what he feared. "Shackle this impertinent outlaw."

As two guardsmen stepped from the hallway at Gilfrey's back, Amicia saw Mag scurry to one side, preventing one of the rough guards from knocking her from their path. By the seeing, Amicia knew how it was that Gilfrey had come upon them so quickly. While the men pulled Galen's hands behind his back and trussed them with stout rope, she blamed herself for not fully realizing the danger earlier, for allowing first the consideration of her mother's words and then the excitement of Galen's arrival to drive from her mind awareness even of the crone's existence.

"You were welcome to them all," Gilfrey repeated, regaining his confidence now that Galen was safely restrained. "Yet, for their taking, for the taking of my justly charged taxes, from you I demand the highest price of all."

Amicia's heart pounded so loud she could barely hear the Dark Lord's gleefully announced penalty.

"One week hence there will be a public execution. Always a festive event, it'll draw crowds from across the fiefdom. The serfs you thought to aid are in reality little more than savages who enjoy a bit of violence. And at the same time they'll learn the lesson of my vengeance for those who dare abuse my property— the example I meant to set with Randolf whom you stole from me."

Gilfrey's eyes burned with strange pleasure, clearly

demonstrating his enjoyment of the prospect, and Amicia found them a horror to watch.

"Galen is a lord, a member of the baronage!" Amicia argued, scrambling down from the bed's gloom into what limited light the windowless room had to offer. "You've no right to pronounce judgment on him!"

"He is an outlaw," Gilfrey instantly responded. A sneer curled his lips into the parody of a smile as he added, "Why, you yourself told me it was so. And no matter the circumstances of his birth, his crimes justify the penalty. Anyone who would *later* argue elsewise would have to argue the matter before King John." He gave Amicia a gloating smile. They both knew the king would never decide against him.

"Put him in the cage so recently robbed of its occupant." He waved his minions off to escort their charge to the dungeon. It gave him joy to contemplate the savage justice in his action and, as he followed the men, cruel laughter resounded against the stone of the stairwell.

"But he'll be killed!" Amicia fiercely argued, dodging around the larger girl, who'd sought to block her way.

"Nay." Kelda would not be so easily overruled on this and again moved in front of Amicia, calmly repeating what she'd already said more than once. "Farrold will arrive with people from Tarrant before it comes to that."

Amicia met the sincerity in dark blue eyes and tried to restrain her impatience. It would accomplish nothing for her to argue that she shared neither the other girl's optimism nor faith in the boy's abilities. "While they may well come in time, what if they don't? What good will it do if they come the next day, the next hour? Can they revive Galen by virtue of the injustice of his death?" Golden fire flamed in her eyes, and Kelda fell back under its heat.

"Surely you should wait until you've some notion of what is happening." Kelda made a last, half-hearted effort to change Amicia's intent.

"Wait? Wait until it is truly too late?" Amicia pulled open the chamber door and stepped out, looking back to add, "I've waited for a night and morn, and I cannot bear to sit quiet a moment longer. But I'll return before the evening meal. I will not be the cause of you or your family's punishment at the Dark Lord's hands. Although now that he has Galen, he's no reason to worry where I might go, even has he called off my crone-shadow."

"Then go." Kelda threw up her hands in defeat. "But what good you think to do I cannot conceive."

Amicia relented, silently admitting that Kelda's concern was for her and the other girl's attitude only a reflection of that worry. To ease Kelda's fear of the unknown, Amicia said, "I go to our no longer secret cave hoping to find Walter, Galen's squire, and ask him to fetch back Carl, Galen's second friend. With their help mayhap we've hope of some rescue, leastways some method to forestall Gilfrey's wicked deed until the people of Tarrant arrive."

Moving back into the room, Amicia lifted a hand toward her friend in a plea for understanding. "I cannot sit calmly and do nothing but wait, praying someone else saves my love. If 'twere Farrold in the dungeon, would you not do your all to see him set free? And do it no matter what others *might* do?"

Kelda saw her point and went forward to wrap her arms about the smaller girl. "Aye, that I would and I am not half so brave as you. So, tell me, what action can I take to help your cause? You've but to ask, and I will act."

"I don't know. I don't know what I'm going to do. For now I ask simply that you allow me to go without argument, without feeling my actions a denigration of your love's efforts. Remember, when Farrold set out he had no knowledge of Galen's danger, no reason to hurry the people he seeks into fast action to beat the deadline later given."

"Then go," Kelda repeated, draping about slender shoulders the dark cloak Amicia had retrieved when changing for her wedding and worn back to the isle the day before. "I will tell lies again on your behalf, if I must. Only make them worth the doing."

Amicia gave her friend a broad grin and whirled, cloak swirling out as she set off down the stairway with the light, quick step of desperation.

Amicia was thankful that the tide was down. The revealed causeway made it unnecessary for her to risk the boat again. She made the crossing with more haste than ever before. Lost in her dark thoughts of what could happen to her love, she hardly felt the strain of the climb and even moved down the cliff face with no thought to her actions. Then, as she stood at the cave entrance she forced her mind's return to immediate matters.

"Walter," she called. Fresh from the daylight, her eyes could find no more than vague shadows inside and a moment of panic held her immobile. What if, when his lord did not return, he'd gone back to Tarrant himself?

"I'm here." Walter rose from his pallet in the dark against the back wall.

The answer dispersed the haze of formless fears in Amicia's mind, and she immediately stepped further into the dim haven, wasting not a breath of time before embarking on the purpose for her visit. "I've come to tell you what's happened to your lord and beg your aid in seeing it undone." The words seemed to tumble over each other in their haste to be said.

Walter heard the desperation in his visitor's voice. For her sake alone he'd have done anything to help, but that it would aid his lord made whatever task was necessary all the more important. "I'll do whatever you ask, my lady," he solemnly swore, moving forward from gloom into the limited ring of light cast by the banked fire.

His form of address briefly diverted Amicia's attention. "You know who I really am?" It occurred neither to her nor to him that the title was hers by virtue of her marriage if naught else.

Surprise tilted Walter's head, and it picked up glints of red from dying coals, allowing them to burn anew on his light hair. "I was there at your wedding."

"'Struth, you were." It was fact she'd lost in the multitude of tangled events and emotions that lay between that time and this.

"But I knew before," he admitted. "From the first day I met you here in the cave."

Amicia had already accepted the uselessness of her dreams and put her trust in Galen. Thus, Walter's revelation that her husband and both of his supporters had known all along she was parading as something she was not aroused in her not anger but embarrassment.

Unable to distinguish her blush amidst the cave's ruddy light, Walter simply shrugged and added more. "Lord Galen told us he thought you a most remarkable woman, and I think so, too. Never met one that would climb down a cliff face or speak to strangers."

Amicia took it as the compliment it was meant to be. She had liked the earnest boy before, but now felt a kinship with him. Aye, he'd not think her asking the impossible just because she was a woman. It confirmed her choice (as if she'd had one) of him as the one to help in her quest.

"Do you know where Carl has gone, and can you fetch him back quickly?"

"I know in what direction he was sent." Walter shrugged again. "But not his specific location."

This news was not good and Amicia felt panic rising once more. With the depth of her concern aching in every word, she succinctly explained the looming danger. "Your lord is in the dungeon, and my step-father says he'll be executed one day less than a sennight from now. I know Farrold has gone to Galen's home, but we cannot be certain they'll arrive in good time when they know neither its limits nor the deadly penalty for delay."

"I'll go and get help, and not just Carl but Will, too." The lady's words had succeeded in imparting to Walter the desperate need for immediate action.

"Will?" In the first instant it was a name unfamiliar, and Amicia was not so certain that bringing strangers into this matter was a safe idea.

"Williken of the Weald, the people call him." Walter straightened with a pride he shared with others of Tarrant. "But he is Galen's cousin. That's who Galen sent the villagers to, and it's Carl who took them."

Amicia spared a tight smile. Will—Williken. She should've realized. Another thought of the recent past deepened her smile. She'd suspected that the boy who'd accompanied her and Galen from cave to abbey for the wedding had, beneath his silent demeanor, been listening intently to every word that passed between them. Plainly she'd either misjudged his curiosity or he'd a very short memory and had forgotten Galen's talk of the same deed.

"Can you fetch them back in time?" she asked. "The Weald is a large place, with few roads and no villages. How can you hope to find anyone within its boundaries?"

Walter grinned. "You don't find Willikin, he finds you. Just enter the Weald at any point and he'll be there. 'Tis a fact the French have proven right well."

Amicia thought back on the tales she'd heard of the knight who held invaders at bay, preventing them from penetrating through the Weald's dense forests. Surely, with his help, Galen could be saved.

"I'll gather my things, fetch my horse from the abbey, and go with all possible haste. It should be no more than three days, four at the outmost, before we return."

"Once you've arrived," Amicia anxiously directed, "send a message with the monk who daily collects alms from the castle. You met Ulric, he stood witness with you at the wedding. His coming and going will go unnoticed, even if the task makes necessary a second trip in one day."

The young squire was already at his packing when her own reference to a monk brought to Amicia's mind something further to question. "Abbot Pieter? What happened to Abbot Pieter?"

"He's back in his abbey, of course." Walter answered without pausing in his chore.

"'Tis surely a dangerous place for him to be."

"Nay," Walter instantly argued, turning to defend an action he'd allowed when Lord Galen had failed to appear. "He says the monks are more than able to hide whatever they must—been doing it for years. Hid three massive warhorses from your stepfather's searching men, so I believe he spoke true."

Amicia climbed the cliff wall behind Walter. They parted company beneath the shielding trees of the river bank at its top, he off to the abbey and she back to the isle in time to keep the promise she'd given Kelda to return before the evening meal.

Three days, Walter had said. Three days to survive while apprehension and the frustrations of inactivity were near bound to drive her mad.

⤜§ *Chapter 17* §⤛

The tension was too great. Amicia thought she could bear it no longer. There was no sign of the promised rescuers from Tarrant, and four days had marched into the past while a fifth was more than half down the path toward its end with still no word from Galen's young squire. Already serfs rounded up at sword point by men from the Dark Lord's garrison were camped in the courtyard and waiting on the mainland's shore to attend the morrow's execution. She must do something, anything but this endless pacing back and forth from one side of her chamber to the other. Hands tightly clasped together behind her back, she gazed down and saw not the path of crushed rushes her footsteps had laid but the caged man several levels below.

What could she do? During the night's dark hours wild plans of hope had filled her restless thoughts, but the light of day had glared with unmistakable clarity upon their crippling flaws. She'd thought to give the entire garrison Anne's wine of sleep to drink, but few among the common soldiers would willingly exchange their fiery ale for a woman's fruit-sweet brew. She'd dwelled upon a scheme to wait until her stepfather was seated at his morning meal and then slide up behind and drive her dagger into him. A plan as unworkable as the first. Hers was a woman's blade and short. Even had she the strength to thrust it to the hilt in the fleshy depths of the thickset man, although it would assuredly render a painful wound, it would not immediately kill.

Amicia sagged against the side of the high bed, so lost in failure that she barely noticed when the door opened. Her visitor would be only Kelda returning to their shared room or Anne come again to try and cajole her into better spirits with assurances of a rescue by Tarrant. A rescue too likely to arrive too late. She buried her face in her hands to hide tears of frustrated defeat.

"They caught him! They caught him!" The words were a wail.

Amicia's hands dropped away, and she stared in surprise at the unexpected woman filling the doorway with her considerable girth.

"They caught him," Orva repeated the hideous fact, advancing into the chamber as she added another. "And they put him in the dungeon."

Perplexed as much by the other's gaze—hurt, reproaching—as by what she said, Amicia tried to make sense of the accusation. "They put Galen in the dungeon days past. You must surely have heard of it before now."

"'Tis my Randolf that's been caged. My Randolf who you promised was safe!" The fine indignation that had carried Orva to Lady Amicia's chamber collapsed on the final damning word. She sagged and would have fallen had Amicia not hurried forward to wrap her arms about the worried woman and help her settle atop the steady support of the sturdy chest at the bed's foot.

"It can't be so." After climbing free of her initial shock an overwhelming guilt washed over Amicia, guilt for the certainty that Randolf's position was her fault.

"It is, it is," Orva sobbed. "I saw him dragged through the great hall and thrust down the stairwell." Tears of grief filled the lines of age Amicia had never before noticed on Orva's cheeks.

"But Galen swore Randolf had been sent to a safe haven." Numbed by the incomprehensible, as if a repetition of solid facts known of the past would change the present, Amicia said, "A sennight gone by Carl took him to—" Sudden understanding broke the flow of Amicia's words. A mind by hope revived to quickness darted through a welter of confusing thoughts to arrive at a heartening end. If Randolf had gone to the same destination as Carl yet had returned, then likely Carl was back. Proof that Walter had accomplished his task, bringing others to aid in Galen's rescue. Assuredly if they were to set Galen free, they would free Randolf as well!

"I don't know how Randolf was taken, but I am certain that an attempt will be made to save him." On her knees beside the chest, Amicia took Orva's hands in her own. "Please trust me."

Orva held a strong affection for the maid, but her impulsive habits had never been conducive to trust. Just see what sorry disappointment trusting the girl's earlier assurances had brought.

"I don't blame you for finding it difficult." And truly she didn't. How could she when so many times she'd been sent to fetch something and forgotten, had promised to return by a certain time but come near too late. "Unthinkingly have I broken many promises in the past." The brown eyes that met a tear-soaked gaze were dark with regret. "But I've grown up enough to never do so again and in the future I mean to prove it. There's little I can say at this moment to convince you we've reason to take heart except that this time the health of my love rides the same dove of hope. Although I've been near despair, now I have faith that an attempt will be made to free them. The manner of its end I cannot promise. Success is in the hands of God. Pray, Orva, as I will pray and others as well."

Following her mother's example throughout the past days of forced inaction, she'd been praying for divine aid in a successful rescue. Her mother, too, had been praying, and Amicia had a great belief in the power contained by that woman of faith's heavenly supplications. She'd learned that it was in part due to their power that she was wed not to Farrold but to a man greater than her dream hero. Surely the strength of her mother's prayers would help to see him saved.

The only good that had come from these desolate days in a fortress crouched beneath cloudy skies full of gloom were the lengthy talks she'd shared with her mother. Amicia had heard again that her mother's reason for holding distant was not lack of love, nor disappointment in her offspring but to save her daughter from pain. On the one hand that reassurance had given Amicia a peace of spirit that both soothed and lent sufficient emotional strength to survive the chaos of impatience and trepidation which rose on the other.

"We will all pray." The quiet statement came from a door left open and drew the attention of the two huddled at the end of the bed. Once more Anne had stood as witness to the comfort Amicia gave their cook, and in the maid's resolution heard a note of sincerity which she believed had transformed it to reality. At last, the girl had grown to maturity—still adventurous mayhap—but with greater sensitivity to the effect her actions would have upon others.

"Anne—" Amicia's one whispered word held a question that needed no more to be understood.

As Anne nodded a slow smile warmed her solemn face. "Aye, the message you've been praying for has arrived."

Amicia stood, relief swelling out in a deep sigh.

"Moreover," Anne added, "I believe God has truly

blessed us. As I set out to bring the news to you, Sir Oswald stopped me to say that the overabundance of activity your stepfather has indulged in during the last fortnight has brought on an exceptionally painful attack. Swollen knees have confined him to his chamber. He can nowise manage the stairs tonight."

Anne saw the flicker of gold in Amicia's eyes that doubtless heralded a spark of hope that the execution was to be postponed. To douse the flame quick before the loss of its bright warmth would leave a gloom too chilling, she quickly said, "But already has the baron given a command that two of the strongest stable serfs be ready to carry him to the courtyard at dawn."

Despite Anne's apprehensions, now that others had come to her aid, Amicia was not so easily disheartened. Although the possibility of a postponement was lost, the path for a rescue had been made infinitely smoother by the news of Gilfrey's ill health. A laugh of pure joy broke from Amicia's throat and rose on the wings of rising hope. She could go from the fortress without even the remote threat of the Dark Lord's interception to hinder her path. She could go and meet her cohorts to form the plan his ailment eased by preventing the possibility that he might see something suspicious, enabling him to foil their surely successful scheme.

The sound of footsteps on stone brought Galen to his feet. In the utter black of the dungeon it was impossible to judge the passage of time, even the few meals a surly guardsmen had thrust through ever locked bars seemed irregularly spaced. Still, he believed some considerable time had passed since he'd been dumped in the locked cage. Left in a void of darkness the frustrations of an active man held immobile, a warrior held powerless could only grow. At the first he'd confidently told himself that the final scene was near. He had only to patiently wait it out. Yet, as a man used to controlling his own fate, the feeling of restraints, of being forced to wait for others to act proved a finer punishment than any the baron could've designed.

Initially, each time a gleam of light broke the gloom, Galen's hope had soared only to crash into greater depths when a guard descended and proved it unwarranted. Thus, when appeared a fresh spot of light, small and too inadequate to fight the power of the lower level's great blackness, Galen refused to pay more than cursory attention. It was the dragging noise and sound of blows landing as the light wavered down the open stairway that brought Galen cautiously to his feet. Not until three figures drew near, two guards hauling an awkward giant in the middle, could Galen be certain he'd recognized the prisoner.

One guardsmen opened the cage door, while the second shoved the fresh captive into the barred enclosure.

"In then, dolt. Plainly you lack the wits even to know that coming back to Wryborne was daft." Metal clanged shut a moment after Randolf's body thudded to a floor strewn with moldy straw.

Galen sank to his knees beside the hulking man and quickly rolled him face up, intending to check for injuries before the light disappeared up the steps. By the now distant taper's glimmer he saw a grinning Randolf wink. Sitting back on his heels, Galen waited for the shutting of a door at the stairway's top to close them into the privacy of utter blackness.

"Why are you here?" He asked the instant it was safe, questioning not only Randolf's presence in the cage but on Wryborne at all.

Not too surprisingly, Randolf heard only the obvious meaning of the question. "I come to tell you that we're going to rescue you."

"If you're here to rescue me, you've taken a strange avenue," Galen said, a dryness to his tone that totally escaped Randolf. "I've never known anyone to be liberated by another's joining his imprisonment."

The meaning of Galen's last words sank slowly into Randolf's understanding and when they did his low laugh rolled. "Nay, I've not come to do the saving, just to tell you the plan afore it begins."

"Whose plan is this?" So far as he knew Walter was the only supporter he had left in the near vicinity, and he'd no real faith in the boy's as yet half-developed talent for strategy. But then Randolf wasn't supposed to be here either, which brought back the even bigger question. "And why are you here when I sent you to safety in the Weald?"

"The women and children of the village stay safe in the Weald." Taking umbrage with the apparent suggestion that they'd done elsewise, a stiff response rumbled from Randolf's still prone chest. "But we men come back to free you."

Unseen in the darkness, Galen's fists clenched. He was getting nowhere except to learn that matters were even worse than he'd thought. Forcing himself to patience, Galen tried again to win some sensible explanation. "How did you know I was here?" One question at a time, one simple question, requiring only a simple answer.

Randolf sat up, anxious to impart the news. "Lady Amicia sent Walter to fetch Carl. It was he who told us the baron had locked you up for wedding Lady Sybil's daughter."

"And you decided to return and rescue me?" Although initially vexed with Amicia for starting this campaign, Galen reminded himself that he should have known Amicia, unlike the average female of his acquaintance, would never meekly stand by uselessly wringing her hands while he was in danger. 'Twas in part why he loved her. Moreover, had he not of recent times realized how very difficult it was to wait helplessly for others to take action? Nay, he couldn't fault

Amicia for her efforts on his behalf but that fact laid the entire load of guilt on his back. He'd specifically kept the people of Brayston ignorant of his true identity. Even had he sent a message with Carl forbidding his cousin Will from talking of it. By such actions he was to blame in their return to danger for the sake of helping him, unknowing of the others he had to call upon.

"I'm sorry that you've all risked so much when likely there is little need." Galen told the other man, voice as vivid a reflection of his sincere regret as a glimpse of his solemn face would have been. "I'm not who you think I am and have powerful friends who are sure to come to my aid."

"Nay." Nothing could be seen, but a movement in the air made it clear that Randolf was emphatically shaking his head. "You are Galen Fitz William, heir to Tarrant." Randolf produced this piece of information with the pride of one who has worked to memorize a difficult passage of script. "We know who you are and that your family comes—but we intend to make certain they don't arrive too late. You saved us, now 'tis our turn to save you. We all agreed, 'tis only just."

Galen's heart was warmed by the knowledge that they were willing to tempt the spiteful baron's fury on his account, yet it merely increased his alarm for them and his frustration in being held powerless when the danger in poor timing was very real. What possibility of else than ignoble defeat had weak, ill-fed farmers against the baron's trained warriors, few though they be? Keeping his voice utterly free of the emotions roiling inside, he asked another simple question. "What is this plan you've come to tell me?"

"'Tis a good one," Randolf was quick to say, plainly pleased with his part in the scheme although he gave credit where it was due. "But if it hadn't a'been for Willikin we'd a'been lost."

251

"Willikin? My cousin Will is the source of your plan?" Excitement vibrated in Galen's tone. Will had turned a crowd of common folk into the most effective defense in the country, and if Will was involved then he'd nothing to fear for the gentle people of Brayston.

Stepping from the ledge with its light of cloudy day into the dim cave, as always Amicia paused, waiting for her eyes to adjust. Slowly her surroundings came into focus, and the shadow directly in front of her resolved itself into a man—a stranger yet not a stranger.

"You are my cousin's bride?"

The voice rumbled from the chest of one whom she'd have known was related to Galen even had he not told her so. He was as tall, as powerfully built, as dark. But where Galen's eyes had the penetrating power of green crystal shards, this man's held the depths of night. Amicia's first urge was to step back from the impact of his presence, just as she had the first time she encountered Galen on this very spot. But she'd learned enough from the first experience to prevent herself from a dangerous repetition.

Walter came forward to stand at the man's side yet Amicia would not allow her attention to shift, a certain betrayal of her nervousness. Long moments passed in silence while dark eyes slowly moved from honey-hued tresses to toes. Under his prolonged examination, she proudly tilted her chin, anxious to prove herself worthy as Galen's choice.

"Galen has always been a fortunate man, and I see his luck has held true." The flash of the man's white smile was unmistakable even in the cave's eternal twilight.

After a lifetime of Wryborne's seclusion, Amicia had limited experience to draw upon and, unfamiliar with such flattering manners, had no notion of how to respond properly. She simply stated, "I am Lady Amicia of Castle Dungeld."

"And honored I am to meet Lady Amicia of Castle Dungeld," the stranger responded, an underlying thread of amusement warming solemn words. Before she realized what he was about, he'd gallantly lifted her hand and brushed a kiss across its back. "I am William and naught but a simple knight."

Amicia heard Walter choking on the understatement and gave the too modest claim a prompt reply. "Ah, then you are not, as I had heard, the great Willikin of the Weald whom the whole country has reason to thank?" Having spoken without forethought, still she was pleased with her response. How better to prove the possession of quick mind and tongue, the very things that might convince this leader to allow her a part in the rescue of her love.

William laughed outright, a free and open sound. "There are those who call me that. But, in truth, I am only a knight with friends among the common folk who lend me their aid, not a great lord with armies at my command." He liked this maid who showed fear of neither his much lauded strength nor of offending his pride.

"It would seem you had little need of an army to forestall more than one powerful foreign lord with all their great legions," Amicia answered, then drove right to the heart of her reason for coming. "But can you halt the wrongful punishment of an innocent man held in the dungeons of a well-fortified castle?"

"I alone cannot, but with the men of Brayston I can and no doubt will."

The grimness of his tone prevented Amicia from taking his answer as an unjustly flip response. Nonetheless, there was a problem with his reasoning, a major flaw. "There are no people in Brayston. The village is empty."

"Is it?" The laughter was back in his voice. "I think you've not considered the matter. Where did those people go? Why to me. However, when they heard of the danger to their savior, in part because of his work on their behalf, they chose to return and help me see an end to the tyranny. And an end it will be—not by my hand nor theirs alone, but by the coming of their true lord."

By sworn oath Will was forbidden to tell the secret that he'd heard had caused a major rift between his cousin and this lovely lady. But, if he could prod her to ask pertinent questions, how could he fail to answer honestly? Soon he discovered his efforts were of little use. She had a goal of her own and nothing would turn her aside. That of itself was reassuring. Her unwavering concern for Galen must mean the bond between them was stronger than others thought, strong enough to hold despite the strains laid upon it.

"You talk in riddles, when all I want are facts." It seemed that Will was trying to tell her something, but Amicia was impatient with anything that did not move Galen's rescue forward and promptly asked, "What is to be done, and how can I see it hastened?"

"We were discussing that very matter, come and sit with us." He motioned toward the firepit about whose outer perimeter, Amicia was surprised to note, a group of men were gathered.

Walter had returned to their number and sat beside Carl, whom she should've expected to see. On his other side she found the solemn village leader, Edgar. And next to him Sir Jasper who'd gone unpunished although Galen had successfully crossed the sea and freed the abbot while he was standing at watch. Gilfrey had too few guardsmen in a garrison depleted by the king's demands. In this they were fortunate, for he couldn't afford to be without even one, which meant they'd already a friend planted inside the castle's defenses, a friend able to loosen its protective shield from the inside out.

As Amicia settled down at Walter's side, her confidence bloomed in the smile she gave the dark man who'd begun to speak. With such a diverse group of leaders, surely they could not fail in whatever plan Will had devised.

ᵉᔑ *Chapter 18* ᔒᵉ

The dark of a cloudy, moonless night lay heavy atop the ramparts of Castle Dungeld, and Amicia's heart pounded. For another long moment she quietly watched a lone guardsman from the shadowed doorway between tower and the parapet walkway where he stood, back to her. This was her part in the plan, small enough yet all the rest might be impossible were she to fail. Summoning her much practiced facade of bravado, she put a smile on her lips and stepped out.

"Sir Oswald—"

The called knight turned toward the maid in surprise, eyes narrowing with suspicion as she approached.

"I hoped you might appreciate some fruit wine to warm you." Amicia extended a chalice filled near to overflowing, holding it perfectly steady by effort of will alone.

Doubtful of the motivation for a deed never done before, Oswald took a step back, on the brink of refusing the too sweet brew.

Amicia forced a potent warmth into her smile and a honeyed blending of regret and pleading into her tone as she explained. "In recent days I've had time to consider the foolishness of childhood dreams and have realized that 'tis past time to grow up, heal old wounds, and start anew." These words at least held the unmistakable ring of truth, enough to cover the insincerity of those that followed. "This," she said, and the engraved pattern on the silver goblet gleamed even in the cloud-restricted light as she raised it a little higher, "is my attempt to make peace between us, to bridge the gap of the many cold years since you dropped my unicorn from this very place."

Still, Oswald hesitated. In his position he was not privy to all the castle gossip, but he had heard enough to know something about the battle of wills being waged between her and Baron Gilfrey. Yet, how could he reject the symbol of conciliation offered by his lord's smiling stepdaughter, the woman who almost certainly would someday be lady of the castle (a probability made more important by the baron's worsening health.)

Amicia restrained an urge to laugh her exultation when the knight took the offered vessel, tilted his head back, and drained it in one long draw. Accepting the emptied goblet from his sword-callused hand, she gave a pretty curtsy and promptly turned, anxious to hide the grin she feared was bound to break free.

Oswald watched her graceful retreat and shrugged his puzzlement for the mystifying doings of women before turning his attention back to the chore at hand.

An uncounted length of time passed between her leavetaking and the moment he found himself dozing against the tower's stone wall and shoved away to stamp his feet. The evening chill had failed to hold back waves of drowsiness, and he shook his head to rouse himself before marching to the opposite end of the walkway. That wine must have been more potent than he'd thought possible.

He leaned out to gaze across endless stretches of a sea faintly seen but heard roaring against the rocks below, too dazed to hear another's approach or protect himself from the blow that gave a justifiable excuse to sleep. The dark figure behind caught the falling man and quietly dragged his senseless form into the tower, then hoisted him over one shoulder.

"You could've avoided the headache you'll awake with, Oswald, had you allowed me to take the night watch." Jasper's words were a nearly inaudible whisper as he deposited the unconscious man in one of the upper level's empty chambers. But then, Oswald took his duties as guard captain seriously, not surprising considering how well acquainted the man was with his lord's black temper.

When the baron's swollen legs had prevented him from descending for an evening meal at the high table, a worried Sir Oswald had insisted on taking the night watch himself, although Jasper was to have done the duty. That decision had threatened to block the path of their plan for waylaying the morrow's execution. It was unfortunate but understandable that Oswald had feared he'd be blamed for any possible wrongs while the baron was immobile; and, therefore, had done his best to see all went smoothly.

Jasper had entertained grave doubts about the only alternative that seemed open. As the only male supporter of the plot who could safely enter the fortress before sunset, he'd thought it possible to overcome Oswald alone on the parapet. Yet, too likely Oswald would've been able to successfully summon help from below before the deed was complete. Jasper could only be thankful for Amicia's resourceful suggestion and use of the sleep-inducing wine.

After efficiently stripping off Oswald's uniform, Jasper lost no time in securely binding the man hand and foot then affixing a gag in his mouth. Lifting the resin-soaked torch left waiting by the door, he quickly slipped from the chamber. In no more than a moment, he'd lit the torch from the flame in one of the stairwell's oil-fed sconces and stepped back onto the ramparts. His purpose, unlike Oswald's, was not to hold the fortress against invaders but rather to wave an invitation with broad sweeps of the bright beacon in his hands.

By the time the pre-dawn's dull gray had crept into an unwelcoming eastern sky, the once empty chamber on the castle's highest level was full and a man wearing an odd-fitting uniform stood guard outside its barred door. The dreadful hour appointed by the baron was rapidly approaching, and the courtyard was astir with a milling crowd of uncomfortable serfs.

Amicia stepped from the castle's outgoing door. 'Twas a portal she so seldom used that she paused uncertainly at the top of the long flight of wooden steps leading down from the great hall, one level above ground, to the courtyard below. Her mother was already waiting at its foot and to one side. She beckoned to her daughter, and as Amicia descended, she took note of an important lesson in the other woman's serene face. Despite the anticipation for a happy conclusion bubbling inside, she must control the smile on her own.

Of all the times she'd sought to emulate her mother's composure, and failed, this was indisputably the most important and she must not fail this time. At first it was a difficult task, but by mentally stepping back and taking a realistic view of the coming scene, she found herself caught between excitement over what was planned and fear for the shadows of unknown possibilities.

By the time the Dark Lord, carried atop the joined arms of two strong stable serfs, was brought from the shadowy tunnel through the castle's thick wall, she'd tamed her expression with remarkably little effort into the deep anguish she knew he would expect.

The baron was glad that dark clouds hovered above

to restrain the sun's power. Any brighter light would surely have sent knives of pain through a head already throbbing from a night spent in solitary celebration of the coming victory—leastways a victory in part. With Galen Fitz William dead, a Tarrant without heir would lie in defeat. At the same time, Gilfrey had no doubt but that Farrold would come crawling back in the end, returning to his hand the weapon with which he could stand evermore triumphant over Wryborne —an heir. In preparation, he meant to keep Amicia safely locked in the tower from the moment the execution was complete until that day of the marriage he'd long planned.

As he was slowly lowered to the ground next to the maid who was source of the many wrongs perpetrated against him, Gilfrey gave her a look of such loathing that Amicia's confidence took a battering. Only could she comfort herself that he'd never suspect the coming deeds by her reactions.

Gilfrey braced himself upright on his two swollen legs, and the resulting agony was distraction enough that though he saw men wearing his livery, he gave no particular attention to those he sharply commanded.

"Fetch the prisoners up from the dungeon to face my justice." The satisfaction in the command burned like acid, and Gilfrey was pleased by how quickly the guardsmen departed to fulfill his words. He'd trained them well by use of the only instrument they respected—fear. The same fear that had enforced his hold on the fiefdom for close on two decades. Even now its dark stain filled the wide eyes of the summoned audience, who glanced apprehensively at the beheading block and quickly away. Aye, by this day's work they'd all learn the deadly folly in rebelling against his rule, in seeking to claim any part of what belonged to him.

Amicia watched a cruel sneer spread thin lips wide as the baron studied first the terrified people and then the thick oak slab placed amidst the courtyard, ominous brown splotches soaked into its chop-marred surface. That symbol of what Gilfrey had planned for her Galen sent a cold shiver through Amicia.

Feeling his stepdaughter's involuntary reaction lightened Gilfrey's mood. It was gratification enough to make up for the failure of his prediction that the serfs would enjoy an execution, leaving him to compel their attendance. But then, he'd rather enjoyed proving he could.

Striving to regain her composure, Amicia stared at the earth beneath her feet, hard packed by the anonymous comings and goings of endless daily traffic. Slowly it seeped into her awareness that despite the vast number of people crammed within the courtyard's towering walls, a strained silence of amazing depth had fallen.

Sir Jasper had arrived behind the baron, and he, too, was sensitive to the unusual quiet. 'Twas as if even the stones of a castle taken by treachery waited impatiently for that wrong to be put right. Having accepted Galen's right as Amicia's husband to speak or withhold secrets, he'd said nothing of the end purpose of the coming scene.

Footfalls on stone, though no heavier than others, seemed to echo from the castle's exit tunnel. Although every eye lifted to the two guardsmen and the prisoners they escorted through its archway, only one of the four held the attention of all. From the stairway top, utterly unfazed, silver-green eyes coolly scanned the crowd before dropping to the plainly exultant baron with a chill that gave even him a moment's pause.

Gilfrey, impatient to secure his coming triumph, took an unwise step forward and grimaced in renewed agony, but didn't allow it to hinder the start.

"To demonstrate what befalls any man who seeks to steal what is mine, take the big lout's hands off first." Gloating contempt filled the order that scraped past the growl of pain lodged unheard in Gilfrey's throat. "Let the outlaw have a taste of what awaits him."

The half-fearful brown eyes Amicia had lifted to the black-haired man warmed to honey when he met the look with a sudden merry smile and a wink.

The growl that now rumbled in earnest from the baron was born not of pain but fury. "Nay, take the Wolf's Head! The Wolf's Head dies first!" The new command was reinforced by a glare of such vicious animosity that 'twas a wonder it failed to kill of itself.

With no notice given the fuming baron, Galen descended the steps unaccompanied and unimpeded by the guardsmen who'd escorted him from the dungeon. He moved to stand directly in front of Amicia and raise her hand to his lowered lips.

In a temper beyond pain, beyond reason, Gilfrey pulled a dagger from the sheath at his waist and leaped at the outlaw others had failed to halt.

Cheeks blush-warmed, Amicia lifted adoring eyes from the black head bent over the palms he'd turned upwards for a more intimate caress. She caught a glimpse of the flashing blade and instinctively threw herself sideways against an unprepared Galen while a scream she never remembered giving resounded across the courtyard.

Sprawled flat on his back by the small burden that spread protectively atop his chest, Galen's startled gaze rose to see Will restrain the vindictive baron with ease. Relieving Gilfrey of both dagger and sword, the far stronger man had no compunction against tossing an again pain-ridden body to the wooden steps as if it were so much refuse—which, from the view of those who'd loved Baron Conal, he was.

"Love, hah!" Will grimaced down with mock disgust at his prone cousin. "What fools it makes of normally sane men." He tucked the baron's dagger into his own boot, then, holding a sword in each hand, returned his attention to their crumpled foe.

The dark velvet laugh Galen gave in response to the man's jest at the expense of his romantic but foolish action held a quality of unrepentant joy. He felt no need to offer an excuse when in his arms he undeniably held the perfect reason for the daft deed—soft, honey-sweet, and his own reckless guardian.

Of a sudden Amicia realized that despite the distraction of the fallen baron, they'd an audience of their own, and she made to rise. Galen merely wrapped her more firmly in his embrace as he sat up and then rose to his feet with his claimed treasure still tenderly cradled in loving arms.

When blind rage cleared from Gilfrey's vision, he discovered himself lying limp and defenseless on the ground, surrounded by the sword points of men dressed in his colors yet not his guardsmen.

"I am the king's man, you filthy blackguards!" Gilfrey sputtered and, as always when under adversity, snarled threats. "The king will not stand for this attack!"

"The king will have to hear of it first." The wry smile that accompanied William's words increased Gilfrey's frustration.

From the safety of Galen's strong arms, on the outer edge of the men encircling the Dark Lord, Amicia watched the deep frown that furrowed his rage-reddened face. Almost she could see his thoughts— Who was this man? And then when his narrowed eyes shifted from Will to Galen and back, she saw him recognize another of Tarrant lineage and his impotent fury increase.

"And 'twill be difficult for his ears to hear your cries from the dungeon's depths." The circle around Gilfrey widened, allowing Galen and his welcome burden to move to the front and squarely face the incapacitated baron. "Gentle Lord." The title was awarded with a mocking grin. "I doubt your royal friend finds your contributions to his cause worth the

loss of those rendered by Williken of the Weald."
Galen graciously nodded toward his cousin, who
swept an elegant bow.

Before Gilfrey could do more than stare at them
dumbfounded, a murmured breeze, begun at the
gates, grew in force to a stormy wind. It seemed to
part the crowd with its roar as it swept through their
midst, leaving clear a broad path to the smaller group
gathered about the stairway.

A sizeable force had filled the open gateway and
advanced, but Gilfrey saw only the horseman in its
lead who bore the shield of Tarrant. It was an unnecessary emblem of identity after one glance into the
freezing gray eyes of the famed Ice Warrior.

"Ah," Galen whispered, a pleased smile warming
his face as he steadily met his father's gaze. "They've
come. Although, if not for you," he gave Amicia a
gentle squeeze, "likely not quite in time to save my
life."

The stark realization of how narrowly her love had
escaped death momentarily robbed Amicia of breath
and a measure of the warm happiness of success in
which she'd been reveling.

Galen felt the soft woman once pliant against him
go tense and his attention instantly dropped to her.
"By your actions in summoning Carl and Will, you
saved my life." He gazed into eyes gone dark with fear
until the green flames in his melted hers to golden
honey. "And I thank you for the gift." Heedless of the
curious, gaping crowd, even of the approaching army,
Galen bent to take Amicia's mouth in a kiss of fire
that she'd neither will nor wish to resist.

"Nay!" Gilfrey's open hand made a loud cracking
sound as it slapped down on a use-smoothed step,
demanding and receiving attention. "I'll not be defeated by the hand of Tarrant! Not again!" In his
overwhelming frustration and anger, he made the
belligerent declaration without regard to his clear

inability to back the words with action, and all the while glared from the force's leader to Galen and Will.

"'Tisn't Tarrant that surrounded you with the sword," Galen flatly pointed out, lowering Amicia to her feet as he met the baron's gaze with eyes gone to green ice.

For the first time Gilfrey closely examined the faces of the armed men who'd initially surrounded him—triumphantly smiling and serfs of Brayston all.

"You've been defeated by the people of Wryborne who were driven by your poor stewardship to bring you low. By your own misdeeds you've lost—just as your king has lost near all of a once mighty empire through his own greed and arrogance."

Gilfrey fell coward beneath the power of truth in a steady green gaze and turned his face toward the three men who'd dismounted to draw nearer on foot. His gaze skittered away from a clash with eyes of silver frost and fell on—Farrold. Farrold! The blame for this dreadful event could rightly be laid at Farrold's door!

"You're a fool," Gilfrey reviled his son, "and I disown you! Who now will hire a knight known to have betrayed his own father?" He put every drop of his helpless wrath into the poisonous brew he poured over Farrold in belittling words. "The craven, weak-wit you are could never have sprung from my loins. You threw away your chance to found a great dynasty through which we'd both live on; threw away your chance for position as lord of the great fiefdom of Wryborne!"

"Nay, he could never be that." The quiet statement was firmly made by the third figure who now stepped in front of Farrold. Calmly he removed his helm and doffed his coif, to reveal thick, tawny hair. "I've come to claim my own."

The Sybil who had stood in tranquil prayer all through the earlier tumultuous events nearly collapsed. Only a brightly beaming Anne held her up-right. Forcing back her own shock, Amicia rushed to her aid.

"It cannot be!" Gilfrey gasped. "I killed you and the dead do not rise in daylight."

"You tried," the newcomer responded. "But though you succeeded in your mortal attack on my father, you failed to see me dead."

Sybil's breath sighed out and even that faint sound came to the speaker of these incredible words. He turned toward the sound and slowly approached, head tilted to one side.

"Mother?"

Sybil shook her head in stupefied amazement until Anne spoke. "It's true. He is your son, Amicia's twin. He was carried from the cradle by Mag, then left to die alone and helpless in the forest." The cold horror of that past hour filled Anne's voice and compelled Sybil to look up and into the confirmation of her steady gaze.

A deep silence had settled over the courtyard again as every ear strained to hear Anne's explanation of unbelievable events. "I saw the deed from the window in your chamber and sent Jasper to rescue the babe. We knew Gilfrey would find a way to kill your son before he reached an age to protect himself. Thus, in secret Jasper took him to safety with Conal's friend, the Earl of Tarrant."

A groan of final defeat came from the vengeful man who'd wickedly taken another man's home and family. Sir Jasper, with Edgar's help, lifted and hauled Gilfrey away, none too gently, leaving the victors in a peace long years awaited.

"We've held him protected and raised him with our own family." The earl had come to stand behind Sybil's lost son returned and laid his hand on one shoulder while he continued the tale. "He's grown to be a fine young man of whom Conal would be proud."

Sybil looked from the long unseen but familiar face

of a friend to another familiar face—a young version of her dead husband. Silent tears dripped down her face. She'd prayed for her daughter's safety and been granted a miracle. Amicia was safe and wed to a fine man—and Conal lived again!

"Conal?" she whispered, tentatively reaching out to brush a lock of tawny hair disarrayed by the helm and coif he'd worn.

"Tiernan, mother." The response was near as emotional as the question. He'd waited a lifetime for this moment.

"Tiernan—your father's second name. A fine choice." Face glowing with a happiness near too great to be borne, Sybil smiled up through her tears at Garrick, the man who'd stood as foster father to her son, just as she had once stood foster mother to his. A double bond between their families to be added to those of friendship and marriage.

"We feared to risk giving a name too recognizable for fear we'd alert Gilfrey," Garrick quietly explained, and as he mournfully shook his head even the gray light of a cloudy day gleamed on the wings of silver that flowed from his temples down amidst the black. "Nessa and I wanted to come to your aid immediately when we learned Conal had been taken. But then your marriage was performed and the boy arrived so soon after that we feared to put him at risk."

"Once I arrived," Galen had come to stand close behind a still stunned Amicia knocked off balance by the utterly unexpected arrival, "I saw the way things were, with a garrison near stripped of men." He told how he'd arranged to give the tale its happy ending. "And by that I knew the time had come for a wrong to be righted. The people of Wryborne deserve their own just lord."

A ripple of agreement passed through the crowd of serfs pressed tight together to make room for Tarrant's guardsmen.

"And now, mother," Tiernan proudly stated, raising his voice to be certain all would hear, "I am able to claim the lands by my own right. Even King John cannot deny me my blood heritage."

A resounding cheer shattered the silence and settled into the dull roar of marveling serfs each trying to tell another of their joy at one and the same time. In the happy confusion of the many actions that followed, Anne enlisted Will's help. Together they escorted Lady Sybil to her chamber. She was still weak from the long fast Gilfrey had imposed and near overmastered by the draining maelstrom of the morn's widely varied emotions and events.

Amicia gave her departing mother a loving smile but, once the older woman had turned to go, she immediately fell back into new worries. Since the moment she'd looked upon the face that was a masculine image of her own, Amicia had been sorting through the many facts that had suddenly changed complexion. Foremost among them, was the realization of how unjust she'd been in accusing Galen of ulterior motives in wedding her. She was no heiress. Indeed, she had nothing at all to offer the great and wealthy lord he was.

Tilting her head and glancing up from the corner of her eyes, she caught a glimpse of his flashing smile and crystal eyes. Still near behind her, he was telling a father he closely resembled of the morn's earlier events. The earl, with the silver streaks so great a contrast to his black hair but so perfect a match for his eyes, had an altogether striking appearance. No wonder Galen, with his midnight hair and green crystal eyes, was so stunningly handsome. And she had once worried he would think himself unequal to her social standing. She cringed at the remembered thought when in reality it was she who was lacking.

Galen felt the touch of brown eyes; and, as always, they summoned his attention. He wrapped his arm about her, drew her back against his chest, and glanced down. Fresh from talk of the fine victory over a foul man, and this woman's, his remarkable wife's, action in setting into motion the plan that had accomplished it and kept him in one piece, Galen was elated. It deepened his shock when he saw her horror in new knowledge. Before he could speak to her, another did.

"Amicia?" Tiernan softly called her attention from his foster brother. "Farrold said I would recognize you immediately and now I see why."

He was taller, broader and masculine, but as Amicia looked into golden brown eyes, she felt as if she were looking into her own. "I—I welcome you to Castle Dungeld." She forced her mind to the present and for the first time put into practice a lesson of good manners Anne had taught her long ago. "I welcome you to Wryborne—" She stopped abruptly. That was wrongly said. One did not treat a castle's lord as a visiting stranger. She weakly added, "—your home."

"My home." Tiernan nodded, realizing that somehow he'd brought discomfort to this reverse side of himself and sorry for it. "But your home as well." He'd no wish to bring aught but good to her life. "It always has been and always will be."

"Oh, no," Galen objected with a friendly smile, emphatically shaking his head above the girl's tawny hair, for once restrained in neatly coiled braids. "You exchange homes. By your action today Dungeld Castle becomes yours, but by marrying me days past hers became Castle Tarrant."

"And you'll be amazed by the enthusiastic welcome you receive there, and not for your saving of Galen's life alone." The earl smiled a first greeting at his new daughter-in-law. "Nessa and I, as well as the whole of Tarrant, have been waiting for this addition to our family far too long, and I fear your greatest problem will be keeping yourself from being smothered by kindnesses."

Looking into the older man's warm and open smile,

Amicia instantly responded. "In truth, it would be a pleasant change, but I fear my tongue, too long trained to sharpness, will offend."

"Ah, then you'll be comfortable in your new home." By her choice of words she'd instantly won Garrick's unqualified approval. "I had worried you might find that my demand for honesty in all things creates too harsh an environment for you to flourish."

"Don't let him scare you," Tiernan said. "I've lived in Castle Tarrant for more than seventeen years and have yet to see anything more threatening than a healthy training to right ways cushioned with abundant love. Nonetheless, I hope you'll not depart too soon."

Tiernan looked up into Galen's face as he gave his reasoning in a gentle plea. "I'd like the opportunity to build a relationship with this twin sister I've never known before she's taken away from me again."

"A sennight, no more. Then I take her away where we can spend time together *alone*—" Galen gave his father a meaningful stare before bending near Amicia's ear to whisper, "with a real bed and unthreatened privacy and endless time."

Amicia blushed and quickly glanced at her brother, who held his expression too innocent to be sincere. The earl made no effort to hide his amusement with his son's words. Abashed, before strange men only just met, Amicia shrank deeper into Galen's hold and turned part way around to hide her yet peach-tinted face against the broad chest from which a deep laugh rumbled.

"I'd never have believed my adventurous, willful, brazen wife would withdraw from a challenge had I not seen it with my own eyes!"

Hours later in the chamber long shared with Kelda but which now and for the length of their stay had been devoted to her and Galen, Amicia tried to talk seriously with a man who was having none of it.

"Really, Galen." Intending, even by her stance, to demonstrate her determination, with hands on the first gentle flare of her hips, she stood a pace back from the opening of parted bedcurtains. But the position required her to gaze down at the comfortably prone man already half-undressed, leaving the magnificent planes of his chest bare and inviting. 'Twas an unfair weapon if ever there was one and too likely successful against her apparently futile words. "It is wrong of you to take me as wife. I've nothing to offer you, nothing."

"You may have forgotten, wife, but 'tis too late for second thoughts—you *are* mine!" Sitting up, Galen pulled her down across his lap and nuzzled the vulnerable curve of her neck.

"But I made such dreadful, groundless accusations about your motives!" A true and deep regret was there in her tone but the voice that delivered it was disgustingly breathless.

"Aye," Galen gave a mock growl that sounded more like a satisfied purr. "And I've methods of my own to see you pay for them." He bit teasingly at her ear lobe. "Besides, you also gave me your trust even though I'd withheld truth from you. So, you see, the fault rests with me, not you."

With firm resolve to lay a measure of distance between them, Amicia put both hands on his chest and pushed back. A mistake of epic proportions which she discovered when she felt the firm texture of skin and black curls above a heart whose accelerating beat matched her own. "Whose fault anything is makes no change in the fact that I have nothing to bring a great lord."

"What nonsense you speak." Galen shook his head and thick black strands brushed her throat as he leaned forward to kiss the dip at its base and moved back again, but only a breath away. "Though you've had no chance to know your brother, you may be certain that Tiernan is an honorable man and would doubtless see his sister well provided for—were I to allow it. And make no mistake—I will refuse any offer of dowry he extends."

Amicia opened her mouth to argue, but Galen laid a restraining finger across their soft, tempting curve and then lingered to brush teasingly as he continued. "You'd no wish to be wed solely for the sake of what you possessed. So, by the reverse of the same logic, why should my choice of bride be dictated by what I possess? I married you knowing you were not an heiress, and I want nothing more than all that your sweet self is—too adventurous, dangerously independent, and a beguiling wanton."

"But I've sworn to reform!" Amicia argued, then sighed as Galen gave her a tormentingly short kiss. "Never again will I put another at risk with my wild ways." The declaration that should have been forceful, though no less sincere, faded into a pause of anticipation as he kissed her once more but still with heat enough only to demonstrate the depth of her need for one more satisfying.

"I'm pleased you don't mean others to suffer for your deeds, but I hope you'll not change too much—" Tangling his fingers into tawny silk, he slowly pulled her close and filled the void he'd created with fire. "I like your wanton ways all too well! Just swear you'll never pursue another man as you pursued me, shamelessly seducing me when I meant to leave you pure."

"You didn't want me?" Amicia maintained her hold on rationality long enough to secure an all-important answer.

While eyes of pale crystal held Amicia willingly in their thrall, Galen quietly told her what he'd longed for almost from the first moment when she'd come to him in the cave. "'Struth, I intended to protect your chastity," a smile of wicked potency appeared, "but only until I could come honestly and claim you with no secrets between us."

Amicia found it a most satisfying answer, but not half so satisfying as what came after she allowed her lover to again lead the way into a blazing reality far, far better than ever any fantasy could be.

☙ *Epilogue* ❧

November of 1216

So, we've further confirmation—King John is dead, a victim of his own gluttony." Galen's quiet statement was flat as he laid the parchment from Dungeld Castle which he'd just read to Amicia on the table beside the big, soft-padded chair where he sat.

Contentedly curled across the lap of the strong, handsome man she loved even more than before, Amicia felt the low thunder of his voice reverberating in the chest beneath her cheek as he continued, a wry twist to the words.

"I doubt that so much as one living creature seriously mourns his passing. Except—Gilfrey, mayhap. What say you?" With a gently mocking smile, Galen tilted his dark head to look down at the sweet maid lying soft and warm in his arms.

Amicia returned his smile ruefully but a slight shrug was her only answer. Her black days under the Dark Lord's hold had receded into the remote past, and she preferred not to let their unpleasant memories spread a shadow over the bright present. In the weeks since she'd come to Castle Tarrant, Amicia had easily adjusted to life in a castle where laughter and love reigned.

For all that the Earl and his lady, as well as their

youngest daughter also lived within, she and Galen had every opportunity for privacy. They'd the massive fortress's entire West Tower to themselves and inhabited the level where, before his peaceful death at a ripe old age, Galen had told her, resided Lord William, the grandfather he shared with Will. The whole floor was divided into only two chambers of incredible size and this one had luxuries of the sort she'd only heard about—a massive fireplace and glass windows! At day's end, as now, they sat in tranquil harmony before the warm glow of a crackling blaze.

"You've the right of it. It makes no difference now," Galen absently agreed, stroking the sun-streaked waves flowing down her back. "Nonetheless, I take joy in the guarantee of our peace that comes in knowing that Gilfrey loses all hope of support by the death of his royal cohort and equal in treachery. Why even has William the Marshal been named regent and protector of John's nine-year-old heir. The Marshal and Gilfrey have been foes near as long as he and my father."

While Galen went on about the shifting politics sure to follow the change in monarch, Amicia's thoughts drifted to another bit of information gleaned from the short letter, and when his words drifted into silence, she mused aloud.

"'Tis amazing how time seems to flow in a circle—Sir Jasper as guard captain under my father, then reduced to mere guardsman by Gilfrey, and now returned to his position of honor by my father's heir." She paused before adding another example. "Then, too, our parents were dear friends until one wicked man broke the pattern and unknowingly divided a pair of babes between them, yet it was healed when you and I were wed."

"Aye, all in a circle." Galen agreed with the perceptive woman whose hair, even skin, were gilded by the fire and stroked by the green flames beginning to glow in his crystal eyes. "Still, I was surprised to read

275

Jasper pled Oswald's case and won the right to keep him as guardsman."

"Beyond the one hurtful deed done while sotted and repented many times, Oswald merely fulfilled his duty for the lord who employed him and did it to the best of his talents. No one can fault him for that." Amicia glanced up into a sardonic gaze and instantly defended her position. "Jasper has a strong sense of justice. Adding that to his awareness of how very difficult 'twould be for a man of Oswald's age to find employment elsewhere—particularly after the ignoble end to which his former lord came—his action is not surprising at all."

Having heard from Amicia the story of Oswald and her unicorn, Galen hugged his lady of the soft heart and brushed a kiss across the top of her freed tresses. Although now she strived to live up to the expected image of a well-bred woman by keeping them restrained, he preferred them loose.

Amicia felt guilty about accepting approval for a generous reaction not totally innocent and sheepishly admitted a personal reason for her compassion. "And, truth be known, because my trickery of him is what brought the whole down, I'd feel badly if he paid a price too high."

Galen laughed, greatly amused by the pleasing honesty of spirit to be found in his impetuous bride. But Amicia, not wanting to dwell on her motives, shifted their talk to a more cheerful topic.

"I pray you will not forget your promise that we'll return to Wryborne in the spring for Kelda and Farrold's wedding." She felt Galen shaking with a further, though silent, laugh at her ploy yet resolutely continued. "With Jasper's encouragement and training, Farrold will make Tiernan a fine guardsman."

"That Farrold would join Tiernan's garrison was only to be expected. How else but that two young men gravely manipulated by the same man should strike up a friendship, and the one begun when Farrold came here to bring them back sounds to be flourishing." Galen commented, but added, "Go to the wedding we will, but we've other merry times to come sooner—a visit by my sisters, Eleanor and Odlyn, who with their ever growing broods will shatter the peace of Tarrant. An uproar that can only grow louder when my Uncle Reynard and Aunt Aleria arrive from Swinton."

Amicia smiled. "Yuletide." The one word held bright anticipation, yet it was mixed with a tinge of sorrow that Galen, sensitive to his beloved wife's every mood, clearly heard.

Galen gently broached the subject that assuredly was its source. "My mother will be overjoyed when we tell her that this letter confirms her old friend will accompany your brother on the Christmas visit."

"I, too, am glad Mother plans to stop here before she enters St. Margaret's cloistered halls. She'll enjoy meeting her namesake." With the mention of Galen's youngest sister, Amicia sighed and snuggled closer against the man who'd taken tender care to ease her every unhappiness. "And I look forward to enjoying Tiernan's company again."

In the days they'd lingered at Dungeld, the twins had discovered an inbred rapport. Then, when she and Galen had arrived at Castle Tarrant, as the earl had predicted, Lady Nessa had welcomed her with open heart and arms just as had the youngest of Galen's three little sisters. If the older two were half so nice as young Sybil, then she looked forward to meeting them as well.

Gazing into the twining flames of yellow and gold, lost in the circle of warmth bounded by Galen's loving arms, she found a quiet strength and responded to his oblique reference.

"Truly, I am happy for my mother. I know 'tis her heart's desire to retire into the peace of the abbey now that both Tiernan and I are happily settled in our new roles. It's only my selfish desire not to lose her so soon after I've come to know her at long last. But then, I can be generous for already am I blessed overmeasure."

With one hand she lightly traced the firm plane of a bronzed cheek, explored the crease his slow smile brought, and brushed tantalizingly across lips that parted.

Nibbling at the teasing fingertip, Galen gazed down into melting brown eyes. Nay, he was the one who'd won the golden prize, and she was his to claim again and again. Fire light gleamed on the black head bending to uplifted and welcoming lips that tasted of the honey in her eyes.